Praise for *The Black Series*

Not for the faint of heart, Jennifer Odom's debut novel, *Summer on the Black Suwannee,* is a stark reminder of the spiritual forces at work around us. A must-read for those who enjoy a page-turning thriller that will leave readers looking nervously over their own shoulders.

Marian Rizzo
Bestselling author of
Angela's Treasures and *In Search of the Beloved.*

Jennifer Odom has crafted an amazing story of betrayal, intrigue, and the power of faith. *Summer on the Black Suwanee* is a must-read and will keep you turning pages well into the night.

Mark Mynheir
author of *The Corruptible*

Jennifer Odom has a fresh, innovative voice that captivated this writer's soul. A reader cannot help but to be enthralled with the power of Jennifer's dynamic command of the elements of storytelling. Her characters come to life on the page and capture the imagination and the heart of those turning the page.

Fay Lamb
author of *Everybody's Broken* and *Stalking Willow*

Summer on the Black Suwanee is a captivating, fascinating, suspenseful tale geared for teenagers navigating the complexities of life.

Sonja Lonadier,
Missionary

I could not put *Summer on the Black Suwanee* down! The words flowed as if I was standing right there beside the old black river itself. All the characters were well defined and the setting was so well described that I could almost hear the flow of the river and see the faces of each person, whether they portrayed good, bad or evil itself. I hardly ever make time to read a book in one day. *Summer on the Black Suwanee* was an exception!

Cheryl Cannon
elementary education teacher, retired
multi-year recipient of Teacher of the Year

This jaw dropping, emotional roller coaster will surely touch your heart. Not only does it teach you the value of friendship and family, *Summer on the Black Suwannee* radiates the awareness of God and His presence, as well as exemplifying that no matter what circumstances you may face He will always be with you through the trials of life.

Abigail Lonadier
Reader
15 years old

Summer on the Black Suwanee is not only a thrill ride of a story for young people, but it also addresses very real issues of spiritual warfare, occult practices, demonic activity, and the power of prayer. It is at once enlightening and encouraging without skirting around the issues of consequences of making ill-advised decisions.

Dr. Ricky Roberts
Senior Pastor, True Light Ministries

Jennifer Odom has hit the jack pot again. *Stranger with a Black Case* offers young adults (and older ones) tantalizing mysteries, gripping suspense, and a heartwarming story of friendship and community. At the same time it acquaints them with faith, forgiveness, prayer, purity, and redeeming love—all essential keys for triumphing over the pain of parental absence or abuse, as well as the dangers and disappointments of their everyday lives. What a difference in our world if teens everywhere could absorb and apply these truths!

Elsie Bowman, MSW, LCSW
Owner and lead psychotherapist
Common Sense Counseling

In *Stranger with a Black Case*, Jennifer Odom has written a worthy successor to *Summer on the Black Suwannee*.

Earlene Carte
Principal
First Assembly Christian Schoo

Not fair! Where's Book 3? Tears and cheers caught me up in the book's home town family drama where I wasn't quite sure what would happen next. *Stranger with a Black Case* kept me guessing. With so many books and movies that end badly or sad this is a joy to read and become involved in. The life lessons are well taught and the prayerful depictions had me reevaluating how I personally pray. I have a feeling the adventure has just begun.

Sylvia Swain
Educator

GIRL WITH A BLACK SOUL

Also by Jennifer Odom

Summer on the Black Suwannee
Stranger with a Black Case

Girl with a Black Soul is a work of fiction. All References to persons, places or events are fictitious or used fictitiously.

Girl with a Black Soul
Copyright © 2021
Jennifer Odom

Cover concept and design by David Warren.

ISBN: 978-1-952474-63-7

Published by WordCrafts Press
Cody, Wyoming 82414
www.wordcrafts.net

GIRL WITH A BLACK SOUL

A NOVEL OF SUSPENSE

JENNIFER ODOM

WordCrafts Press

Dedication

To all decent young men everywhere—because the enemy of your soul would like nothing better than to take you down.

Chapter 1

Christmas Vacation, Sunday Night

The demon's senses prickled. He sat up straight in the passenger seat as the boy's Jeep slowed near the edge of town. He tittered as Chad brought the wheels to an abrupt halt beside an abandoned Texaco station and backed in behind the building.

Yes. The location.

His and Murdo's assignment.

The boy shut off his lights and engine and climbed out.

Destroyer glanced up at the moonless December sky. *Oh yeah.*

Behind the vehicle, across the weed and gravel-covered lot, his demon-partner's dark form bent low behind the oil drum, busy with tonight's business.

Destroyer hopped out behind the boy and waved his hands around the fifteen-year-old's head. He breathed into the boy's face. Not a flinch. *Pfft!* The kid had no clue the demon was even there.

At the back of the Jeep, Chad swung open the hatch and folded back the quilt.

Destroyer snorted and propped his fists on his hips as the boy lifted out a tall mounted figurine. The boy's latest trophy. Its glimmer brought a grin to the demon's scaly lips.

He snorted as Chad Montgomery dug out more of same and piled them in his arms like so much junk.

This chump was his and Murdo's special assignment, their

Get Out of Hell Free task for a while. Anything to get away from those flames.

The demons' assignment had started back at the kid's house where Chad stuffed all his trophies under the old quilt in the back of the Jeep. His mama's family treasure.

Treasure. Destroyer spat. *Sentiment! Well, too bad, Mama. You're both headed for a surprise.*

What made this job so delightful was their little buddy Chad was about to destroy his own prizes. He tapped his claws together. And, *whoo-ee,* was this kid going to be sorry.

Score one for Destroyer.

He loved it when people trashed themselves.

Chad hauled away a load of trophies and came back to the Jeep—where he loaded up again and paused as if to think.

The demon leaned into his ear. *The box. Get the box. Above all, get the box.*

Chad eyed the long narrow shape still buried under the quilt.

Yank it out. Burn it.

Still no movement.

Slam it against the building.

The boy adjusted an arm under his load.

Destroy it all.

Instead, Chad stepped away from the Jeep.

Destroyer cursed.

A hiss behind the gas station drew Destroyer's attention to his partner-demon squatting near an old rusty drum with a wide smirk across his face.

Ugly skunk. Destroyer pointed a crooked finger at Murdo and brought it straight down then to the left. Even stupid old Murdo could figure out the big capital L. "What are you staring at, Murdo? Get back to work."

Loser.

Across town in a simple three-bedroom house, Myrtle Montgomery knelt beside her only son's empty bed. At her side, Brilliance the angel awaited The Holy Creator's command. *Just give the word.* Then and only then could he intervene.

Brilliance waited.

He tensed.

But the request must come from the woman.

"God, open Chad's eyes. Bring him home," the woman prayed. "And in Jesus' name, send your angels to help and comfort him."

That's all it took. Words were everything.

"Go!" The Father's word cut through Gaskille's night sky with Brilliance in its wake.

Finally. He had his orders.

Gravel crunched under Chad's sneakers as he stepped away from the Jeep and crossed the barren ground to the brush pile he'd previously gathered. No one would notice the flames behind the abandoned gas station. His arms opened and a dozen trophies clattered into the pile of brush.

Destroyer leaned close to the boy's ear. *Jake and his friends can't call you names anymore, can they? This will finish it.*

Chad blinked as if he wanted to block out the thoughts.

Worthless trophies—luck, not talent. That's what it was. Luck. You have no talent.

Destroyer leaned closer, refusing to let up on the boy. *Crazy people hear voices in their heads. Maybe you're one of them.*

Chad clutched at his ears. "All right, all right, all right!"

Brilliance the angel slipped into place behind Murdo's hunched form near the oil drum. He caught Destroyer's eye with a steely stare and fingered the hilt of his sword. "Get away from the boy's ear."

The demon eased backward.

Beside the angel's foot, Murdo punctured the rusty base of the drum with one of his long, jagged fingernails. A stream of black oil snaked toward the boy's pile of sticks.

Brilliance raised his sword and brought it down across Murdo's claw.

The demon screamed and backed away, clutching the stub. "I'll kill you for that."

Brilliance laughed. "What else is new?" He brought the hilt up under Murdo's chin like a sledgehammer Its loud impact ricocheted through the night, and Murdo landed in the gravel like a scaly sack of rocks.

Brilliance wrinkled his nose at the demon's rotten-carcass odor and wiped off his fist. These foolish demons always said the same stupid things.

He drew his foot across the gravel and made a line. The oil would run into the weeds now.

The boy, busy beside the fence, scooped up an armful of dead grass and threw it onto the heap of brittle branches. Because of his mother's prayer he was now under Brilliance's full protection, but not control—only demons controlled and manipulated.

Chad lit a match and dropped it in. Sparks flickered and brought the dry material to life. Flames grew into lapping tongues, and smoke lifted, curling into the canopy of the overhanging oak.

Murdo, still bent on trouble, dragged his own black toenail over the ground to coax the oil toward a flaming stick.

Brilliance hadn't missed it. *These fools never quit.*

Crack! Brilliance served him a hearty kick, and Murdo rolled away howling and clutching his knee as Brilliance once again redirected the oil.

These demons never seem to get enough.

The boy turned away, hearing none of it, of course. His ear was un-tuned to the frequencies of the demonic or angelic. Brilliance stood by while Chad gathered twigs.

Destroyer cupped his hands and continued his taunts from a safe distance. *You sure don't need company right now. Be alone. You have no one, Chad.*

Brilliance slashed at Destroyer's neck, his sword gouging a fresh crevice in the pus-oozing flesh. "And you have no rights to this boy. Stay away."

The orange flames licked upward, illuminating the boy's legs. Wood smoke mixed with the acrid fumes of the trophies as their plastic figures turned from gold to black—then dripped away.

Brilliance hated the sight of that. This was not the best place for Chad right now.

The boy squatted, mesmerized by the melting trophies.

Destroyer cackled and taunted. *A mess, just like you. Remember what the kids at school called you?*

Brilliance knew this boy. He wasn't one of the sodomites. And Chad would destroy every last shred of his past before he'd let anyone call him that again.

Destroyer taunted. *You're a loser with a dead father. You ride a school bus and live with your mommy.*

"Shut up, Destroyer," the angel said. "You can't have the boy. And you won't destroy him."

Then he sat down and rested an arm across Chad's shoulders. *What did your mom say? Don't listen in at every keyhole, or you'll hear yourself whispered about. The devil whispers. But God shouts! You are a child of the King. And He loves you.*

Behind them Destroyer edged a little closer with his singsong tune. *They said you're gay-ay. They said you're gay-ay.*

Brilliance swung the sword and connected with a loud *thwunk*. Destroyer screamed. Brilliance couldn't help but smile. *Fool.*

But his focus never left Chad. *Kids talk about everyone. They make everyone the butt of their gossip. It's a coverup of their own problems and not about you.*

Chad pressed the tears out of his eyes with his fingertips.

Destroyer kept it up. *They said you're gay-ay.*

"Shut up. Just shut up!" Chad screamed.

Brilliance glared at the demon. "You heard what he said."

Destroyer backed away.

Somewhat relieved after his outburst, Chad exhaled and picked up a broken stick. He stirred the red embers, feeding the flames. He blinked away the burn in his eyes. And it wasn't from the smoke.

"Jake the Snake Jackson. Jake the Jerk." He mumbled the words, trying them out for effect. Jake—the one who'd started the rumors. Didn't matter that they weren't true. Chad's reputation—ripped apart by a creep with a fancy black Camaro.

A tap on Chad's shoulder. He whirled around.

Electra, his new girlfriend—her smooth skin as orange as

his in the flames—stood in sharp contrast to the black night around her. *How'd she sneak up like that?*

"Who in the heck are you talking to?" she said.

With his sleeve, he wiped his eyes. Good thing it was dark. "No one."

"What's up with the campfire? It stinks."

"Just some junk."

"Are those *trophies*?"

"It's nothing."

She dangled a keychain and key in front of his face. "Fine with me. I brought you this."

He reached for it. "You sure your uncle doesn't care?"

"It doesn't matter, does it? It's all about perception. He thinks we're doing club meetings down here, like once a week."

"Club meetings? In an old Texaco station? Right."

"Club. So, don't use flashlights, or he'll figure out you're staying here. You might even get arrested for trespassing."

"You're a smooth liar, Electra."

"Skills, Chad. You've told a few yourself." She settled criss-cross beside him with her over-sized purse in her lap. "So, what did you tell your mom?"

"I'm staying with Andy while I get my head on straight." Mom had no idea he'd be living alone.

"And she said—?"

"What do you think she said?"

Electra stretched out her toes and fingers for him to see. They shined to match the red on her purse. "Like my nails? I just hit up Tippy Toes at the mall. Forty bucks doubled."

"Expensive."

"*Pfft!* Good old Dad."

"You always look beautiful."

She dipped her chin to her shoulder and batted her aqua-blue eyes. They sparkled like gems in the firelight. That's what drew him to her in Mr. Garrimore's art class. Like a black-haired Barbie, this girl was perfect in every way. And when she'd told him she liked him on the way into class, he'd tripped and knocked over his easel. Perfect girls like her didn't hang out with zit-faces like him. It couldn't be his wealth, since he had none. But who was he to question fate? He'd make sure to work in more Zit-Fix before he woke up from the dream—before she figured out her mistake. Or got glasses.

"How did you get here, Electra?"

A friend dropped me off.

"Kind of a bad side of town, don't you think? Isn't your mom worried?"

"Mom, schmom. She's in Paris."

"You're kidding."

"Anyway, I knew you'd take me home."

With barely twenty dollars in his pocket, he'd planned to go light on the driving. Because he was an underage worker, Tires-R-Us hardly paid him anything at all. Youth wages. Odd-job money.

Electra reached into her purse. "Want gum?"

"If you've got some to spare."

"Oh, yeah, yeah, yeah. I forgot about this." She pulled out a tee-shirt with a picture of a bass on the front and a crude rhyming word. "A present to you from the mall."

The shirt wasn't one he could wear at school or at home. Not quite him. But he wasn't at home now, and he had an image to change. A shirt like this would help him look tough.

She threw it across his lap. "And here's another one," she said, extracting a second one. "Free."

She'd been thinking of him in the mall? "That was nice of you."

"Think nothing of it. Like I said, a gift from the mall."

From the mall? Strange wording. But never mind. "You think I could use your phone?" he said. "I promised to touch base with Mom."

"Are you kidding? Does she even matter?"

"I told her I'd stay in touch. I haven't run away, Electra."

This seemed to disappoint her. She picked up her phone and handed it backward across her shoulder. "Suit yourself, bucko, but your mom should be the least of your worries."

He wrapped his hand around the heavy rhinestone-laden device. A promise was a promise, whether Electra liked it or not.

Chad stepped away from the fire for a small measure of privacy. He leaned against the musty gas station wall and dialed home.

"How are you, son?"

"Doin' okay, Mom."

"You could change your mind and come on home. We could spend the Christmas break together."

By the tone of her voice, Mom wasn't even trying to make him feel sorry for her. Not like the last summer when he'd left for Andy's when Dad was so sick. What a coward. But he'd come back home. Getting through the death of his adoptive dad had been tough. Twice fatherless in one lifetime. It was a lot to digest. And worry about. He could end up twice motherless, too. A real possibility during his life. Maybe he was being a mama's boy by thinking about it. "Yeah."

"Are you eating well? How's Andy's family? It's so nice of them to let you stay there."

"Trust me, Mom. They're feeding me good."

"Come back home anytime, okay? And get me Andy's number."

"This is a borrowed phone. But I told you I'd call, and so I did. I can get it later."

"You're a good boy, Chad. I want you to know I love you, and I miss you."

"Love you, too."

He waited for her to hang up first.

"By the way, Chad. When you get a chance, would you come by and pick up the mustang quilt I made you? Trade it out for the antique quilt you took with you. That one's special, it was my Great-Great Grandma's."

Yeah, the one he'd grabbed off his bed to cover up the things inside his Jeep to keep prying eyes away.

"It's not that I don't trust you. But I'm a little worried about your rough guy friends. Not Andy, necessarily, but boys who might come in contact with my antique. I know how guys are. Would you mind?"

On one hand, Mom was trying not to hover, to give him some leeway, but at the same time, she was doing anything and everything to get him back to the house. The quilt was special, though. She'd said that a bunch of times in years past and had always taken extra care of it. They wouldn't be having this discussion if he'd grabbed something else.

"Soon, Mom. But I gotta go now. Love you."

Chapter 2

Monday Late Afternoon

Tony straightened the new poster against the stucco wall and centered the tack. He and Emily were nearly done arranging their new daycare office, a refurbished janitor's-closet, next to the play yard while laughter and chatter of daycare kids trickled in through the open doorway.

Emily sat just outside, with her eye on the kids. Today was the first day of Christmas vacation, and kindergartners, fresh out of school and full of vinegar, now packed the Faith Church daycare near downtown Gaskille.

Last summer, after Tony's dad got shot, the rector, a friend of the family, offered Tony the after-school job, and Tony had snapped it up. Considering the wealthy clientele, Tony figured the church might also be able to hire Emily. Nothing ventured, nothing gained. It would be a great excuse for Tony to spend more time with her. So, he persuaded the rector to hire Emily, too—a two-for-one opportunity.

Thump. Thump. Thump. Before he could hammer the tack, the wall vibrated under his hands. He glanced through the open doorway. Emily, in her chair next to the wall, sat with her jeans-covered legs stretched out into the swiftly-fading rays of late afternoon sunshine—such long pretty legs. "Hey, Em. Could you get whoever that is to quit bouncing their ball against the wall?"

"Levi, over that way," she said. "You're rattling the office wall."

She peered back inside. "How does our poster look?"

"Come see." Mike, their friend from Larry's Restaurant, had snapped their picture a while back using the school's green screen, and they'd had it enlarged. He'd filled in a background with the state capitol in Tallahassee. In the photo, Tony and Emily stood back-to-back in a pose that showed off their new look-alike outfits, at least the part they'd been able to afford so far, like two spies with guns. The photo was their interpretation of the armor of God. Their money jar and wish list for more pieces of their outfits sat on the corner of their office desk.

Emily rose and craned her neck inside. Her fingertips clutching the doorframe. "Pretty good."

"Is that all? Just pretty good?" He stepped outside to help watch the kids.

"You don't think Mrs. Sanders cares if you tack it on the wall?"

The director, an old grump, was always throwing kinks into their plans. "Not in a janitor's closet. She did call this ours. You'd expect—"

"One never knows with her, though."

Tony waved off Emily's comment. "Don't worry about her. She'll be fine." He leaned against the doorframe and crossed his arms. "I wish it were the same with Dad, though."

Emily glanced up. "He's still scared to death to meet Robert? Why? I just don't get it."

Robert, a New Yorker, had entered Tony and Emily's lives only a few months back during his trip to Gaskille. But the musician wasn't always from New York, and according to Dad wasn't new to the family. Somehow, he and Dad had crossed paths long ago. Yet Dad wouldn't say how. And he refused to meet the man these few days Robert was back in town seeing his new girlfriend.

"Dad thinks Robert might have been the shooter."

Emily shook her head. They both knew Dad had created quite a few enemies during his life. But Robert wasn't the type to hold grudges.

"If they'd just shake hands and say hi it would absolutely make my Christmas." After all, since Tony had first met him, Robert had been giving Tony free music lessons via Zoom. "It only makes sense that Dad would want to meet my favorite music teacher in the world. Mom did. And she loved him. He's only in town for a few days."

"You'll just have to be persistent, I guess," Emily said.

Tony blew out a breath.

Robert couldn't be one of Dad's enemies. Tony knew better.

Persistent. Tony turned the word over in his mind.

It sure summed up this daycare job. Up until this week, he and Emily'd operated out of the back corner of Mrs. Sanders's office.

But the elderly woman had tired of them sharing her cramped quarters. She wanted her space back.

"Listen, guys," Mrs. Sanders had said. "I can't even get into my own desk anymore. I reach for something, and all this crazy donated stuff is in the way. Brother Ed hired you to play games with the kids, not teach school. Box this stuff up. This pile of junk's gotta go."

"Junk? It isn't junk," Tony argued. "We're using it for lessons."

"I've talked to the rector. You two can have the old janitor's closet and remodel it into an office. He'll give you a desk and two chairs."

Tony and Emily had grinned and high-fived—until they peeked inside the new space.

There was barely enough room for a person to squeeze around the desk and sit in the chair.

"Look at all the shelves, though," Emily had said. She was always so positive. "The kids adore the projects. We'll just jam in the supplies until we run out of space."

They did. While Mrs. Sanders rolled her eyes.

Right now, the playground was empty but for half a dozen swinging, sand-digging children. Emily swatted Tony's shoulder and stepped inside to take a good look at the poster.

With one eye on the kids, Tony spoke over his shoulder. "Any progress with your mom?"

Emily spoke from inside. "Looks great, Tony. Good job."

"What about my question? What's up with your mom?"

"Mom's the most stubborn human being I know." Emily propped against the doorframe with a sigh. "All she'll let Dad do is sit on the porch and visit with me. He's not welcome to come inside. Or eat. Or talk to her. He's trying so hard. I guess that's the one thing I wish for Christmas—for her to give a little. Give him a chance."

She stepped outside. But instead of sitting, she gasped.

Her gaze was turned to the street side gate where Ben, their friend, entered.

Blood ran from his clasped hands and dripped off his elbows.

Tony jumped to his feet. "Ben! What happened?"

The teen, born with Down's Syndrome, held up his injured right palm and then quickly returned it to the grip of his left.

Ben lived a block away in an assisted-living facility. Aged out of the foster-care system, he'd never been adopted and was now on his own. Tony had no idea where the kid's parents were.

And right now, Ben's left hand was not stopping the

flow. Tony grabbed him by the arms and guided him inside. Emily followed.

"Get Mrs. Sanders and her first-aid kit," Tony said. She was their first-responder.

He lifted Ben's wrist and studied the hand. "What'd you do to yourself?"

A shadow appeared in the doorway. Mrs. Sanders's broad silhouette. Tony breathed a sigh of relief. How'd she get there so fast?

Like a pro, she slid her first-aid kit onto the desk and slipped on a pair of latex gloves. She'd obviously been through this before, but nothing like this had come up before under Tony's watch. And Ben's hand was pouring blood.

She lifted Ben's hand out of Tony's grasp. "Get him a chair," she said.

Tony dragged one over to the doorway. Ben sat while Mrs. Sanders elevated the hand again.

"We've got to get that bleeding stopped. Now look at me, Ben," she said. She took one glance at the boy's pale face and frowned. "Oh, dear. Look at you. What cut you? Was it metal? Glass?"

Ben nodded.

"Talk to me, Ben. Which one?"

"G-g-glass."

"Tell me, is there any glass stuck in your hand?"

He shook his head.

Tony had to ask. "Mrs. Sanders, how'd you get...?"

"Watched him come through the gate."

Her eyes and attention remained on her patient, and she winced as she lifted the flap of skin on Ben's palm. "I guess you're right, Ben. I don't see any glass."

She poured a lid-full of peroxide over the cut and dabbed lightly at the skin. "It's not that deep, just a bleeder." Ben leaned away as her brow wrinkled, and she pressed the folded gauze against the wound. But, as she would treat a little child, Mrs. Sanders reached around and drew him back against the chair. "It's okay, Ben." After a minute of pressure, she checked the wound again. The oozing had slowed. But Ben's hand trembled. She moved the first-aid box to her lap and dug through until she found a tube of ointment. Dabbing with a cotton swab, she applied the antibiotic then wrapped a mitten of gauze and white tape around his hand. The first-aid supplies went back in her kit, and she threw away the used bandage wrappers.

"My picture frame broke," Ben said.

Tony nodded. "You dropped the frame?"

"It broke." Ben stared at the floor. Was Ben protecting someone?

Other residents could sometimes be mean to Ben. He had a tender heart, and unless someone pressed the point, he tended to protect his oppressors from getting in trouble, even if they'd done him wrong. Tony tried to clarify. "You mean someone broke it?"

He nodded. "Yeah."

"Why didn't you tell someone at your home?"

Ben shrugged.

"Why not, Ben?"

"Everybody's busy."

Ben was always looking for excuses to visit them at the church. He loved to hang around the playground during aftercare. The kids loved him, too.

Mrs. Sanders perched on the desk and shook her head.

"We don't mind bandaging your hand," Tony said. "We're

glad to help you anytime. But if you're bleeding or sick, you should tell the people at your home, so you can get help right away."

"But I like you, Tony."

"I know. But next time, just tell them, please. Promise me? What if you pass out or something on the way over here?"

"What's *pass out*?"

A handful of curious kindergarteners now clustered at the door. Jimmy, a freckly tow-head with a worried expression, studied the huge white bandage. "What happened?"

"Ben had a boo-boo. But he's okay, now," Tony said, stepping toward the group to gently guide them back to the enclosed playground.

The kids, apparently satisfied, shuffled out. "Bye, Ben!"

But Jimmy hung back. "Can we give him a hug?"

Tony shrugged. "Sure. Go ahead."

Jimmy's friends, overhearing his words, filtered back in, and after a big group hug, they headed back out to the play area, content that they'd done their part to help.

Still, Jimmy hung back. Before Tony or Mrs. Sanders could respond he leaned around and kissed Ben's bandage. "I hope it feels better soon."

Mrs. Sanders scolded him. "Jimmy, we don't kiss bandages."

"Mommy does."

"That's at home. You can't do that here, honey."

Ben patted Jimmy's head. "Thank you, little buddy. I'm okay now."

And Jimmy, his mission now complete, skipped away.

Tony turned to Mrs. Sanders. "I'll walk Ben back to the group home in a little bit. He shouldn't be walking alone, and I can explain everything to his director."

Mrs. Sanders gathered up her box as Ben stood. "Tony, you and I need to have a little chat when you get back."

What could Mrs. Sanders find to complain about this time?

Monday Evening

Right now, out by his pool, Vinnie felt like cussing. His wife and son Tony, standing to his left, were about to get a dose. Words rose in his throat as he clamped his hands on the chaise's armrests and ratcheted the thing upright. Yet those old words didn't feel right anymore.

Yeah, he'd gotten religion last summer. But right now, the two of them were teaming up on him. They wanted him to meet Robert.

Hmph. No way, Jose.

He swung his feet over the side but they stopped in mid-air as he grimaced—then nice and easy—and one at a time—drew them back on the chair again. His fingers clutched the spot below his right collarbone, and he sank against the chair.

Nerve damage, the doctor had called it.

He held his breath and pressed against the scar. "Stop buggin' me, please," he gasped. "Both o' ya'll. I ain't doin' it."

It took a minute, but the fireworks between his new metal rib and the plate in his back—where the bullet had blown a hole through his shoulder blade—subsided. He hated getting mad. Setting off the pain like that. It felt like getting shot all over again.

Well, not the getting shot part. That memory was wiped clean. As well as him coming back to life in the medical examiner's van.

The hole in his chest—and the physical therapy—were both a pain.

The last thing he remembered was sitting across the pool from the hedges—and wadding up the letter—then waking up in the hospital, hearing he got shot.

Beyond that he drew a blank.

Nancy leaned in and patted Vinnie's hand. He drew it back. His wife was always trying to settle him down. "This is not something you need to decide right now," she said. "He's only here in town for a few days. So, calm yourself, and just think it over."

Vinnie turned from her gaze. His wife shouldn't have to cope with his stupid after-effects like he was some kind of baby.

He took another minute to line up his thoughts, then looked up at his son who'd started this whole thing in the first place with his constant pressure to *meet the guy, meet the guy, meet the guy*. Alright already.

News flash, everybody. Vinnie *had* met the guy, twenty-five or so years ago, and that was enough.

"I ain't doin' it, Tony."

And here was Vinnie all shot up and his sins breathing down his neck.

"But Robert's been wanting to get with you since last summer."

"I ain't meetin' no guy." Vinnie said. "Not after what I done to him. There ain't no way he ain't still boilin' mad about what I done."

Tony shook his head. "It's not like that, Dad. Believe me."

The cops had long-since caught Vinnie's shooter. But Vinnie was still getting the whispered phone calls saying, *I'm gonna get you.*

Now Vinnie kept a look-out over his shoulder, even at home, wondering what was next. Never mind going out in public—which was rare these days. Even Vinnie's new-found religion hadn't taken the mortal fear out of his life.

Maybe this violinist Robert had something to do with all that. Didn't matter that the guy lived in New York. He could still be Vinnie's caller.

Tony nudged Vinnie's toes at the end of the chaise. "You read his letter Dad. Robert's not out to get you. He only came last summer to let you know that whatever happened back then is alright now."

Vinnie shook his head and pulled his foot away. *That ain't the way things work, buddy.*

Robert, some big-shot in New York now, was back in town on a visit. He'd been teaching Tony all this violin stuff over the Zoom-thing, and getting all buddy-buddy with him—probably just to get close to Vinnie.

And come in for the kill.

Worse than that, though, Robert was courting Eve. *Eve* of all people, their neighbor from back then. She'd seen it happen. Robert might just end up marrying the girl. Before you knew it, he'd be moving down here to *stay*.

Vinnie's chest tightened. He couldn't live in the same town as this guy. He squeezed his eyes shut and opened them with a sigh.

Though it wasn't the solution he wanted, Vinnie could actually fix the problem.

He could sell his house and move to the country. Lock, stock, and barrel.

Never mind that he'd lived here in Gaskille all his life. He couldn't have Tony finding out about his past. Vinnie had never told his son what he'd done to Robert as a kid. That would be stupid.

The farther away from Robert they could get, the better.

Oh, yeah, sure. Jesus forgave Vinnie. For all of it. That day he got shot and Lusmila the maid had prayed for him.

But a *victim* couldn't forgive it.

Nobody, but nobody could look past such a thing.

No victim would wanna come look Vinnie in the eye and tell him he forgave him.

Robert still had to be secretly mad at Vinnie. And those phone calls—they'd increased to once a week now.

Had to be him, had to be Robert.

Vinnie dropped the chaise down flat and turned over on his side, away from his wife and son. "Just go. Leave me be."

Robert was ready for the kill.

Ready to look Vinnie in the eye—and stab him.

Vinnie closed his eyes.

On the other hand, maybe that was okay after all. At least Vinnie would go to heaven and wouldn't have to worry about it anymore.

Tuesday Morning

"C'mon, Mom, be reasonable," Emily hollered over her shoulder. "Can't you cut Dad a little slack?" She unlatched the front screen door and turned, facing down the hall toward the kitchen. Mom was still back there cooking breakfast. "It's not like he ran out on you."

Emily had only asked her a simple question, and now Mom was yelling and kicking up a ruckus. How could Mom say

Dad was absolutely unwelcome here in this house? Mom definitely had a problem with unforgiveness.

Grandma, in her bacon-scented apron, had followed Emily through the house and now waited beside the stairs so she could latch the screen door behind her. Grandma never meddled in her and Mom's arguments, but she did try to keep the peace.

A wink, scowl, or furtive poke from Grandma usually revealed whose side she was on—and it was usually Emily's. Right now, Grandma raised a finger to her lips. *Shhh!*

Emily paused, waiting for some indication that Mom was coming around to her way of thinking.

No sound. Just the angry clatter of silverware being dropped into the sink.

Emily nudged the screen door with her heel. Its metal springs squeaked as it opened partway behind her. Nearly all the big homes in this historic district had front screen doors like Grandma's that allowed fresh air to pass through, a luxury Emily never ceased to be grateful for. Grandma's two-story home was a far cry from their sweatbox of a cabin up on Orange Lake, and Emily hoped she'd never have to leave Grandma or her home. And normally, the wonderful morning sun that now bathed Grandma's hallway, dining room, and stairway would make Emily want to sing. Except for Mom's negative attitude toward Dad.

"No!" came Mom's sharp answer. Emily sighed. A few months back she and Mom held a similar conversation about Dad coming to sit on the porch to talk with Emily. That one hadn't begun so well, either.

It took her a while, but Emily prevailed. And now, at least, Dad was allowed to visit Emily on the porch.

Mom still needed convincing, but Emily needed to get to work. This job, an easy one at a daycare with her boyfriend Tony, was her first, and she didn't want to get fired. He was probably already there. Emily took a deep breath, and Grandma, standing next to the stairs, winced as she yelled past her one last time. "I'm not asking you to remarry him, Mom, just invite him to dinner as part of the family. He's harmless."

"Not on your life!" came the quick retort.

What a shame Dad had to lose his family before he tried to fix his situation. He'd gained back Emily's trust since last summer. But not Mom's.

Not yet, anyway.

"Patience, Emily," Grandma whispered, patting the air as if to calm Emily. "One thing at a time."

"Okay, okay."

But Mom wasn't done yelling. "Give you an inch, you ask for a mile. No. No. No. And double-no again."

Emily shook her head and stepped away from the door to kiss Grandma's soft cheek. "Gotta go."

Grandma squeezed her tight and let go. She patted Emily's arm. "Give her credit, she's already letting your dad sit with you on the porch."

Emily nodded. She and Dad had shared some good conversations out there.

So much had changed since Dad had showed back up. He'd grown strong with Alcoholics Anonymous and church, and was well on his way to being all straightened out. He'd taken on a full-time mechanics job—and was even reading his Bible and praying.

But Mom was not convinced. She'd remarried once since the divorce. And that guy, Bill, was in prison now—and wasn't ever coming back. No way, Jose. Then ever since the Suwannee incident Mom didn't trust anyone anymore. She'd bought a handgun, carried pepper spray in her bra, and signed up for a gun-carry class.

Grandma winked at Emily. "Patience and prayer. You think about it."

"I guess you're right, Grandma. Bye." She kissed her a second time and scooted out the door to where her bike leaned against the porch, hidden behind the hedges. It was the only logical place to stash it. Nobody would ever see it from the street.

She glanced back at the screen door. Grandma blew her a kiss and disappeared into the house. Why couldn't Mom just forgive Emily's dad and move on? Accept Dad as a person? All Emily'd wanted was to invite him to dinner.

Tuesday Morning

Across the street in the historic district, the squeak of a screen door alerted the young man to the girl as she stepped out of her house. He knelt along his path in the middle of the overgrown vacant lot. Over the years a scattering of old limbs, white-flowered Spanish needles, broom sedges, and other tall weeds had taken over the place. He peered through the overgrowth as the girl crossed her porch.

He narrowed his eyes—*that face*—then he snapped his fingers. *Yes.* She was that chick from last summer, the girl with the ruffled shorts. The one he'd taken all those pictures of—and then lost every single one.

Yeah, he'd tried, back at his aunt's booth that day—to find out where she lived. But she wouldn't tell him.

She'd probably wanted him to guess. And he'd tried. He could tell by the way she responded she had a crush on him. Had to be his dimples. She liked them. Every girl did. All he had to do was turn on the charm, and girls swooned.

But then she'd started asking all those questions—about his name and his school. Hemming him in. Cornering him.

His chest tightened even now thinking about it. He reached up and tugged his collar away from his skin. Massaged his neck. Took three deep breaths. Just the thought of being questioned made the shirt feel like a noose. The one thing Axelrod couldn't stand was being hemmed in. He crossed his arms and clenched his hands.

Sometimes those hands had a mind of their own.

And right now, they wanted to wrap around something.

He took a few more deliberate breaths. Closed his eyes. Calmed his breathing. His hands relaxed. His neck and chest relaxed. That's what the counselor at juvie suggested, anyway. Picture something different. That could settle him down.

So, he did. He pictured the girl's ruffled shorts and the picture she'd drawn at his aunt's booth. That bulldog picture. But the one question returned. The one every girl asked him. The question filled the front of his brain like a water balloon—a thick headache—a tumor—and pushed aside every other thought—

"*What is your name?*"

He shook his head to break the tumor loose. Ran his fingers through his hair. Under his collar. Oh, *gahhh!* There it was again. He hated this feeling. Hated his stupid name. Hated his mother for picking it. Of all the ugly names—it didn't matter it was some old family name. Who cared about that?

He deserved a handsome name like everyone else. Not *Axelrod.*

Mama should have given him a nice name. Why did she have to make him an Axelrod? If he could only be someone else.

He shut his eyes, and the capital letters of his name, large and bold, drifted over the screen of his mind. They swirled like bats across the vision of Mama's rolled-back eyes. He pressed the heels of his hands against his own eyes as the girl from last summer's booth reappeared. He sighed and relaxed. His breathing slowed. Much better.

What had he told the girl? The same stupid lies he told all the girls.

Hadn't his teachers always said he could be anything he wanted to be? And he wanted to be Eric who went to med school. Girls went crazy for that. He couldn't very well tell them his name was Axelrod, could he?

He hated Axelrod.

His hands clenched and opened again. He raised them in front of his face. His mother's dying face came back. He stared hard at his fingers and forced the image of his mother away. He refused to feel bad about that. Mama deserved what she got. He wouldn't let anyone stick him with a name like that. Nobody. Not even her.

He snorted and glanced back toward the house. But where had the girl gone?

Yeah. He recalled her fake boyfriend that kept hanging around her that day at the town square. He was sitting with her—*Axelrod's girl*—on the bench and sharing her lunch.

Of course, she preferred Axelrod over that *poseur.* She had to. She *loved* Axelrod.

He glanced up at the two-story house where the girl had come out. He'd guessed right about her last summer. He'd always had the feeling she lived here.

But then that night when he'd tried to snap those pictures…

Hmmm. Rats to that. He'd never forget the old man with the hat and glasses who'd messed it all up. He'd caught Axelrod holding his phone/camera—right out front there on the sidewalk—in the middle of the night. And he'd beat the living stew out of him. He'd stomped the phone and told Axelrod to get out of town. Leave. Vamoose.

Since that time Axelrod had avoided the streets in this area. Avoided the old man. Oh, he knew the garage where the old man worked. All his hours. Enough to give him a wide berth. And make this trail so he never had to cross his path again.

But Axelrod couldn't very well leave town. Nope. They may have cut him loose from juvie last spring, but he was still stuck living with his aunt and helping her at that stupid art booth.

He frowned and pictured the old man with his hat and glasses—nobody was going to tell Axelrod what to do. Not the old man. Not Axelrod's aunt. Not Mama. Not anybody. Not here; not anywhere.

A movement across the street caught his eye and he refocused.

There she was again. Right before his very eyes came Miss Ruffle-shorts pedaling down her sidewalk on her pretty pink bike. He ducked a little lower as she turned and rode away toward town.

He ran his thumb and fingertip along the corners of his mouth and scrambled to his feet. Now that his cute little chickie was back on the radar, he'd have to find out where she hung out every day.

Tuesday Morning

Axelrod backed up under the cedars' low-hanging branches and shimmied off his backpack. This would be Axelrod's new hangout. Right across the street from Miss Ruffle-short's two-story house in the historic district.

Back here, along the vacant lot's back and western edge stood a row of twenty-year old cedars, long-since forgotten by their planters—the final high school ag students to ever meet in this neighborhood. County politics had built a new high school, and turned its former halls—situated two blocks away—into a prestigious elementary school, one that had no use for agricultural work or this field.

Axelrod glanced down the street where the girl had long-since disappeared on her pink bike. She'd been way too quick on that bike of hers for him to follow. So, Axelrod, to avoid the company of his bossy old aunt, had napped, drunk from his water bottles, peed a bunch of times, eaten half a pack of crème-filled chocolate cookies, and napped some more. Between dreams he watched the house across the street to see what else was going on.

He raised up one more time, peering above brittle brown broom sedges, invasive cogon grass, and other tall weeds to check the house across the street, then propped the backpack under his head and stretched out.

Even in December the weather in this town was pleasant.

The creak and slam of the house's screen door alerted him. He sat up. Got up on his knees. The woman of the house, probably the girl's mother, was heading out front to her little blue Honda.

Axelrod, too lazy to jump up and follow, brushed away a crawling bug and watched as the woman backed out of the driveway. He eyed the car as it eased north along the street toward the school. Much too slow. Just like his aunt.

But instead of disappearing beyond the traffic light near the school, the little Accord pulled into the elementary school's parking area around the next block. Oh yeah? He craned his neck. A second car pulled in beside it.

Hm, then. He'd walk that far. Take a gander at what everybody was up to down at the school. He stood, knocked the sand off his jeans and tee shirt, then stepped along his private path that cut through the center of the lot and out to the street.

By the time he reached the cluster of wild sabal palms at the corner of the school's parking area, the drivers had disappeared through a side door of the building.

So, he waited. Stood right there among the palm fronds and waited. He knew a thing or two about camouflage, and nobody would notice his legs among the trunks.

Late Tuesday Morning

Axelrod held his position in the cluster of sabal palms. The main thing was not to move. Just listen in. Watch and see what was what, and not hurt anybody. He didn't plan to hurt anybody in this town. He had only one enemy.

The girl's mother exited first from what appeared to be a side-office door. In her arms she carried three fat folders. A stretchy key-ring encircled her upper arm.

A second lady came out behind her and locked up. Maybe she was the boss.

"Thank you," the boss-lady said. "Charlene, I don't know what I'd do if you hadn't agreed to take care of these folders for me. There's no way my family would ever let me forget it if I brought that stack of papers to Aspen." She shook Charlene's hand.

So, the girl's mother's name is Charlene. He'd learned something already.

"It's my pleasure." She gave boss-lady a hug and backed away. "You can't bring this work to your son's wedding. Don't be ridiculous."

"I never in a million years would have asked you to do this—you know that."

"Just go on. Climb in that plane tomorrow, and forget about your worries," Charlene said.

The other lady dropped a long, narrow envelope on top of the stack of folders. "And there's a little Christmas bonus."

A look of surprise crossed Charlene's face, and she brought one hand up to nudge the envelope back to the other woman. "No, no, I couldn't. You keep this. I don't mind helping you any way I can."

Had to be money in there. Axelrod would never refuse cash. *Stupid woman.*

The boss-lady raised both hands and turned, refusing to take back the envelope. "Good-bye. You enjoy your Christmas break. I'll see you back here on January 6th. How's that?" With that the boss lady slid back into her nice sports car, cranked the engine, backed it out, and sped away.

Charlene waved and watched her drive away. But as Charlene turned to her own vehicle, her eyes flitted over the young sabal palms. She startled—demanded, "Wh—who is that in the bushes?" She shifted the weight of the folders and reached into her bosom as she stood firm beside her driver door. A small bright green object now gleamed in her extended hand.

"You come out of there right now," she ordered as she eased the folders onto the ground. She stepped across them. Closer to Axelrod. "Get out of those bushes."

Her thumb bent on the green thing. It had to be a trigger. Had to be pepper spray. Axelrod didn't need that. He stayed put. No woman was going to tell him what to do.

"Come. Out. Of. There!" Her voice came out firm and bitter. Sounded just like Mama. And his bossy aunt.

Axelrod waited.

"Don't mess with me. I. Do. Not. Like. Sneaky. Step out!"

He stepped out and crossed his arms. How could a complete stranger look so much like Mama. Had Mama come back to life?

"Who are you? What is your business back there in those bushes?"

He clammed up. No woman was going to interrogate him. He'd give her a little of her own what-for.

"Well, what were ya'll doin' breaking into a school?" He smarted off back.

"Wh-what? Breaking into a school? You've got to be kidding. Listen here, buddy. You better get the heck out of here. I don't want to see that face of yours back at this place again. Don't you come near this school."

"Whatcha got there little lady, a little green squirt gun?"

"Come close and find out. I'll burn your beady little eyes."

Oooeee, this one was full of venom. He turned to walk away. But not before he caught a motion out of the corner of his eye. She'd reached for that keychain on her upper arm.

Meeep Meeep Meeep Meeep Meeep! Meeep Meeep Meeep Meeep Meeep!

An electric current shot through his brain. *No cops, no cops, no cops!* His feet took off sprinting. He raced down the hill, past the historic district, and headed for his own street. He wasn't about to hang around with that car alarm going off and everybody staring at him beside that blue Honda.

The further away he got, though, the madder he got. He wasn't about to be bested by a horn-honkin' woman and a little old pepper spray. Come to think of it, maybe he *would* hurt somebody in this town.

Give it time, he'd get even.

Chapter 3

Late Tuesday Afternoon

Chad braked his Jeep at the stop sign on First Street located near the old phone company. He glanced across the seat to Electra and gave her a wink.

She dipped her chin and fluttered her eyelashes at him.

Until she came along, he'd thought the eye-flutter thing was only in the cartoons. He grinned. "The way you bat those eyes at me—it's so Betty Boop."

She returned the smile, clearly pleased.

"You think I'm pretty, then?"

"Most beautiful girl in the world."

"Then, maybe you wouldn't mind ..."

"Mind what?"

She ignored the question and pointed down the empty street instead. "You can go now."

Chad eased through the intersection. Electra had already talked him into cruising around town for a while. As long as the cops weren't out and didn't notice him. Fifteen-year-olds weren't allowed to drive alone, and Electra was too young to count as an experienced other-driver. The law said nothing, though, about owning a car.

Once school started back, he wasn't getting back on that school bus with Jake's friends. He'd drive the Jeep. Or he would walk.

"Hey, up ahead's Faith Church and that daycare. Rev your motor."

Before Chad could think, Electra had stood and squirmed her body out the window and stretched her arms across the top of the Jeep. She hollered down to Chad inside. "Rev it, Chad! Rev it!"

Well, if she said so. He coasted alongside the church playground and revved his motor as loud as he could, then as Electra ducked back inside, he scratched off, burning rubber.

That ought to impress Electra.

She shoved her way across his arms and hollered out his window. "Whoooo! Merry Christmas, kiddoes!"

Chad eyed his rearview mirror as two little girls leaped away from the fence and ran wailing to their teenage baby sitter.

By now Electra had climbed out the passenger-side window again.

Chad kept his eye on his rearview mirror but slowed at the corner to keep Electra from falling out. The big Down's Syndrome kid had climbed off the swing and it whapped him the in the groin. Chad knew that kid. He'd seen him around town. And there he was doubled over.

Chad pursed his mouth. Enough of this. He hadn't meant for anyone to get hurt. "Get back inside, Electra," he hollered. "We don't need to be attracting this kind of attention."

Electra climbed in again, beaming. "Next time, we'll hit the train horn!"

Yeah, the one Dad had helped him hook up just before he started going downhill. Talk about getting a ticket.

She laughed. "That was awesome! Didn't you love all that havoc back there?"

Chad stared at her and shook his head. He should never have done that to those little kids.

Electra drew her head back. "Why are you looking at me

like that? Didn't you like it?" She laughed. "Did you see what happened to that big retard?"

Even Electra knew who Ben was.

Chad circled the next block. "I've got to park. What were you going to ask me?"

"Oh, that." She stretched out her hand to admire her nails. "Just wanted to know if you felt like buying a pretty girl some ice cream."

"Sure. But let's walk." His calculations told him that would be a buck-fifty if he bought her a sundae at Burger King. Eighteen left for gas and food.

Maybe he could stretch the rest of his money until the next paycheck.

He returned to the parking lot right smack across from Faith Church's daycare and pulled in under a small oak. Maybe nobody at the daycare had paid any attention.

"I don't feel like walking."

"Walking's good exercise."

"Why don't you park a little closer to the street?"

"I'll get your door." He smiled as he climbed out and opened it for her. Parking under the protection of this tree was one thing he wouldn't compromise on.

He held her hand and helped her out, making sure the doors were locked. Once on the ground, she elbowed him away. "That's completely weird, Chad, always parking under some special tree. And why in this parking lot? I don't want to be staring at Faith Church every time I get in or out of your vehicle."

Too bad. This was non-negotiable. Especially with that box in the back.

No sunny parking places, not even in December.

Tuesday Just Before Closing

At the daycare Tony nearly trampled Emily's heels as they moved around to calm the cluster of crying children. Emily cuddled the two most traumatized girls in her arms. "Here, here. It's all right."

He squatted beside her with another one. "Don't worry about that ugly old Jeep. It's not going to hurt you. It's just loud."

In fact, now that he thought about it, this might be the same Jeep he'd bumped into last summer—in the middle of the night while he was sneaking around down by The Rock—clearly one of the stupidest things he'd ever done.

The kid driving it looked a lot like someone he'd seen around school, too.

The girls whimpered against Emily's shoulders but seemed to be calming down. She patted their heads.

"I'll go check on Ben," Tony said.

Ben seemed better after the blow to the groin and was helping a younger boy back into his swing. But his bandaged hand complicated things.

"You okay now? Let me help you." Tony lifted the five-year-old into the seat. "There you go."

Ben pushed the swing. "Thank you, Tony. That car was loud, huh?"

"Yeah, it was. Electra and her boyfriend are the jerks of the century. Two losers with nothing to do but scare little kids."

"I liked it," Ben said.

Tony stared at him. Surprises never ceased. "You what?"

"Yeah." Ben grinned, despite his earlier injury.

Tony laughed and waved him away.

"I'm sorry, Tony."

"What's to be sorry about?"

Ben hung his head. "It scared everybody."

"Yeah, but you didn't do it."

Emily returned to the sandbox with the two little girls, and they started their digging again. The majority of the children had resumed playing, and it seemed little harm had been done. Parents would be off from work soon and dropping in to pick up their kids. It would look awful if they were all upset and crying.

Tony strode back over to Emily where she helped the kids pat sand into a castle.

She glanced up with a grim expression. "What they did makes my blood boil. No regard for these little kids."

"Losers." Tony paused. "I'm sure I've seen that guy." He snapped his fingers. "Yes. algebra class. That's it."

"Oh, yeah. And that Electra girl, I've seen her around, too. And I'm extremely unimpressed." Emily dumped a bucket of sand upside down. "So glad *he's* not your twin."

"Don't even suggest it." The kid in the Jeep looked nothing like Tony. The dirty blond hair ruled him out. "I'd give anything, though, to find my twin." He ran his hands through his hair. "I feel like I'm going crazy, looking at every new face and thinking, 'Maybe it's him, or him, or him.'"

Only last summer he'd learned of his own adoption and had been given his grandfather's violin and case. The note inside mentioned his twin. Talk about surprises. The only other thing that Tony wanted for Christmas besides his dad meeting his friend Robert, was to find his twin. But lately, things hadn't been going so smooth.

"Me, too, but I haven't seen too many new people with your dark hair and complexion." Emily clapped her hand over her mouth and her eyes grew wide. "Oh, no. What if your twin is her? That girl, Electra?"

Tony made a sour face. "What?"

"She's got that dark hair."

"No, no, no, no, no! Not Electra. Forget it. She may have the right coloring. But even if she was my twin, I'd never claim her. Don't even joke about it."

"Tony, how can you say that about sweet little Electra? Didn't you see how she wished all the kids a Merry Christmas? Truly, she's a girl with a kind and merry heart."

"Very funny. Ha ha." He waved the thought away as he walked back to the office. "You're crazy."

The last hour at the daycare passed quickly. Tony had taken a few minutes to walk Ben to his group home before they had to start cleaning up for the arrival of the parents.

Once the parents picked up their kids, Tony and Emily locked the office door. When they popped into Mrs. Sanders' office to sign out, she already had her car keys in her hand.

"Bye, Emily, Tony. I'll lock the gate tonight. See you tomorrow." She pointed at Tony. "And remember," she said, her eyes zeroing in on his. "We still need to have that little talk."

He nodded and stepped around to the breezeway where his bike leaned against the wall. Emily reached hers first and pulled it upright. Darkness filled the breezeway. Tony had meant to remind the custodian about the burned-out bulb. Well, tomorrow. Anyway, he despised it that the days were becoming shorter and shorter, and night came so early. The darkness drained his energy, like it was already bedtime. At least after December 21, the days would start getting longer again.

He grabbed the handlebars of his bike. "I'm so glad Mike gave me his old bike when he got that new one for his birthday. Now, there's someone who would make a good twin. Mike."

Emily laughed and followed behind. "Think about it. He sort of looks like you. The hair color, the eyes, and even acts like a brother. Maybe he's the twin, right under your nose. Imagine the headlines, 'Friends Realize They're Twins, Living Right in the Same Town.'"

He shook his head. "I wish. But his birthday was in October, remember? Wrong month."

"What if it's not really his birthday? What if his parents changed the celebration date for some reason?"

"I really, really wish that was the case, Emily." It would be perfect. "But that's farfetched. My twin might not even live in this town."

Tony pushed his bike out of the breezeway and around the corner, nearly running over Mrs. Sanders.

"Whoa, sorry."

It almost seemed as if she'd been eavesdropping.

Tuesday Night after Work

Emily sat beside Dad on Grandma's front porch swing. Tony had escorted her home and taken off after a call from his own dad. It was still early evening, but the dark came early in December. She stuck her toe out and gave the swing a push, wishing the sun was still shining, wishing everything was back to normal in her life. "Dad, I'm sorry Mom is not more friendly."

"Don't worry about it, Little Bit. What's meant to be will be."

"But how do you know what to expect?"

"Trust God. Ask Him to have His will. That's all we can do."

"I am. You won't believe how hard I am praying. Every morning, every night. I'm praying so hard."

"I'm really proud of you."

"But Mom is so rude to you."

"With good reason. You can't expect her to just forget all the wrong I've done. To just up and say, *Oh, never-mind.* Can you? Give her time. She probably thinks I'm faking it. If I were her, I'd certainly have questions."

Emily shrugged.

"You can't make things happen. God's in control." Dad winked. "He's changed me, hasn't he?"

Emily leaned her head against his shoulder.

Mom's cowbell rang from back in the kitchen. *Suppertime.* The bell was Mom's way of not having to step outside to call Emily inside. Her way of communicating with Emily, and not Eldon. And the rudest thing of all—she was letting Dad know he wasn't invited to supper.

"I've gotta go, Dad." She stood and waited for him to stand so she could give him a hug.

Tuesday Evening

In the dark, Axelrod rose from his place under the cedars. He brushed off his pants and shirt where he'd been sitting criss-cross on the trampled weeds. On the porch across the street the girl and man stood. His eyes followed every move as they hugged and parted ways. The girl disappeared inside, and the old man clambered down the steps and headed down the hill away from town and into the neighborhood. Maybe Axelrod would follow him one day. But not today.

The blue vehicle remained in front of the house. That meant the woman was at home, the one who'd tried to tell him what to do. He'd make sure it was there when he decided to get even with her. He spat. She was so much like Mama. His fingers clenched and unclenched. Maybe he'd hurt both the woman and the girl. Why not? A two for one deal. After all it was plain to see the girl was hanging out with the old man. The one who'd beat him up. His number one enemy.

Hanging out with the enemy made her a traitor.

Traitor. He formed the word on his lips.

Axelrod had no use for traitors.

Later, traitors!

He laughed at his joke and stepped away from the cedars and down his little path.

Tuesday Night

At the corner table of Baskin-Robbins—and not the Burger King, like he'd planned—Chad watched Electra scrape up the last few bites of her chocolate sundae. He angled his shoulders to keep the old folks at the next table from seeing the offensive writing on the front of his shirt, the one with the bass picture and the rhyming word. He needed to look tough. But not around these old folks, just around—

"Ja—I mean, Chad, why don't we go on a picnic?"

"Tonight?"

"Of course not, silly. But soon."

He thought about it for a minute. "We could go after work someday. I'm working the last part of the afternoons during the holidays."

"Tomorrow then. I've got the perfect picnic basket. Plus, I've got gift cards to use up. Why don't I pack everything while you're at work?"

He had no resources for a picnic anyway in that gas station. Not a scrap to eat in that place. And the free meal sounded good, no matter what she brought. "Sure. I get off at five."

"I'll get a friend to drop me off."

"What about your parents? You never mention them. Don't they ever take you anywhere?"

"I'll tell you about it sometime. But you and I have a lot of things in common."

Yeah, hardly. Anyway, the friend dropping her off was fine. It saved him the gas. By the time he got off work, though, it would be getting dark. "Where do you wanna go for this little picnic?"

"Let me think on it. Someplace with lights. You sure you don't want an ice cream, too?" she asked as if she'd bought the treat for herself.

"No, thanks. Not in the mood for ice cream right now." Actually, he was starved and could eat double the ice cream she'd just put away.

"This is so yummy. You're a sweetie."

"Glad you enjoyed it."

The tiny table wobbled as Electra adjusted and stretched her long legs across to the opposite chair. Tony studied the blood red nails on her toes. In Florida, even while most people wore jeans in December, on nights like tonight, it was warm enough for sandals.

She didn't miss his glance and pouted. "My poor little feet are throbbing. You should have driven us down here instead of making me walk."

"Sorry, but you're the one who wanted Baskin-Robbins." If she'd been content with a Burger King sundae, they would already be back to the Jeep by now. And he wouldn't have spent a whole five bucks either.

How was he going to afford food and gas for the rest of the week? If this kept up, he'd better start dumpster diving behind the Winn Dixie.

Or go home.

But he wasn't ready for that yet. Yes, he did feel sorry for Mom, alone at home. But this wouldn't be forever. A man had to work things out.

To be honest, though, this figuring-things-out gig wasn't quite working for him yet. Give it time, though. These days he hadn't even had time to get his perspective. If his thoughts weren't on work or Electra, he was usually just too tired or hungry to think about anything else, and the list of things he'd planned to think through kept getting put off.

Electra did her chin-dip thing with those long lashes. "Maybe when we're done here you'll be a sweetheart and come pick me up so I don't have to walk."

Those eyes were more than he could resist. "Looks like you're about done. Guess I'd better go fetch the Jeep then." It wasn't that far away. But how much gas would it take?

She grabbed his head with a squeal and pecked him on the cheek with her chilled ice-cream lips. "Thank you, Chad.

You're a sweetie. I do need to get on home. I mean a girl's gotta get her beauty sleep, you know."

He rose and strode to the door. With his hand on the bar, he turned to steal another glimpse of the beautiful girl who'd let him sit by her side. How could she possibly fall for him? Unbelievable. He pushed the door open, and cool air blasted him in the face.

His feet led him up the boulevard. Block after block of Christmas ornaments glittered from the light poles around him. But not much glittered in his pockets.

How could he finagle more hours at Tires-R-Us?

He pictured Electra's long lashes and aqua eyes. Whatever it took, he wanted to keep her happy.

Even if she was a little spoiled.

Along the boulevard, night seeped in between the spaced-out streetlights. Behind the electronic sign over Muffy Muffler's roof, stood Brilliance. He peered down at the reprobates in the alley on his right.

One hand rested on the hilt of his sword. The other cradled Snowball against his chest, a purring ball of fluff.

The lost kitty belonged to a city cop's five-year-old daughter. It had wandered off and ended up in the angel's care.

The little girl had waved a tearful good-bye that morning. "Bwing Snowball home today, Daddy. I'm pwaying. Weally weally hard."

Brilliance caressed the downy fur as he studied the two hidden crazies below, Heck-No and Wild-Eye. In anticipation of their approaching victim, they lurked beside the peeling wall of Bueno's Paint Store next door. Their two controlling demons, Murdo and Ruin, clung to their shadows.

Below Muffy's lit-up sign dangled another. Its message, *Merry Christmas,* camouflaged the angel's presence. Demons hated that word Christmas—or anything promoting the Savior's name, and couldn't bear to look at it. Brilliance grinned and gave the sign a tap. Colorful beams shifted back and forth across the demons below.

A light shuffle and the angel turned. Chad approached from the east. The boy, his eyes glued to the sidewalk, was oblivious to the danger ahead.

Wild-Eye scratched his nails through his lice-filled scalp and peered around the building. "Here he comes."

Brilliance tightened his hand on his sword. Murdo and Ruin weren't about to kill the boy on his watch.

The boulevard's traffic was unusually thin tonight. After-work shoppers had driven across town where sales at the brand-new mall awaited.

Wild-Eye held up one hand. ""Shhh. Wait."

Over the hill to the east crept a cop car.

"Cops," he hissed.

Heck-No flicked open his rusty switchblade. "Let 'em pass. Then we'll go."

The crazies flattened themselves against the wall. Chad ambled by. Then, a minute later, the nearly silent electric cop car. By that time Chad was half-a-block away.

Wild-Eye brought his arm forward. "Now."

The men eased out and crept along behind the boy.

Brilliance stepped down from the roof and over to the double yellow lines that divided the six lanes of asphalt. He lowered Snowball between them and flashed his sword to draw the cop's attention in his rearview mirror.

As small as he was, Snowball's fuzzy silhouette, backlit by the hilltop Christmas lights, would be hard for the officer to miss.

Sure enough, the cruiser's brake lights flickered. The vehicle swung wide in a left arc, and with red and blue lights flashing sped back in a one-eighty toward Bueno's Paint Store.

Wild-Eye froze then dove through an alley. "He saw us!"

Heck-No sprinted past him. They blasted through the bushes behind the stores.

Snowball scampered across three lanes, bounded across the sidewalk. and climbed into Muffy's front planter where Brilliance guarded him with cupped hand against the potted poinsettias.

Red and blue lights flickered across the windows as the officer pulled up in front between Muffy's and Bueno's and threw the car in park.

He leaped out, flashlight in hand, and shined it across the hedges and box-planters in front of the buildings. "Snowball? I sure hope that's you. Here kitty, kitty, kitty."

A tiny mew drew the man's beam to the potted poinsettias.

"Great day, Snowball. It's you. I can hardly believe it." He lifted the kitty from between the leaves and looked him in the eye. "Somebody's gonna be mighty happy to see you."

He gathered the kitten against his big chest, and strode back to the car.

Brilliance eyed the bushes where the two crazies had fled. A grin spread over his face.

So much for Murdo's plan to kill the boy.

Chad strolled along the right side of the boulevard and

passed through another patch of streetlight. In a few more yards and he'd cut left across the boulevard and head down a side street to retrieve his Jeep then go pick up Electra from Baskin-Robbins.

Behind him a distinctive vehicular rumble grew louder and louder as it drew near. *Uh oh.* He knew that sound.

Chad turned to verify as the Camaro passed.

Not Jake again.

Brake lights flamed. The car lurched forward and stopped. It backed up.

Chad couldn't seem to get away from this dude. What had he ever done to aggravate him?

Jake pulled up even with him. But Chad walked on, trying to ignore him.

He coasted forward—revved his engine and hollered across through the open passenger window. "Ho, ho, ho! I thought that was you, gay boy."

"I'm not gay, you jerk."

"I don't see you with no little girlfriend."

Chad crossed the street behind the Camaro. He needed to get back to his Jeep.

The Camaro's engine revved in place, blocking one lane of the boulevard.

Headlights approached as Chad crossed the lanes. Streetlights behind the oncoming car outlined its silhouette—a rack of lights on top. A cop car. Chad paused on the south sidewalk, his eyes following the cruiser's nearly silent approach on Jake's Camaro.

Jake caught Chad's grin and the direction of his gaze and checked his rearview mirror.

He slapped the side of his car door and pointed at Chad.

"I'll see you later kid. Watch your back." Then, with his eye trained on his rearview mirror, he slipped into the right lane at a decent speed and moved on.

Chad chuckled out loud. *Looks like you better watch your own back, Jake.*

Chapter 4

Wednesday Late Afternoon

Tony shoved the stack of small flowerpots into Emily's hands. "Hold onto these, and I'll get the bag of potting soil. Once they're planted, we'll let the kids line them up along the far side of the fence next to their lettuce pots."
The gardening projects were coming along great and the kids' lettuce plants were already about five inches tall.

She held up the radish seed package. "These are supposed to grow really fast. Just wait till the kids get back from Christmas. They'll be so surprised."

"Yeah, if we remember to stop by and water them every couple of days."

She glanced up. "Yay, there's Ben now."

Ben stood outside the wrought-iron fence, trading high fives with the flock of kids gathered on the other side. "Come on in, Ben," Emily shouted out. "Ready to help?"

He nodded and slipped inside. "Hey, Miss Emily."

Tony dumped the bag of potting soil into a large galvanized tub and nodded his way. "Almost ready." Tony had asked him yesterday if he wanted to participate.

Ben was game for anything—if it involved the kids.

"Don't get your bandage wet, though," Tony said.

"Okay, everybody," Emily hollered toward the kids. "Line up over here." She waited for them to settle down. "Does anybody remember what we're going to plant today?"

"Radishes!" they yelled in unison.

"Ben, you hand out the pots. We'll help you put the dirt in. Then we'll plant the seeds."

Squeals, pushes, and elbows: children jostled to be first in line. Emily guided two boys to the back of the line. "Here, let's be gentle," she reminded them.

Hemmed in by the little guys, Ben held the box of pots over his head. "Okay, everybody. No pushing."

After a minute, the group settled down. "Good job. That's better," Emily said.

With a clatter, Tony dropped the tub of fresh potting soil near the grassy edge of the playground. On top of the soil lay a half dozen plastic spades. "All right, everybody," he said. "Let's hold up a minute." He reached for Ben's arm and pulled him closer to the tub. Everyone knelt except the kids in the back. "Ben's going to show us how to do this."

"First you'll take one of these." He handed Ben a pot. "Remember how we planted the lettuce?" Kids nodded around the tub. "Then we'll take a spade." He handed one to Ben. "And fill the pot with soil. Go ahead, Ben."

Every eye followed Ben as he filled a pot.

"Perfect," Tony said.

"See how he's brushing the extra back into the tub? You guys can do the same thing." Tony stood and so did everyone else. He motioned them over to the picnic table. "Ben's going to show us how to plant the seed."

As they gathered around, Emily held up the seed pack with a picture of radishes on the front. "Before Ben plants, everybody look up here." She rattled the seeds in the package so everybody was looking at her. "Remember the radishes we're planting? Here's the picture again. And here," she said, pouring a few seeds into her palm, "are the seeds." Do they look like this picture?

All the kindergarteners shook their heads.

"You're right. The seeds don't look anything like the plants. But one day after we plant the seeds, the radish leaves will pop right out of the soil and start to grow. More and more will grow. Just like our lettuce did. They'll get bigger and bigger. And, after a while, at the bottom of those leaves this bright red root will grow big and fat down under the ground. Then at the right time, we'll pull up those beautiful green leaves and find a radish on the other end." Emily leaned down and looked into their faces. "And you know what we're going to do then? We're gonna wash it off and eat it!"

A wave of excitement rippled through the children. Several looked at each other and rubbed their stomachs.

She turned to Tony.

He took the seed package. "Watch how Ben pokes only his fingertip in the dirt." He placed his thumb near the end of his index finger and showed the kindergarteners. "Not too deep, just this far. Ready, Ben? That's right."

Emily reached over and handed Ben a tiny seed.

"Now," Tony said, "he's going to drop it in and press the soil around it a little bit. Perfect. Good job, Ben."

Tony stood back. "Hold out your pot Ben, so everybody can see."

Ben held out the pot and the kids bent close.

"Who's ready for Ben to help you plant your seed?

"Me, me, me!" Every hand shot up.

"Looks like you're the star of the day," Tony said to Ben.

Emily stood by the tub of soil.

Tony motioned in her direction. "Y'all get a pot from Miss Emily and fill it with soil. Then take it over and let Ben watch you plant the seed."

Tony turned as Mike from Larry's Restaurant pulled up on his bike.

"All right, Tony! How's it going? Looks like a dirt party from out here."

"Yeah, we're planting seeds. Tomorrow we'll color some pictures and talk about how seedlings grow. Kids will get a little science lesson. You doing okay?"

Again, the idea of somehow discovering that Mike was really his brother slid through Tony's mind. Would people actually change birthdates when they adopted kids? Anything was possible. He should ask Mike's dad.

"Awesome. Just on the way to work," Mike pointed to his wheel. "But I wanted to show you my new sprocket. Check it out. Xposure Infinity."

The golden bike part glittered in the sunset.

"Wow, fancy. Look at that," Tony said.

"Saw it online and just had to have it."

"Your dad okay with the dirt jumping?"

"You kidding," Mike laughed. "He's all about it. Said if he wasn't so old and stiff he'd be out there, too."

Tony glanced up. Mrs. Sanders stood with her hands on her hips in their office doorway.

She motioned him over.

Uh-oh. This must be the little talk she'd been warning me about.

"Gotta go, Mike. Boss's calling."

"Later."

When Tony reached the door of his office, Mrs. Sanders ushered him in. "Have a seat."

He sank into the closest chair. "Yes, ma'am."

"Now, Tony, you know we appreciate your hard work. You and Emily have been doing a good job."

What was she about to do, fire him? "Yes, ma'am."

"Ben, however, is not a paid employee."

Oh. Ben. Whatever she had in mind, it had to be negative.

"He likes to help out. He's not asking to be paid."

"That's not the point."

"But what's the problem?"

"Something we've overlooked. He's got to have a background check if he's going to come in here and work with the children. That's the rule."

Tony sighed. That hardly seemed necessary. "But everybody knows Ben. He's perfectly safe. Harmless."

"Background check."

Tony crossed his arms. "Can't the school just order one?"

"There is a cost."

"It can't be much."

"I've talked to the rector. The school won't pay for a background check on him."

Tony sighed. "And what kind of background would Ben have, anyway? He's lived here all his life. Never been in trouble."

"Rules, Tony."

He threw up his hands with a sigh. "So how much is a background check?" If Tony had to pay for one, he would.

"Last time I checked it was around seventy-five dollars."

"Seventy-five dollars? Are you kidding?" That was about all Tony had.

"And your friend, Mike, can't be coming in and out of the daycare, either. He's not an employee."

Mike hadn't come in, actually. Tony leaned his face into his hands. Oh, man. This was going to be hard.

When he raised his head, Mrs. Sanders had gone.

Now what? How was Tony going to say good-riddance to Ben?

And if he did pay for a background check, how long would it take?

Wednesday at Closing

Mrs. Sanders stood side by side with Brother Ed and gazed across the empty playground. Tony and Emily had already stopped by her office and signed out for the day, but they'd gone back into their little office. If Tony and Emily would just hurry up and fetch their bikes and clear out, she could lock the gate and go. She had things to do.

She spoke. "It's so quiet here without the kids."

After a long pause, the rector cleared his throat. "Our enrollment's jumped twenty-five percent since school started."

Like Sanders hadn't done her job before Tony and his girl-friend came along. They'd breezed in here like a high-powered fan and showed her up. "I knew that."

"Word's out that our daycare is fun."

She wouldn't give him the honor of a compliment for the teens. Of course, they'd made it fun. They were young and hyper. She could have done the same thing if she'd wanted. But she wasn't hired for that.

But compared to them she looked bad.

Out on the playground, Jim, the custodian, strode into view from the right and headed for the breezeway. He carried a ladder and a paper bag.

She changed the subject. "I'm glad Jim stays late on

Wednesdays. That dark breezeway's been a bother all week. Can't see a thing in there at closing time."

"What was it you wanted to talk to me about? I hate to be in a rush, but I need to go over my notes before the service. We have a baby dedication tonight."

"I'm sorry. I didn't mean to hold you up." How was she going to say this? She turned and pushed a strand of her gosh-awful graying hair behind her ear. She needed this man's help.

Friendship was the only way to appeal to him, because as the rector, he might not—no, he *would* not, identify with her predicament. "Listen, Ed. As an old friend, a good friend, I need you to back me up on this."

"The background check?"

"That and more. Are you aware of what Tony's up to?"

"I can only guess. The boy's trying to find his relatives."

"We've got to keep that whole crew of kids away from here. Something's going to bust loose, and I don't want the fallout to hit me in the face. There's too much on the line."

Behind the rector's head, the playground lit up with a new yellow glow as Jim screwed the new bulb into the socket. Tony and Emily emerged from their office door bathed in yellow from their own dim bulb. Their shadows, long and dark, floated over the playground as they rounded the corner of the breezeway to retrieve their bikes.

Jim emerged.

Mrs. Sanders stepped outside. "Excuse me a minute, Jim."

One hand clutched the bag with the dead bulb and his other the ladder. "All fixed, Miss McDavid."

"Shh," she hissed, glancing toward the breezeway and clamping a finger to her lips. But nothing she said could undo Jim's comment. "Don't ever call me that, Jim. Ever."

He parked the ladder on its end and leaned it on the wall. "My mistake. Sorry. I can't help but think of the good old days back at the courthouse."

"Never again, I said."

"Okay, Mrs. Sanders. No need to get mad. I forgot."

She pursed her lips and nodded tightly. "Thank you, Jim. Good job on the light."

After the kids rode away, Mrs. Sanders locked the gate behind them and swished back into the building. Brother Ed had disappeared.

How dare Jim call her that name. And in front of those teenagers. They'd end up putting two and two together. Oh, forget going to church tonight. Her nerves were shot now.

She could only hope Tony and Emily hadn't overheard Jim.

Chapter 5

Wednesday Evening

Darkness covered the surrounding fields and pastures. And on this special hilltop Brilliance positioned himself in the middle of the only lit-up thing for miles—the Nativity scene. He flexed his arms. Beside him, also in plain view and equally invisible to the kids in the approaching Jeep—or the demons—stood his helper Wisdom. Brilliance fixed his gaze on the dark road that wound through the gate below and up the hill and listened for the vehicle.

The angel filled his lungs with the fresh country air. "It's so invigorating to work at full capacity." A fasting saint always imbued him with a special energy. Myrtle, the boy's mother, had undertaken a three-day fast and had already completed her first day.

"She's a special one, willing to give up her food and pray like that," Wisdom said.

Brilliance shook his head. "Few saints will suffer it, though, even for a day."

"No negative comments," Wisdom warned without turning. "Save all that for the enemy. If the saints only knew what they could accomplish by praying and fasting. She's a brave woman."

"Is it bravery? Or is it familiarity with the Word?"

The woman had her Bible open every day. Some saints were blind to its gems.

"The secret is her confidence in what she reads. Her faith. She follows the wise—"

Brilliance held up his hand and whispered. "Smell that?"

Wisdom went silent.

"Sulfur and dead fish. Destroyer's coming close."

A hundred yards away, the Jeep emerged around a dark copse of trees. Its headlights, closer together than on most cars, were easy to identify. The vehicle bounced along the unpaved road, ascending to the solar powered Nativity scene, the one sponsored by The Christian Garden Club of Gaskille. In November, a city-wide fight with scrapping and arguing had marred the old scene and its location in front of the Chamber of Commerce. Finally, one of Gaskille's citizens loaned the group this hill, loaded the figures into her truck, and set the scene up here. A full 180 degrees of the scene bordered I-75. It shone for miles—much farther—and exposed to a much higher number of people than it would have been in front of the Chamber.

"Destroyer travels alone tonight," Brilliance whispered. "See him there on top of the Jeep?"

"Pride goes before a fall."

Brilliance couldn't help but chuckle. "Look at that. He can't even stomach a glimpse of a plastic Nativity scene. Plastic, no less. Can you believe it?"

Destroyer's eyes blinked green, glowing only in the direction of the interstate.

"Classic."

Brilliance and Wisdom, statue-like in the middle of the Nativity, were well camouflaged and would be undetected by Destroyer, even if he did turn their way.

Brilliance snorted. "Wish he would just take a little peek. I'd love to hear him howl." The angel chuckled. Of course, there was an added pleasure of being up here. Seeing as how they'd gained heavenly permission to be seen by drivers along

I-75, these human sightings of the moving angels promised to stir great excitement.

Wisdom lifted a hand. "Enough. Remember, do nothing until the right time."

The Jeep pulled to a stop in front of the Nativity scene. Chad and Electra climbed out. She retrieved the basket and bottled sodas from the back, and Chad grabbed the quilt.

"There's the quilt. Right on cue," Brilliance said. His mouth twitched as he eyed Destroyer's smoky black silhouette behind Electra. He probably hovered back there to hide his eyes from the Nativity scene.

Together, Chad and Electra spread the quilt in front of the Nativity. "This is great lighting," she said. "Who would have ever thought of having a picnic here?"

Chad leaned inside the Jeep and retrieved a few cans of motor oil. "Listen, why don't you set up the picnic while I drain the oil real quick."

"What? Change the oil while we're on a picnic? That's so unromantic."

"It's the lighting. I don't have any at the station. Nothing."

"I don't get it. You're changing your oil on a date?"

"Electra. My boss gave me the oil, and I don't have any daylight to do this. The bays were full. It won't take but a few minutes. Honest."

Brilliance nudged Wisdom. "That was Compassion's assignment, getting the boss to give Chad the oil. I was there."

Wisdom nodded. "It's all coming together."

Electra pouted and dropped the basket onto the quilt. "This is so *not* romantic."

Wisdom turned to Brilliance. "What's so pressing about this oil change?"

"Chad's dad gave him this Jeep. Helped him work on it. Right up until he got sick and died. One of the last things he told the kid was they needed to change the oil. It's been months now, and things keep coming up. Especially a shortage of money. Kid's on a mission to get that oil changed."

"I understand," Wisdom said. "Wise place to park then."

Chad ignored Electra's pouting and climbed under the jeep with a wide, black pan.

Electra opened the basket and flung out the sandwiches, drinks, and napkins. A frown twisted her face.

Oil trickled into the pan under the Jeep and Chad emerged, wiping his hands on a red rag. He still wore his work uniform from Tires-R-Us. "There, see? It only took a minute to get it started. Sorry you had to wait."

"I'm still mad at you."

Chad gave her a peck on the cheek. "I'm sorry. This has to get done."

"On a picnic?"

"I've already explained. My boss gave me the oil. But I didn't have the chance in the daytime."

"Oh, all right." She nestled crisscross on the quilt and slapped a wrapped sandwich in his hand. "I brought Italian subs from McDuff's, Italian all the way. You like 'em?"

"I love them," he said, settling in beside her. "Thanks."

Chad scarfed down half the sandwich with hardly a breath between bites. He guzzled half the bottle of soda she brought and wiped his mouth. "I was so starved. And this is so good. Thank you."

Brilliance leaned over to Wisdom. "He's skipped a few meals lately."

Wisdom raised his eyebrows an inch, and he gave an understanding nod.

"So, Chad," Electra said. "What is it you want to do when you get out of high school?"

"I don't know. Let me finish high school first. I can't be thinking that far ahead." He took another bite.

"Well, I've been thinking," she said.

Chad swigged more soda then gazed past her shoulder at the oil pan underneath the Jeep.

"Are you listening?"

"Yes, I'm hearing every word. What are you thinking?"

"You and I could buy a mud hole," she said. "Charge people to come in and drive around in their trucks. People love mudding. They'll pay big money, you know."

Wisdom shook his head. "The boy can't even get his cap on straight, and she's asking him about four years down the road. What a hoot."

Chad nodded at Electra.

"I can tell you're not listening."

"That's such a long way off—after high school."

"All right. Forget that. Want to hear the latest?"

He held the last bite of his sandwich out in front of him. "Wonderful picnic. Thank you again."

"The latest, I said." She threw her arms wide. "Do you want to hear it?"

Destroyer cha-cha-ed behind her.

Brilliance nudged Wisdom. "Look at Destroyer. He thinks he's got this in the bag."

"Like I said—pride. Won't he be surprised?"

"Well, I'll tell you," Electra said. "Daddy's talking about moving to a job somewhere else."

Brilliance nudged Wisdom. "Best thing that could happen to the boy."

"Out of town, you mean?" Chad said.

The girl wrapped her arms around her knees and put on a sad expression. "I might not be around much longer."

Chad moved closer to her and crooked his arm around her shoulders. With his other hand, he still gripped the final crust of his bread. "Maybe he's just thinking it over. Checking your reaction. Dads do that, you know. Don't let it worry you." He pushed the bread into his mouth and wiped his mouth on his sleeve.

Electra's shoulders shook. She put on a little crying show for Chad and wiped at her tearless eyes. "I'll miss you, Chad."

He patted her shoulder and hugged her tighter, leaning his cheek against hers. "Let's just see what happens. I'm sure he's just trying to see how you react."

"I hope so."

Chad pointed to the Jeep. "I've got to put a cap on that and put the new oil in. Hang on."

"Hey, not that again," Electra whined.

He pulled out the oil pan, fiddled with something underneath, and crawled back out.

With the black oil pan in both hands, he stepped over to Electra. "You probably can't see it in this light. But that's the dirty oil. Black as can be. If it doesn't get changed, the crud in it ruins the engine."

He set the pan down in the grass. "Just don't get it on you. All I have left to do is add clean oil and pour the dirty stuff into a jug so I can dispose of it at work."

Electra crossed her arms and stewed.

A funnel lay on the ground beside the oil cans. Chad

snatched it up and began pouring the fresh oil into the engine. "It'll only take a minute."

She rolled her eyes. "You should just dump the stuff in the grass."

Destroyer's blackness clung to her like a bodysuit. Except for Destroyer's arms on Electra's, Brilliance could hardly see him.

"Get ready," Brilliance said. "He's about to make his move."

Electra took a deep breath and stood. Then she leaned over with a forced grin and placed two hands on the sides of the oil pan. "You know what I think of all this, Chad?"

The boy stared up at her from under the hood, a blank expression on his face.

She heaved the pan back. "I think you're being selfish and—"

Chad's eyes widened as if he realized what she was about to do, and he reached out his hand. "No. Don't!"

"—practical!" she yelled over him and tossed the contents as hard as she could.

The filthy liquid spread through the air like a shiny-fingered hand.

"Go!" Wisdom commanded.

The two angels flashed between the oil and the quilt before the mess could land.

Interception!

The majority of the oil hit the grass beside the Jeep. A small part hit the quilt.

Electra dangled the empty pan between two fingers and dropped it on the grass. "And I hate practical."

The boy's mouth hung open as the ringing words disintegrated into the sounds of the traffic below. "What did you *do*?"

"What do you think I did?"

He opened and shut his mouth in a vain effort to speak. Finally, he pointed at the quilt. "Electra, that's—that's an antique. My great-great-grandmother's. It's probably ruined."

"Who cares about antiques, Chad? They're just a bunch of old junk. And you're totally ignoring me here." She tapped her chest a half-dozen times. "I'm telling you all about my dad, that we might move out of town, and what are you doing? You're changing the oil in your car."

"It's not junk. It's my mother's grandmother's quilt from her mother. She made that with her own hands. It has actual pieces from General Robert E. Lee's old shirt. How could you?"

"How could I? If you're so crazy about your mother, move back in with her. You certainly don't show appreciation for me. I'm the one who set you up at that gas station. Where else could you get free rent?" She crossed her arms.

"Electra, I'm sorry. I explained this to you. And getting me set up at the gas station was your idea."

"Yeah, after you confided in me. After you shared all your angst about your dad dying and so on. I'm trying to be a friend to you. Trying to help you." She balled up her fists and set them on her hips. "You're obviously not seeing my point of view. And you're only thinking of yourself."

Chad ducked back under the hood, wrapped up what he was doing, and came back out. He slammed it shut. "I'm sorry. I'm not trying to ignore you or anything you're saying."

She gathered up her picnic things without a word. Chad folded the quilt and carried it in such a way that the soiled part would not contaminate the rest of it.

"Good boy," Wisdom said.

"I do care about you. But I care about other things, too," Chad said.

Destroyer dis-entangled from Electra's arms and backed away. The demon gaped at the two angels. "Wh–Where'd—?"

Destroyer quickly regained his composure and rearranged his face into a sneer. He pointed a gnarly claw at the quilt and taunted. "Ha ha! Look at that. You mi-issed. You mi-issed," he taunted in a sing-song voice.

Brilliance flicked his sword back and forth across the demon's naked torso.

The filthy creature backed away with his arms around his body then drew up into a scaly ball like a kid's transforming toy.

His stink was obnoxious. Brilliance wrinkled his nose and blew it out of his nose. "Is that what you think, you sick, fetid creature? You think I missed?" The angel pulled his leg back and kicked the demon like a football. The gnarly bump twirled and smoked, screaming all the way to the interstate where sparks flew high as he hit the asphalt three-quarters of a mile away.

"Good riddance for a while," Brilliance said.

"Don't let your guard down, Wisdom said.

Brilliance strode back to the Nativity with Wisdom and traded a high five with him, a little something he'd learned from the saints.

Chad's quilt had just the right-size stain. The joke was on the demon.

Wednesday Night

After the picnic disaster, Chad dropped off Electra off at her friend's. He tossed the empty oil cans in a dump-ster and poured the used oil into the recycling tank behind

Tires-R-Us. Afterward he'd driven down the unlit backstreets of Gaskille and crept along below the speed limit to save gas and avoid drawing attention to himself. Just one traffic stop would have spelled disaster. And if that happened, he'd be back on a school bus again come January.

But so far, so good.

Chad coasted up to his gas-station-living quarters at the north side of town, the living quarters that might not be his for much longer, thanks to Electra's anger. Across the street to the right lay the vacant parking lot of the Greyhound Bus station, asleep for the time being, where it backed up against the Amtrak station, whose multiple rails passed mere yards from Chad's triangular chunk of temporary real estate.

He shifted gears and backed in between the vine-covered chain-link fence and the side of the building until he was out of sight from the street. He turned off the engine and lights and leaned against the warm camo seat covers—ones he and his Dad had picked out together—ones he'd never get rid of. The darkness settled around him.

He fingered the sharp edge of the keys in his hand, the same keys Dad had placed in his hand two years ago. If only Dad were back. He closed his eyes and pictured the man's gentle brown eyes and graying moustache, back when Dad was well. He imagined the sound of his voice as he promised to spend time with Chad, to teach him everything he needed to know about fixing up the old Jeep. He'd made good on it all, especially after his diagnosis. Not a day went by, even in his pain, that he didn't spend time with Chad out in that garage. Right up until he couldn't stand on his feet.

A weight of sorrow pressed against Chad's chest. If only he could see those gnarled hands again, watch them twist and turn and pry in the depths of that oily engine. Or Dad's eyes as he unbent his frame and stood to say, "Okay, son, now you do it."

Seconds ticked by, the intervals between the clicks and clacks of his cooling engine grew longer and longer. The meager warmth of his vehicle had leaked away, and an uncomfortable cold settled around Chad as his thoughts returned to Electra and her tantrum at the picnic.

What a rotten evening this had been. Except for the food, of course. Electra had pouted all the way to her friend's, leaped out slamming the Jeep's door, and pranced away with her picnic basket over one arm and that big red purse over the other.

What had he done to deserve all that? Were all girls so hard to get along with?

Changing his oil was no cardinal sin. And he'd needed the light. Under the circumstances he'd done his best. Electra should have listened to him, tried to understand what obstacles he was forced to work around.

On the other hand, he should have given her a little heads-up on his plan.

Too late for that now.

If she stayed mad, he'd probably have to move out of here.

He frowned and shrugged and glanced toward the back door of the station. Maybe she'd come around. At least Dad would be proud. Chad had saved the Jeep's engine, after all.

What really nagged him, though, was the quilt. That stain would bring Mom to tears.

And it was all Chad's fault. What was wrong with him? Everything he touched these days turned out wrong.

Chad, the loser.

If he'd only taken her quilt home the other day like she'd asked, this wouldn't have happened.

And if he'd given Electra that simple heads-up she might not hate him. Might not have thrown the oil.

Stupid, stupid, stupid.

Chad ran his thumb back and forth across the key. Beyond the fence a truck passed by, its lights sending shadows of vines crawling across the Texaco's wall. Across the street the bus station's loudspeaker blared an announcement. Incoming headlights and a rumble and *pshhhh!* of airbrakes confirmed their new bus's arrival.

Like the bus station, despite Chad's problems, life moved on. With our without him.

The world would not stop. He didn't expect it to. Still, he couldn't stop either. He'd better get a grip on things. Get his act together.

At least figure out how to fix that quilt.

He squinted his eyes in thought. How would someone clean something like that? Definitely not a washing machine. Long ago Mom said something about a washer tearing a quilt to pieces.

The cleaners would cost more than he had—besides, wasn't that about the same as a washing machine?

A bathtub might work. But whose?

With a groan he shoved open the door and climbed out. He stepped around to the back of the Jeep and lifted out the soiled quilt. In the darkness he felt around for the quilt's dirty corner. He'd folded it over to contain the stain and separate it from the clean part.

The bus station's lights lit up the eaves and the broken-down sign next to the wall. But pitch black covered the back wall and yard. He moved cautiously through it. But a few steps in and the stale scent of ash and the crunch and snap of unburned twigs reminded him of Sunday's fire. He stepped wide but still met debris. His shoes were probably covered in soot. Next time, he'd park a little smarter. If there was a next time.

When Electra showed up the other night he'd allowed the blaze to fizzle out. But those distracting eyes of hers—one look at them and he'd forgotten what he was doing.

Next chance he got, he'd finish the burn. Out with the old, in with the new. Hey, after all, a new year was on the way.

But right this minute his bladder was on the way too—on its way to bursting, thanks to that big soda Electra brought.

He reached for the door knob and hesitated. The building's bathroom was around the left side of the building, but what good would it do with no water or electricity?

Best to visit the tree out back, camp-out style. He felt his way across the yard and gave the waist high weeds by the fence a good watering. Anything more serious would have to wait until he got to work the next morning.

Returning to the back door he inserted the key. It fit both locks.

Like a long-held breath waiting to exhale, the building's ancient odors poured over him as the door swung open— odors of gasoline, oil, and tire rubber. And one other fleeting scent—sort of like rotten eggs. He stuffed the key back in his pocket and sniffed again. But try as he might he couldn't isolate the smell. It had slipped away like sand.

He shoved his curiosity aside. Probably just his imagination.

The bolt locks closed again with two quick twists. With

all the bums drifting around the bus station, Chad planned to take no chances.

He turned around and *Whap!*

He clutched his face. "Stupid!" Star-spangled pain shot from his cheekbone and nose.

He'd left the stairs down this morning.

What other idiotic thing was he going to add to his list?

His plan this morning to prowl around the attic before work hadn't seemed so dumb as it did right now. He'd hoped to discover a little history or come across a cool artifact. But the ladder's cracked rungs had nixed his plan, and he'd left them extended and headed off to work instead. Who would've guessed he'd ram his own head into them?

With fingertips pressed against his skull, he staggered down the hall toward his sleeping quarters in the front room. It didn't take long for the sensation in his head to settle into a throb.

Muted street light seeped into the front room through yellowed newspapers. Some long-ago caretaker had stuck them to the plate glass windows and door. Now their edges peeled and curled. No telling how old they were. And they might hold some historic news. In the morning light, he'd check for dates and headings.

A ghostly sheen of dust covered a metal desk in the corner of the room, the only piece of furniture. Wedged behind this was Chad's sleeping bag where he'd crawled out of it this morning. Pushed up next to the cupboards, it was hidden in the narrow space behind the desk where the sprinkling of oil and gunk had appeared to be the lightest.

He pulled the red rag from his pocket and dusted the grimy desk then draped the quilt across it so the soiled end hung low near his bed roll. He hadn't needed to bring it inside, but at least in here Mom's treasure was safe. Maybe a brainstorm would hit while it hung there.

Ha. Maybe he'd wake up and find it clean.

Yeah, in his dreams.

He tossed his keys into the desk's metal drawer and slammed it shut. They slid and clattered against the back. Aching and tired, he lay down in his work clothes and closed his eyes. One by one his vertebrae relaxed.

Down here on the floor, the scent reminded him of the bottom of a shoe. Awesome. The dust of history in his nostrils. Who'd sat in the chair back here, jumping up every time a car drove in to fill customers' gas tanks and wipe their windows? Where were the old attendants now? Dead? His imaginings gathered then disintegrated into wispy blotches and soon into the dark peace of restful sleep.

For a time…

Scrittch! Scrittch! His eyes fluttered, He stirred, mid-dream. But sleep held tight.

Scrittch! Scrittch! Mixed voices.

His eyes flew open. He froze—ears alert.

What was that?

A muffled curse filtered in through the front door, Male. Deep and husky.

Chad sat upright. His heart hammered.

"Just gimme the tool, Joe. Quit foolin' around."

This was no dream. No joke.

"I told you I can't find it." This snappy voice must be Joe.

Another mumbled curse. "I can't pick it without some kinda tool."

"I told ya already. I done looked."

"You bust that glass, and cops'll be all over this place," Husky said. He sounded like the boss.

Chad rolled to his knees. Raised his eyes above the desk.

His mouth dropped open.

A gasp choked his throat.

Electric current shot through his limbs.

Right outside and sharply defined through the newspapers, crouched the shadows of two hulking men—working the doorknob—*his* doorknob.

Their smooth round heads might have been bikers with do-rags. Thick arms bulged like hams. Stout legs ended in stocky boots. Loops dangled from their hips. Chains.

Chad's heart pummeled like a speed-bag. This couldn't be happening.

Only then did he glance toward the left front window. And there loomed a gnarly silhouette—a cluster of motorcycles, maybe three, with high handlebars.

Chad attempted a swallow. But a dry knot plugged his throat.

Ten measly feet and a puny sheet of glass were all that separated him from these dudes. No need to imagine what they could do to him.

He glanced around for an exit. But his eyes returned to the horror in front of him. His limbs, paralyzed, seemed like disembodied posts.

The palm tree's shadow expanded out by the motorcycles. A hand lowered. Probably a smoker. A man, bigger than the other two, stepped away from the trunk and joined the other two by the door. Chad tried another swallow. Failed again.

Three of them?

Oh, gosh. Oh, man. If they came in here—and they'd be inside any second—he had to go.

He forced himself out from behind the desk, scrambled down the hall, and headed toward the back door. *Whap!* His head snapped back. Stars speckled his vision. He reeled. Grabbed the ladder. Now he had two concussions. A voice screamed inside him. *Never mind. Go up!* He grabbed for the highest rung and scrambled toward the attic like a monkey. Never mind the wood-rot. No time for door locks.

Up, up! Snap! "Oof!" The rung punched through. He dangled, panting. Caught by his elbow. He squirmed back up and got past the next rung. Kept going. Made it to the top. Threw himself inside. Let out a breath. *Whew!*

A broken rung clattered to the floor.

Safe. Chad backed away from the attic's opening. The pulse in his ears hammered as he closed his eyes—and fought to quiet his breath. After a few seconds, he dared move to the edge and peer back down. Nothing yet. Nobody. He leaned back on his hands. *Crunch.* A mass like hairy shredded wheat crumbled beneath his fingers. He shuddered and wiped the hand against his pants.

A rattle and squeak of the door downstairs.

Light poured in along with large shadows, very large shadows, that extended down the hall.

He blew out a long slow breath.

Just in time.

Vapor-like, the angels Brilliance and his helper Radiance slipped in through the back wall of the gas station.

The demons Murdo, Sulfur, and Gloom stumbled in too—through the front door. They trailed the heels of the three biker-Goliaths and dragged along their fumes of cigarette smoke, liquor, and body odor.

Brilliance planted his feet apart and blocked the area near the back door.

So far, Murdo hadn't noticed the two angels.

Murdo's demon-companions hunkered down in the narrow hallway. Idiots. No need to try to hide. These bikers weren't able to detect demons—or angels.

The front door latched behind them, and Murdo glanced around the station. His eyes landed on Brilliance and company by the stairs. He jerked back with a snarl.

Brilliance grinned. "Surprise, surprise."

The demon's eyes flared red. He whirled around and faced the front window. He couldn't stand the sight of the angels. "I'll kill you," he muttered over his shoulder.

Brilliance flashed his sword. He had authority here. Not the demons. Its reflection flickered across the newspaper on the windows, and Murdo shuddered. Brilliance chuckled. *Coward.*

Husky the biker stood by the desk. The boy's quilt dangled from his two meaty fingers. "Lookie here, what some old granny left us. Hoo ha." With a twist of the wrist, he spread it across the floor in front of the window and dropped his backpack onto its corner. Still in his boots, he eased down beside it. Too chunky to sit cross-legged, the biker pulled out a liquor bottle and leaned against the front wall with his legs extended. "Doggone," he said, slapping his thigh with a wide grin. "If I ain't turned into a purdy little girl scout."

His buddies howled and tossed down their backpacks and playing cards.

Biker-Joe eyed the boy's sleeping bag behind the desk. "Well, well, you ain't the only smart one, girlie," he said. He grabbed the bag and dragged it over beside the quilt. "Ya'll ain't got nothin' over us boy scouts." Another round of laughter.

Soon poker chips and wads of cash passed from hand to hand. Bottles tipped higher and higher. Hours passed.

Murdo tossed a smirk over his shoulder to Brilliance.

After a while, Joe's slurred syllables reached out to the mostly silent Cigarette Man. "Been wondering. That dude back in Daytona...we break his neck or not? I didn't see him move none after we threwed him down them stairs."

"Not too sure." Cigarette Man said, stretching out, sleep in his red-rimmed eyes. "Mighta been dead. Looked to me like he was anyways. And I seen a few."

"You think...?"

"Ain't no way those dumb cops gonna find us."

"You sure?"

"Not with all them other bikers in town."

Joe shrugged.

"Think of Bike Week as a Merry Christmas just for us."

Joe dealt the cards again, but before he could finish the play, he dozed off. The cards trickled from his grip. Cigarette Man, at his feet, lay snoring with his mouth open. His drool puddled on the bedroll.

After an hour, Husky woke with a snort. "Huh? What's all the racket?" He struggled to his feet and lunged down the hall. "Hey, I need to use the head." He ran his hand along the wall, locating and flipping the light switch up and down. Ain't no lights, neither," he said. "Man, I gotta go."

He turned left and with his arms extended, blindly headed for the attic stairs.

Brilliance lloosened the ladder's screws and stepped back. Husky tripped against the lowest rung, plunging head-first between the rails. The fragile rungs popped and snapped as if they were pretzels. He landed, face-first against the floor with his knees across the second rung. Try as he might he couldn't raise himself. He rolled to the right and bellowed, "Joe, Joe. Wake up and help me, boy. Get me out of this. Hurry. I'm about to wet myself."

Joe rolled over and crawled off the bedroll. "A-ight. Cool yer jets." He stood, and like the leaning tower in Italy, pitched himself in Husky's direction. Halfway down the hall, he grabbed the wall. Then *Urrp!* The contents of his stomach erupted, splattering across the floor and the walls. He swiped at his mouth. "Don't nobody slip in that."

Husky squirmed. "Shut up and come help me."

While his buddy jerked the rotten rails apart, Husky cursed. "Don't break my neck, you fool."

Joe dropped a board on the floor and helped him up. "Now I gotta go, too."

"Ain't no *fass-silities* in this place."

Radiance renewed his stance in front of the back door, blocking their view.

Husky pointed in that direction. "Coulda sworn I seen a door back there."

"Where?"

"Forget it. They's some bushes out front."

Joe followed him toward the front door. "A-ight."

The door wobbled half-shut behind Husky, where Joe's forehead smacked into it with a thud. He grabbed his head with both hands. "Watch what yer doin', bub."

They stood in the weeds and did their business. A foot away, Brilliance, who'd slipped through the wall, blocked their view of the Jeep.

Back inside, it was only a matter of minutes before their snores again filled the station.

Defeated for the time being, Murdo skulked against the front wall.

Brilliance would take nothing for granted, though. He and Radiance had thwarted Murdo's mission to kill Chad tonight, but their job to protect him wasn't over. Brilliance signaled to Radiance, and they took their places at the foot of the attic.

Chad still had to get free of this place in the morning.

The angels kept watch as the hours passed. They'd surely seem much longer for Chad than for them. Time was a continuum for the angels, marked by so many important historic events, the creation, the expulsion of the evil one, the Son's birth on Earth, His crucifixion.

And the most thrilling event was soon to come, though none of them knew the day or hour. The return of the Son. And the end of the age.

At this thought, Brilliance knelt down and worshipped. Radiance joined him. "All hail, Holy One. Thank You for letting us serve You. Blessed is Your Name, Jesus, Holy Son of the Most High God."

By the time they finished, no trace of the two hallway demons remained.

Up front, they found Murdo doubled over by the windows and clutching his midsection. "No, no, no!"

All demons hated the praise. Convulsing violently, he toppled over and the top of his ugly head hit the floor. The essence of rotten eggs leaked from his putrid flesh and stunk up the room even more than before.

Brilliance made a face and waved the smell away with his sword.

"I'll kill you," Murdo said, looking up with blood-colored eyes.

Brilliance chuckled and stretched tall, back on duty. He and Radiance grinned at Murdo, and twisted their glittering swords left and right, shooting sparks of light around the room. Murdo heaved and balled up, covering his head and hiding his eyes.

Radiance traded a smile with Brilliance, and every time Murdo tried to peek, they flashed him again. It went on all night long.

Dawn finally broke, its dusty rays cutting through the station's high back windows and illuminating the wooden ceiling.

Time for Chad to get to work. The boy needed his job.

Brilliance reached through the ceiling and gave the boy a nudge. Chad would have to walk to work today or fall into Murdo's trap.

Chapter 6

Thursday Morning

After fitful rounds of dozing and waking, Chad had eventually dropped off to sleep. He woke with a start, the sense of danger still immediate. He placed his palms on the plywood floor, grateful for it and this hiding place. After last night, when the biker wrecked his stairs, his main worries devolved into not falling through the hatch or snoring too loud. And thanks to the bikers' drunken state, he'd made it. But right now, he had to get out of here. And get to work.

He crawled to the opening and peered below. Forgotten crumbs of last night's dried animal rained down in front of his knee. They landed on the scattered wood below. Loud snores floated in from the other room.

If these guys were as drunk as they sounded last night, they were probably passed out cold from all the liquor. He'd heard that drunks slept hard the morning after. If Chad stayed quiet, he could sneak out the back door.

His keys, though.

They were still in the desk. And whether the bikers had found them or not was anybody's guess. So far, they'd mentioned nothing about keys.

Chad placed his hands on the opposite side of the opening. He swung out and dangled, debating where to best touch down.

No matter how he landed—left, right, or any direction—he'd have to dodge the debris and land without a sound. If he missed, he'd better make a run for it because the pile of wood would make a lot of noise.

With his toes aimed at a wide place between two broken boards, he held his breath and let go.

His shoes landed perfectly, like cats' feet, between the boards, almost like hands had guided him.

He tiptoed through the rubble and checked down the hall. Pinching his nose he exhaled through his mouth. *Gross.* The wall and floor were covered in puke.

He placed one foot in the hall. The snoring was louder down here. It should be pretty easy to get in there and get those keys.

With his eyes narrowed he squinted into the dim front room at the two pairs of feet. Not good. There had to be more in there.

Nevermind. This was a dumb idea. He turned.

The feet weren't moving, though.

And he needed those keys. If Chad didn't get down to Tires-R-Us, they'd fire him.

The bikers were knocked out cold. They'd never hear it if he eased the desk open and lifted out the keys. Chad could be very quiet when he wanted to.

But then, the desk was metal, unpredictable. It might squeak. Too much of a risk.

A loud snort filled the front room. Chad froze.

Forget it.

A new kind of noise filled the space behind him. The *pshhh* of an arriving bus. And way too loud. He turned. Light shined in between the back door and doorframe—not there a minute ago. How…?

Time was ticking. Maybe he should walk to work. He

could. If he left this minute. It wasn't all that far to Tires-R-Us. He could jog there if he needed to. Whatever he decided, he needed to get a move on.

As he stepped through the debris that feeling returned, the sense of being helped along—like a touch on his back—almost a push. He stepped into the sunlight and closed the door quietly behind him.

Last night was a night he'd never forget.

He shook his head and as he strode by his vehicle, brushed the dew off the taped-up tail light and made a mental note to get it fixed soon. The last thing he needed was the cops stopping him.

What he hated more, though, was leaving the Jeep behind with those bikers in there.

He cupped his fingers and dragged the dew off its hood as he passed. Out on the sidewalk he flicked his hand and took off walking. Hopefully, the bikers would clear out soon. And hopefully before he came back to the station.

"Lord, please don't let them notice my Jeep or the stuff inside."

And then there was the quilt.

Would they roll it up and haul it off?

Thursday at Lunch

Tony knocked on the doorframe of Brother Ed's office.

Brother Ed looked up from the papers on his desk.

"Could I ask you something?"

"My door is always open, Tony."

The man laid his pen down as Tony stepped inside. "It has to do with Ben."

"The background check?"

"Yes, sir." Tony creased the bills in his pocket. He'd only go through with this if he had to. "Is there any way we could get around having to do the background check? Ben's absolutely no threat, and everybody knows that."

"You have to—" A rustle at the door drew Brother Ed's attention.

Tony turned. There stood Mrs. Sanders, in her long gray dress and matching hair, leaning against the doorframe. Where'd she come from? She was the last person he wanted to bump into right now. And he'd caught that shake of her head as she signaled her *No* to Brother Ed. Something was going on. She stopped, touching her chin to cover her actions. Tony'd seen it, though. Couldn't he even get a private word with the rector?

He offered a polite smile and eased closer to Brother Ed's desk. This was between the two of them, and the rector might actually see things his way.

In low tones, he hoped Mrs. Sanders couldn't hear, he pressed on. "Ben needs to be here as much as these kids need him."

Brother Ed ignored Mrs. Sanders and returned his gaze to Tony. "You have to understand. We're bound by the law. Volunteers have to have clearance. No matter how nice they are."

"But is there any way the church or daycare could pay for it?" Ben certainly couldn't afford it himself.

Mrs. Sanders barged right on in and swung around by Brother Ed's desk to face Tony. "Tony, I already answered that for you. So why are you in here going over my head, trying to get your own way? That's not right."

"I—"

"It's all right, Mrs. Sanders," Brother Ed said. "He's just trying to help Ben. I agree. Ben needs the kids. The kids need Ben."

Mrs. Sanders' mouth dropped open. She raised her chin and skulked out of the office. Tony watched until the sound of her footsteps diminished down the hall. He shut the door and pulled a wad of bills from his pocket. "Take this, then." He laid the seventy-five dollars on Brother Ed's desk. "Emily and I've been saving up for something, but we can do without it. We've talked it over and agreed to pay for Ben's background check."

Brother Ed leaned back in his chair without touching the money. "This came out of your pocket?"

"And Emily's."

"All right, then," Brother Ed said, straightening the bills and sliding them toward his side of the desk like a deck of cards. "I'll see to it that Ben gets his background check."

At least Brother Ed had a heart.

Tony could do nothing about Mrs. Sanders' disapproval. It didn't matter to him, though. Ben was more important.

Tony paused with his hand on the doorknob. "Just to let you know, Emily's covering me for lunch. I have to run to the courthouse and tend to some personal business."

He scrambled away before the rector or Mrs. Sanders could change his plans.

Mrs. Sanders burst from her office. *Tony was headed for the courthouse?* She marched through the rector's door again and thumped her fists down on her hips. She glared down at the rector. "You're letting him go there? The courthouse!"

Unbelievable. What if Tony went looking for answers he shouldn't see? "Real families in this town are going to hate me. Maybe even sue me. I'll be ruined for the rest of my life."

Brother Ed waved it away as if it were nothing. "No, they won't."

"Please, Ed, you can't do this to me."

"Yes, I can. And I did."

"But they'll—"

"It's not that big of a deal. You're making too much of it."

"Easy for you to say. It's my guilty conscience, not yours."

"Tony's free to do what he wants on his lunch hour."

"But—"

"Look. He's a free citizen, he can go to the courthouse, Mrs. Sanders. Anytime he wants."

She practically wailed. "Everybody will—"

The rector raised his palms as if to say, "It's out of my control."

She grumbled her way back into her office and dropped into her swivel chair.

No. No. No.

Call. She could do that. *Call the courthouse.*

She snatched up the phone and punched in the familiar number. The one that long ago had been her work number. Back when she was Miss McDavid. Now someone else warmed the seat cushion at her old desk. Her ex-sister-in-law. Man, she hated dealing with Mildred Sanders. But she had to. This phone call would save her neck.

If Mildred cooperated. Which she wasn't known to do.

Several rings later, Mildred picked up. "County Adoption Services, how may I help you?"

"I need you to do me a favor, Mildred. Really fast. Can

you go out to lunch right now? Right this minute? Close the office for just as long as you can. Drag it out. The whole lunch hour. I'll call you tonight and explain. Please."

"Well I'm fine, thank you, Mrs. Sanders." Sarcasm dripped from Mildred's voice Just like the last time and the time before that. Mildred was no better than her. She just thought she was. "Long time no speak. And how are you today, honey?"

She imagined Mildred smacking her gum and twirling her pencil in her polished fingers. "I'm so sorry, Mildred." There was no time to put up with this woman's antics today. "It's just a little emergency, and I didn't mean to be rude. Can you help me? Please, please, please. I'll owe you a lunch. At Larry's or anywhere you like."

"Okaaay..." Mildred said. "So what do you need again, hon?"

"Just—just go out a while. I'll explain when there's more time."

"Okaaay..." Mildred would agree. For a lunch at Larry's, of course.

After the line went dead again, Mrs. Sanders leaned back in her chair with a sigh. At least she'd bought herself some time. Things were closing in, though. And these families would find out what a bumbling jerk she had been.

Chad stuffed his red rag in his pocket and jogged away from Tires-R-Us toward his temporary gas-station home. Thirty minutes for lunch was not much if you had to run across town and back.

But he needed to reclaim his Jeep. Food first, though, to quiet his raging stomach. He'd already skipped breakfast today.

He darted across Burger King's parking lot and plunged

inside. The only one in line he ordered two burgers from the budget menu and drummed his fingers on the counter as he waited. The food had little variety, but it kept him alive.

"Thank you," he said to the cashier and grabbed the bag and small cup for water. He unwrapped a burger as the cup filled under the spout. Despite strange looks from the workers—he knew all their faces—he stood right there and lit into his meal. Delicious. He grabbed a napkin, wiped his mouth and took out the second burger. There was no time to waste. Every second counted.

On the way out he tossed all the trash, polished off the second burger, and gulped down the water before he even left the parking lot. Then he took off jogging. Maybe by now the bikers had left his place.

His imagination roamed to what might have happened to Mom's quilt, but he quickly pushed it aside. He couldn't afford those kinds of thoughts.

His shoes beat a rhythm on the sidewalk. Houses, bushes, and trees zipped by. "Lord, please, please, please," he begged, "let my stuff be safe. Please. You know what it means to me. And Mom's quilt. You know what it means to her."

A cramp stabbed below his ribs, and he powered down a little. How far was it to his place, anyway? He'd never checked. Was it a mile? More likely two. Or three.

He limped for a block or two until the pain in his side eased, then he pressed on.

Close to home it returned, and he paused again, panting and bending low to catch his breath. Boy, did that stitch hurt. He should get in shape. Or something. Not run after eating. Or eat more often. All of it. Or quit leaving his Jeep where bikers could get hold of it.

What if those bikers found his keys? It stood to reason they'd search the desk. What if they left and locked them inside?

Nah, bikers wouldn't bother to lock up.

"One more favor, Lord, please. Don't let the door be hanging open." Even if the bikers were gone, the hoboes could come in and rifle his stuff.

And what about his Jeep? He picked up his pace.

Within minutes he rounded the corner, and there, on a pole between two ancient sabal palms, rose the familiar blue Greyhound bus sign with its white racing dog. And across the street, barely visible above his vine-covered fence still sat the sun-baked roof of his Jeep.

He let out a slow breath, slipped around behind the overgrown span of chain-link fence, and with trembling hands yanked open the vehicle's back end. *Yes!* His box was still there. He checked under its lid. The bikers hadn't found it. "Thank you, God. Thank You."

Clutching his ribs, he crossed the gravel to the back door of the building and turned the knob. Open. *Another miracle.* He shoved it wide and stepped in.

But he froze. Mid-doorway. Muted voices. They were still in there somewhere. He backed out and closed the door, his heart battering his chest like a punching bag. *Idiot.* Why hadn't he thought of that? He'd never even checked for motorcycles out front.

He hoped they hadn't noticed the open door.

Glancing left and right Chad crept past the sidewalk and crossed the street. Sneaky behavior was not his style. But there were things he had to know. And quick. He'd act like a pedestrian and cross the tracks out front.

If motorcycles were there, he'd beat it back to work. If that wasn't them in there, he'd grab his stuff.

And he'd still be late. *Late!* He was already on the boss's *"you're walkin' a thin line"* list.

Of all the employers in the world, Chad's boss was no one you wanted to mess around with. He frequently reminded the guys that the other kids in town would love to have their jobs. He cut no one any slack. And Electra had already called Chad at work. On the company number. Several times.

He passed the Greyhound sign, walked another few yards across the tracks and turned back to catch a glimpse of the Texaco.

The door hung open and sure enough, three giant men in do-rags and leather vests stood talking and smoking next to their motorcycles.

If any of them had them had turned and glanced back, they would have seen straight through the station to the back door. And seen him burst in just now. But at the moment they weren't acting disturbed in any way.

Chad let out a sigh. He eyed the motorcycles and shook his head. *Man, that was close.* A few more steps inside that station, and he'd be dead meat right now.

He turned and re-crossed the tracks. Forget the Jeep. Now Chad would never get back to work on time.

Better to call in with a problem than to show up late and get fired.

He squeezed the spot in his side again and circled back to the Greyhound station. Maybe they'd let him use their phone.

Thursday After Lunch

Tony parked his bike in the daycare's breezeway. He kicked down the stand and ambled over to the playground. A CD player on the sidewalk played a tinny version of *Deck the Halls.* Red and green tablecloths fluttered over picnic tables, and Emily poured red punch into Christmas cups. Mrs. Sanders arranged Oreos on a platter. Clustering near the table, kids jostled against each other as they waited to be called. Everything seemed to be going along as usual at the daycare, but Tony was getting nowhere with his search. Nothing was turning out right. Especially at the courthouse.

"Hey," Emily waved. "Tony. Look. Jimmy's mother dropped off some treats."

Mrs. Sanders eyed him as if he were late, which he wasn't. She tossed her empty cookie bag in the trash and hustled away. "I'll be in my office, guys. Let me know if you need any more help."

"Okay, everyone, line up on this end and no pushing," Emily said.

Emily offered Tony some punch. "Any luck at the courthouse? You look like you struck out."

He shook his head. "It's Christmas break. And *closed for lunch,*" he said, making quotation marks in the air.

Emily frowned. "I'm sorry. It's going to work out, though. I just know it."

She plopped a large container of hand sanitizer on the end of the table for the kids. "Listen up, everyone. Clean your hands first. Then take a napkin, two cookies, and a cup. In that order." She made them repeat the directions to her.

Tony chugged his own drink and crumpled the cup, pitching it at the trashcan. "Easy, guys," he said, stepping between two shoving boys. He guided them toward the back of the line.

Emily turned his way. "The courthouse is closed?"

He threw up his hands. "Might as well be. The woman in adoption records is on vacation. Her helper was at lunch. The sign said to come back later." He threw up his hands. "There's no *later* for me. I'm stuck here. And we close at six.

"I should have taken an early lunch. Or gone after it was over."

Emily offered a sympathetic shake of her head. "How could you know? We'll just have to pray."

"At this rate, I'll be a hundred years old before I find my twin. I want to find him now." Emily raised a brow. "Or her."

Sure. Maybe. But he was not going to claim that Electra girl. Even if it was her.

Thursday After Work

For the second time today, Chad counted out his change and paid for bargain food at the Burger King counter. Good thing payday came tomorrow. One thing he'd learned about money, it slid through his fingers like sand. And he wasn't even wasting it. Well, aside from Electra's ice cream.

That didn't count, though. It was for her, a romantic expenditure and well worth the price for his beautiful Barbie.

"Two burgers, please. And a courtesy cup for water."

He took the order outside and, once again, ate on the go as he headed west. The trees ahead of him were black silhouettes against the setting sun. No running this time. Thank goodness for this warmer weather.

And, thank goodness, the boss hadn't fired him. The call from the bus station had helped, and the man only docked him for ten minutes.

As Chad devoured his food the possibilities of what he might find at the gas station played through his mind. The image of a vandalized Jeep struck first, and he quickened his steps. Took a bigger bite. Wiped the back of his hand across his mouth. Then the possibility of a missing box. And a missing quilt.

He stopped long enough to chug down his water, swallow that last bite, crush his trash and stuff it into his pockets. Even as he swiped his mouth he took off running toward the station. The crick in his side reappeared like a nightmare, but he plowed on, leaning into it, clutching and limping.

Across from the bus station, the roof of his Jeep appeared. But was it still okay?

This time, instead of being stupid, he passed the building first. He crossed the tracks like a pedestrian, then cut his eyes back toward the building. No motorcycles. The door was shut. He crossed back over the tracks and headed for the Jeep in back.

Leaning close to the vehicle's windows he cupped his hands and peered inside. Seemed okay. He opened up the back end and checked for the box. *Yes!* How had they overlooked this vehicle right in front of their noses?

He crossed the backyard and twisted the back doorknob. Unlocked, just like before.

Shoving it open, he stepped across the broken stairs and the dried puke and moved down the hall.

Whiskey bottles and stray poker chips cluttered the room. And there behind the desk lay his quilt and sleeping bag— two wadded piles. He stepped across them and yanked open the metal desk drawer. His keys slid to the front. "Thank You, God! Thank You."

How'd they miss them? If he'd been one of those bikers, he'd have searched the desk first. Looked for old forgotten money.

He glanced back at the quilt and bedroll. But instead of carrying them to the Jeep he shook them out and rearranged them. Might as well. The sun had set, and it wouldn't be long before he'd be back to hit the hay.

What were the odds the bikers would return? Probably slim to none.

At Dark

Three blocks from his abandoned gas-station home, Chad pulled the Jeep into a parking space in a quiet neighborhood near Tuscawilla Pond. A circle of streetlight brightened the corner in front of him. Most of the craftsman-style homes lining these streets displayed large front porches and sat off the ground on high brick pillars. Some had lattice-covered crawlspaces underneath. But others were completely open, and if one bent low enough they could see clear through to the backyards. Such was the building two lots back. It wasn't a home, the windows were black, and the sign out front said Veterans Outpost—meaning right now nobody was there.

The other day on the way to work Chad spotted a water hose in back—perfect for a cleanup after dark. And Chad was desperate for a shower.

But he'd have to be careful.

He sniffed an armpit and blew air out of his mouth. *Gag a maggot.* No more of this going without a bath. He wasn't sure why she hadn't already, but any day now, Electra would complain. Or she'd just disappear.

He pushed open the Jeep's front door and stepped out with his bar of Ivory soap he'd bought at the five and dime, the cheapest soap he could find that didn't smell like flowers. In his other hand, he held a wadded shirt and clean undershorts.

The door clicked shut behind him.

Here goes nothing.

Just to be careful, he strode the opposite direction of the VO, down the right side of the sidewalk and passed the corner house where matching Christmas trees twinkled inside its front windows. Behind the building he turned left. The aroma of frying pork chops and who-knows-what-else filled the crisp air and brought up the saliva in his mouth. Just like home. He missed Mom's cooking. And this neighborhood food sure smelled better than budget burgers.

Brittle grass, dead from an earlier frost, crunched underfoot. Nothing else stirred but the *shwww* of an occasional car along the boulevard two blocks away. Not even a dog. He held still, searched for any movement then eased toward the darkened back yard of the VO. Five steps and a railing led up to a landing and plain back door.

A coiled hose hung from a spigot on the left—the same hose he'd noticed the other day. A covered galvanized trashcan sat next to it.

Most homes had a hose, sure. But not every place was safe. He'd heard the vibrating pipes inside his own home whenever Mom ran the sprinklers outside.

With the VO closed tonight, though, he'd be fine.

He laid the soap and clean clothing up on the steps and knotted the hose up high on the rail so the stream would point down toward him. Good thing it was dark back here.

Trees and overgrown hedges blocked the view from the windows next door. Those in the distance didn't matter.

Off came his old clothes. He wrinkled his nose, lifted the lid on the trashcan, and dropped in his underwear. *Good riddance.* He chuckled and turned on the water. Imagine the person's face when they found that underwear in there.

He glanced at the lid and shrugged as he turned the faucet. Maybe he should bury it.

The hose's cold water made him gasp, but he held his breath and stayed the course, grabbing the soap and lathering his hair.

The water, though brisk, was still warmer than the outside air. Amazing. He considered this as he scrubbed the rest of his body. Cleaning up was a thing he really missed about home, the hot running water, the fresh towels, the clean clothes. But tonight he'd have to put his dirty jeans back on until he could rummage through the Jeep and find some more in the daylight tomorrow. If he'd been smart and planned ahead, he'd have taken care of it this afternoon.

He finished up, set the soap on the steps, and closed his eyes, allowing the water to pour over his head, his shoulders, and his body. This was the best he'd felt for days. What a great location to clean up. He'd make sure to come again.

A dog barked in the distance. Hopefully indoors. Or tied up. He didn't need to be seen fleeing naked through the neighborhood.

The sound of a car's engine and strong white light across his lower legs jerked him to his senses. He froze.

Headlights!

He didn't dare move, or the driver would spot him. The same way he'd spotted the dangling hose the other day. Only his eyes moved as he searched the dark perimeter for a place to hide.

Wait, the water spigot. He reached around and turned it off.

A car door slammed. Then a second one. Faint voices. Conversation, shuffling. His legs lost their brilliance as the vehicle's headlights turned off.

The voices out front indicated no sign of alarm.

Good.

Within seconds, lights glowed from inside the building. The whole building. Must be one big room in there. They blazed through the naked windows and onto the backyard grass. He was glad to be hidden within the wedge of darkness beside the building. With wet arms he snatched up his clothes and clean underwear and trotted to safety behind the border of tall unkempt hedges. Shivering, he dried with the dirty shirt and felt his way back into the other garments. At least he was clean.

He slung the damp shirt across his shoulder, took few steps toward the Jeep and stopped.

The soap. He backtracked and parted the hedges. Its small white form gleamed bright and white at the top of the steps— and the hose—there it was knotted around the rail. If he didn't go back his location would be busted.

The two lone figures moved around inside the building dragging furniture, talking, and straightening for what must be some kind of meeting coming up.

It's now or never.

He sprinted through the shadows, untied and dropped the hose in the grass, grabbed the soap, and slipped back into the trees. With a pounding heart he cut through the hedges again, and strode back to the sidewalk, as if nothing had happened.

Back at the Jeep, he reached for the handle.

What about the dirty underwear in the bottom of the trash can? Nah, forget it.

He swung the door wide and hopped in.

Thursday Night

Across from the daycare, Chad turned off the motor and rested his elbow out the open window. An acorn dropped out of the tree above and pinged his hood. Electra, in the passenger seat, immersed herself in the licking and nibbling of her double vanilla cherry cone from Baskin-Robbins. But right now, Chad's mind focused on the Jeep and where he ought to park it from now on. And for the first time during the break it centered on that looming January 4th algebra test.

A fall-like breeze passed through the Jeep. He breathed deep and let it out, thankful to be right here, right now. This atmosphere was worlds apart from the desolate silence of his old gas station, or even the bustling boulevard two blocks over—and just the peace he needed right now—a haven apart from bikers or nutcases behind the bus station. The next time his Jeep might not be so lucky.

He clamped his lips together and nodded. Starting tonight, the Jeep would stay here, and he'd walk to the station.

Dead leaves twirled across the asphalt in front of him, but his gaze passed beyond to the other side of the street where six abandoned swings hung motionless under the faint glow of the streetlights. The place Electra hated. With the people Electra hated—that kid from algebra class and his girlfriend.

Chad wondered if the guy who worked there even

recognized him. Someone like him would probably study the whole Christmas break.

Algebra wasn't Chad's best subject. Nothing was these days. And he hadn't even touched his own book.

He let out a sigh. If he didn't do something fast, he'd flunk.

A figure with a familiar lumping gait rounded the street corner on his left. The big kid, Ben. Chad watched as he ambled up to the fence, eyed the empty playground and dark windows, and turned away with a dejected slump.

Probably lonely. Out looking for someone to play with.

Inside the Jeep, Brilliance squeezed himself into the space between Electra and Chad. Destroyer, who'd followed along beside Electra this whole day long, was going to get nowhere with Chad—not on his watch.

These demons had such basic instructions—kill, steal, and destroy. They were always switching out and trying to catch the humans off-guard.

Well, it wasn't going to happen. Chad had too much prayer cover.

The blood of Jesus was this kid's protection.

Destroyer stepped in through the Jeep's passenger window. He embraced Electra from behind, then, with a giggle, squirmed and slipped into her skin as smooth as a foot in a stocking.

Brilliance shook his head. Unprotected humans like her saddened him, and he could do nothing for this one right now. If only she had a mother or a friend to pray for her. Destroyer could do what he liked with Electra. The pathetic girl had no backup.

The demon glanced at Brilliance. He popped his hand out of her skin with a rude gesture.

Brilliance drew back his fist. "Keep it light, or I'll treat you to some of this."

The demon dropped his grin and clammed up, tucking the hand back inside the girl's.

Chad stared out the Jeep's window. His other concern was that quilt. He needed to get it back home, but that spot—it would crush Mom. He had to get it out. At least the bikers had left it unharmed.

Electra fluffed her napkin against Chad's ear to get his attention. "Why, Chad? Why are you always parking under this stupid tree?" She caught a drip with her finger then raised it to her lips. "Mmm. This was so delish. You should have gotten one for yourself."

"Not today."

"So, what's on your mind?" she said. "What can we talk about?"

Across the street, Ben had passed under streetlights and disappeared around the corner again.

"Stop ignoring me, Chad. Let's talk."

What wasn't on his mind? The possibility of getting stopped. Of getting some kind of ticket. A situation that would force him to ride the bus again. He shrugged. "My Jeep needs a new tail light."

She licked her cone. "Really?"

"My left one's got red tape over it, and I'd like to get it fixed soon. Make it look nice. I could get stopped for that."

"Why don't we talk about what you hate?"

He frowned. "Who'd want to talk about that?"

"Me first, then," she said. "I hate parking under this tree."

"There's a reason for parking here."

"And that dufus over there, the one that walked by a minute ago? I hate him and those religious do-gooders that work over at that playground. I despise them all."

That was nothing new. Electra had a pretty big hate list. He'd never just sat around and thought up things to hate. He took a deep breath. "Ranch dressing. I guess I hate that."

"You hate ranches?"

"I didn't say that." Ranches had nothing to do with ranch dressing. But if she wanted to stretch the point. "I guess."

"You hate like stupid old cowboy hats and boots? All that?"

He shrugged. "Maybe." It wasn't something he'd ever considered. But if she didn't like it—neither would he.

"See, you've come up with your own stuff to hate. That wasn't so hard, was it?"

"Okay, I guess I hate the ranch style, too. Cowboys, boots."

She smirked and crunched a bite off her cone. "Your mom's house is ranch style."

"How'd you come up with that? It doesn't look like a cowboy house. It's plain. Ordinary."

"I agree. Ranch is totally boring. And like you said, your mom's place is the pits. She could do better for herself. I'm glad you had the sense to move out."

"Wait. I didn't say all that. You're twisting my words around." And the gas station place was clearly worse, not better than his home.

"No, I'm just sticking up for you And I hate how she made you study and turn off the TV. And practice. That's so not fair."

Come to think about it, Mom was pretty strict. He'd forgotten about that. "Yeah, speaking of that, I should start studying for that algebra exam right after Christmas."

She threw her wadded napkin at his head. It hit the window. "Are you kidding? Don't you hate that, too? Studying over Christmas break?" She turned her whole body, suddenly animated. "Here's what you should do. You and everybody in class should get together and flunk that test. Show the teacher how unfair he's being. Make a statement."

He gaped at her. "Nobody would go for that."

"And your mom? She's way too—" Electra squinted and leveled her index finger at him "—religious."

Words failed him as Electra's pupils widened into scary deep pits and she stared him down like an alien. The blue had disappeared.

He shuddered and turned away, back to his battered steering wheel. Maybe it was just a trick of the darkness—or his imagination. People's eyes and faces couldn't change like that. Pupils didn't dilate like that. It had to be the darkness—the distance of the streetlights.

"Let's change the subject," he said.

Electra poked the last of her cone in her mouth and turned the mirror down to dab at her lips. She posed and smiled as if for a selfie.

"Okay, tell me. What do you like?" she said, with her gaze still riveted on her reflection. She fluttered her eyelashes then turned to him. Her eyes seemed normal now. It had to have been his imagination.

"I like you."

"That's what I wanted to hear."

She smiled and pooched her lips out like all the other

girls did in their selfies these days. "*Mwah.* I like you, too."

He leaned over as if to kiss her, but she pushed his chest away. She patted his t-shirt where the bass met its rhyming word. "Chad, just keep up all that good work of standing up for what's right in this world. Maybe one day you'll get to leave this Podunk town."

He started to speak, but she clapped her hand over her mouth as if a bad thought had just occurred to her.

"What?"

"Something Daddy said. I forgot to tell you."

"Well, I'm waiting."

"He's still talking about leaving," she said.

"Remember what I told you."

"I don't know. He sounds serious. I think he's really going through with it." Electra checked the mirror again and dug in her purse until she found her lipstick. "Will you miss me?" she asked as she ran it over her lips a few times and made more self-admiring faces at herself.

Too bad. It almost sounded like *will you kiss me.* "If you leave, I..."

She threw her forearm across his bicep as if a fantastic new thought had suddenly occurred to her. "What kind of going away present will you buy for me?"

Present? With what? He'd just spent a whole hour's wages on a single cone for her. "I'll come up with something."

"I have an idea. Let's walk over to the jewelry shop. It's just a block or two."

Well, it didn't look like he'd get that kiss. He shut the window and opened his door. "I was tired of sitting anyway."

The crisp air felt good out here. Circling to the passenger side, he opened her door and led her by her slightly sticky hand across the street. At the curb, Chad checked up and down, but Ben was nowhere in sight.

"You walk on the inside, Electra. I'll protect you from all this dangerous traffic."

Of course, there was no traffic.

She laughed and dragged her fingertips along the black wrought-iron fence of the daycare. Behind the fence sat a long row of small identical pots filled with soil. Clearly some kind of daycare project.

When they passed the gate, Electra let go of Chad's hand. "Wait. I hate these people. Let's just show those two jerks who's boss around here."

Then, before he realized what was happening or could stop it, Electra had kicked her leg through an opening in the fence and overturned half the pots.

"Electra. What are you doing? You're ruining the kids' stuff."

Streetlights defined the sharp contrast between the pots and dark soil scattered across the white play sand.

Electra kicked a few more pots.

"Stop it."

"I told you I hated these idiots."

No doubt there. He pulled her away from the fence. "See that security camera up there? You didn't need to prove it to them, did you?"

"Do you think I care? You think the cops are going to arrest us over a few pots of dirt?"

"Your dad will care."

She whirled and faced him with burning eyes and tight lips. "You really think so? He's too busy out chasing some new skirt. I can't even pretend to think he cares."

"Well, I care, Electra. I really do. I don't want you to get in trouble."

She crossed her arms and blew steam.

"So let's get out of here," he said. He sure didn't want to get arrested for vandalizing a church.

Chapter 7

Friday Morning

Chad tucked the rolled-up quilt under his arm. He was half pedestrian now and on his way to pick up his Jeep in the parking lot in front of the playground. He rounded the corner toward the front of Faith Church and slowed to watch two kids with watering cans beside the fence. Their water sprinkled over the same pots of dirt Electra had kicked over last night. The sight was a welcome one as rivulets ran down the sidewalk. Someone had gotten hold of the pots and finished putting them back together.

Last night, after his and Electra's walk to the jewelry store where she pointed out a gazillion dollars-worth of rings and bracelets she wanted, he'd dropped her back at her friend's. Then he'd stopped by here on his way to the station and done his best to reach through the fence and set things straight. Most of the damage was out of reach, and now, at least someone else had intervened. The kids didn't look too distraught.

At least Electra hadn't ruined everything.

If he hadn't tried to be a gentleman last night and walked on the inside instead of on the outside, none of this would have happened. But how could he have guessed?

From the far side of the play area, joyful kids spotted him. They hollered a Christmas greeting from the swings and then belted out the words "We Wish You a Merry Christmas" at the top of their lungs.

Funny, here they were looking at him and wishing him

well, and he was half the cause of their upset morning. He waved back, and they giggled.

Inside, next to the gate, the guy from his algebra class leaned over to tie a little guy's shoe.

Unlike Electra, Chad didn't hate this guy or his friend. And why would Electra hate him anyway? Did she even know him? Chad paralleled the fence. "Morning."

"Hi. Morning."

Seemed like the guy was a pretty decent person—just doing his job. And Chad himself wouldn't mind a nice clean job like daycare-keeper or whatever you call it.

He crossed the street and wove his way through the parking lot, which was already filled with employees' cars from the church, the phone company, and other nearby businesses.

Under the tree, on the other side of a large SUV, sat his Jeep right where he'd left it. He opened the back end and checked under the laundry he'd piled on top of his box. Yep. Still there. He tossed in the quilt. He'd show it around at work today. Surely somebody could give him advice on how to clean it.

He'd made the right decision to leave his vehicle here. It was a whole lot safer here than behind the station.

Come to think of it, maybe he would be too. Even if sleeping was a little tight in the Jeep.

Friday at Lunch

Two hot dogs and a drink, the daily special at *Stoppat-tamart* today. Chad handed the clerk the last of his paper money. He'd sure eat better if he could find a second part-time job. But this close to Christmas? Fat chance.

So far, he'd gotten away without having to dumpster-dive. The boss was supposed to pay him this afternoon. Hopefully, he'd remember. Checks had been late before.

As he pocketed his change and eased his catsup-laden food off the counter, the door-indicator dinged behind him, but he didn't turn.

He didn't need catsup all over his clothes. As far as spots went, though, he still needed to get the quilt clean before he could take it home.

This morning at work he'd asked advice, but the guys had laughed, hadn't taken him seriously. They told him to throw the piece of junk away.

Right. He'd given Mom his word. There had to be a way to get that grease out.

By some miracle, maybe the cashier knew how to clean oil. He turned back slightly and checked the guy's nametag. "Say, Jamal, you don't happen to know how to get dirty engine oil out of a piece of cloth, do you?"

The teen shrugged and offered a blank look.

Forget it. Jamal probably didn't even know what engine oil was.

As he turned, he stumbled, nearly dumping his lunch over a guy crouched down at the candy rack. It was Ben. Chad knew his name, of course, but had never spoken to him before.

"Sorry," the boy said as Chad regained his balance.

"No problem, I wasn't looking where I was going." He moved around him and took a seat at the empty tables by the front windows.

The disabled boy presented his candy bar to the cashier

while Chad bit into his hot but greasy roller-food. Food had never tasted so good. Not that this was very healthy, but Chad's stomach was growling.

Over at the counter, Ben emptied out his pockets and laid his coins on the counter. "Here."

The cashier shuffled the coins around. "You almost have it. But you need ten cents more, sir."

"That's all I got."

"I can't give you the candy bar. Not unless you have ten cents more."

Chad bit off another bite and set his hot dog in the wrapper. Didn't the store have a penny dish up there? He wiped the back of his hand across his mouth as he watched the scene at the register.

Ben's shoulders slumped. "Okay." He left his candy bar as well as his change on the counter and headed to the door.

"Sir," Jamal called after him, "you forgot your money."

The boy hesitated at the door as if confused.

Chad stood, gave his mouth another swipe, and reached into his pocket. "Wait," he said, still chewing. "Here." In two steps, Chad snapped a dime down in front of the clerk and scooped up the kid's Hershey bar.

He held it toward Ben at the door. "Here. Take the candy."

The boy's face lit up. "Thank you." Then he brightened. "Can I sit with you?"

"Sure. Help yourself."

The kid slid into the seat opposite Chad, tore open his candy bar, and bit off a hunk of chocolate. He smacked a bit, then said, "I know how to get it out of the cloth."

"Yeah? Okay, tell me. But first, my name's Chad. What's yours?" Of course, he knew, but he wanted to make conversation.

"Ben."

"Okay, Ben. What's the secret?"

"Use lots of soap. Hot water. Hot, hot, hot."

Naturally. "Thanks. That's a good idea. Wish it was so easy, Ben. This spot might need a little chemical help, too." They polished off their food, and Chad gathered the trash and stood. "Want to go outside and see the quilt?"

Ben nodded vigorously. He licked his fingers, wiped them on his thigh, and followed Chad out to the Jeep.

"Well, there it is," Chad said as he swung open the back of the vehicle and stepped back.

Ben leaned in and took a good long look at the spot. "Wow. You're right. It's really black."

Chad closed the Jeep. "All I can say is I need a serious miracle."

A loud engine pulled to a stop behind them. Chad's heart sank as he turned. *Jake.* Not him again. Him and that Camaro—following Chad around. First at school, and now here. Why? The only thing he knew about Jake was his name.

The black Camaro's engine revved, and down came the passenger window. Jake leaned toward Chad with his arm across the back of the seat and yelled. "Fancy seeing you here, gay boy. I didn't know you had a retarded brother!"

Before Chad could come up with an intelligent reply, Jake's tires had squealed out of the parking lot, leaving behind the scent of burnt rubber and echo of his mocking laughter.

Chad shook his head.

Ben reached over and patted him on the back. "It's okay, Chad. I'll be your friend."

Tony parked his bike in the daycare breezeway again. He kicked an imaginary rock out of the way. Another dead end at the courthouse. Every single day.

Emily rounded the corner with a stack of plastic stepping stools. The kids at this time of day were mid-nap with the director, Mrs. Sanders, inside. "What's wrong, Tony? You look like someone stole your goodies."

He pressed his lips together and shook his head.

"What?"

"I could bite an iron spike in two right now."

"I'll get our lunch from the office, and you can tell me all about it."

He slumped down on the bench in front of the office.

Emily returned within minutes. She dropped his brown bag and bottle of iced tea in front of him. This was her week to fix their lunches, and he enjoyed the daily surprise. "So, what happened at the courthouse?"

"Nothing. Nada," he said, unwrapping an egg salad sandwich. "That's the problem. I even got down there early this time."

In the fellowship hall window, beyond Emily's shoulder, Mrs. Sanders' face peered out then disappeared again.

"They handed me some records all right. But—"

"But?"

He leaned back and stared at the clouds, the sandwich in his hand all but forgotten. "All the important stuff like names and cities was redacted."

"Blacked out?"

All he was finding were obstacles. "I'm not sure what to do next."

"I know it's hard, but you shouldn't quit looking. It's your brother you're trying to find."

"Maybe for some strange reason, it's not God's will for me to find my brother. Or sister." Yeah, and hopefully not that Electra girl.

"Did the paper even say if you have a brother or sister?"

He leaned with his elbows on his knees. "I don't even know what I'm looking for. I can't get help. It's such a losing battle." He paused. "There was one signature. Just one. Miss McDavid. Maybe I could look her up. Maybe she would remember something."

"What about Brother Ed? Could he help?"

"That's a thought."

"Things might get easier after Christmas with everybody back from vacation. You can bet I'll be there."

"Thanks, Em." He took her hand in his.

It didn't help that school would be starting, though. Add that into the mixture. Christmas vacation should have made things easier. But it hadn't. And that was drawing to a close.

Friday Mid-Afternoon

Mrs. Sanders stood beside Brother Ed and studied the scene across the street from her office window. "Look at that boy, sitting there on that curb. It's just pitiful. The concrete's gotta be cold."

"Feeling guilty?"

If only he knew. Ben had been sitting across the street, watching the kids on the playground for the last hour.

"Why don't we just run him off?"

"You'd want that? In all good conscience?"

"Well, he can't come in the fence. Regulations."

"Well, who brought up those regulations?"

"Just the other day, he came in here with blood all over his hands. He's a walking hazard."

"Is he?"

"Covered in blood."

"I heard it happened up the street, though. He came here for help."

"Well, here or there, it's unimportant. He's simply a hazard."

"Is that so? A hazard to whom?"

"Tony went down to the courthouse today."

"Can't say I'm surprised. He's a determined young man," Brother Ed said this with a touch of amusement in his voice.

"But according to my friends he didn't find anything."

"I see. And you'd like to leave it that way?"

She ran her fingers through her hair. "This is such a mess. I should just move out of town."

He grinned down at her. "But the truth will set you free."

"Ha! It's a cage full of monkeys. If it opens, I'll be ruined."

Brother Ed chuckled.

"Cut it out," she said. "You think everything's so funny, don't you?"

"Granted. It might cause a few problems. And then it might not."

"He'll hate me."

"So, you'd rather see him suffer?"

"He might sue me."

"Not likely," Brother Ed said. "But that would be his issue, not yours."

"Maybe between the Lord and him, but what about down here in the practical here and now? I can't afford to get sued."

"He's a good kid. You don't think he has the right to find his twin?"

"Humph." Mrs. Sanders sighed. "At my expense."

"What if it were you trying to find a twin? Not just a sibling. But a twin?"

It wasn't something she could begin to imagine with her own sister and brother-filled childhood.

"Better for you to come out with the truth than someone to discover it later and bop you over the head with it."

Mrs. Sanders shook her head then pointed to the street. "See there? Look at that."

Emily had unlocked the gate and was taking cookies and punch across the street to Ben. "They shouldn't be encouraging that boy. He needs to go on home."

Brother Ed raised his eyebrows. "That boy? Wish we could get some of that boy's good will to spread around the town."

She gaped at him. "Whose side are you on?"

His eyes twinkled above that grin of his. "Do you remember when Tony came to see me about Ben?"

"What do you mean?"

"He and Emily are paying for the background check."

She shook her head. "They never stop, do they?"

He laughed and walked away.

She pressed her forehead against the cold glass. "It's not funny, Brother Ed."

His voice echoed down the hall. "I told you. Tony's a good kid."

Of course, she knew that.

"And so is Ben, Mrs. Sanders. A wonderful kindhearted boy."

Oh, this was all her fault. On the one hand—if she'd just waited. And on the other—if she'd only acted sooner.

Then, maybe it wasn't too late.

Friday After 5:00 p.m.

An hour before closing, Tony yelled across the playground, "Christmas carols!"

Cheers and chatter rang out as children leaped off swings and piled out of sandboxes. They raced toward Emily, the keeper of the stepping-stool seats.

Tony ducked into the tiny office to get his violin and book as Emily headed for the breezeway to grab the stools. His book, a seasonal one assigned by his Zoom teacher from New York, was full of new unmemorized Christmas pieces. And so far, he'd earned a hundred percent on each one. He snapped open his violin case and lifted out the instrument.

Emily, back now, stood outside the office door and handed out the stools. Once they were passed out, she grabbed a folding chair and leaned inside. "This is for Ben. We're setting up by the gate. He's out there, and I don't want him to feel left out."

Ben's background check hadn't come back yet, and in the meantime, nobody had said anything about him standing outside the fence.

Tony tuned up outside the door as Emily guided the kids' formation of a curved line with two extras in the middle for her and Tony. She got them seated. "Be right back," she said, and darted back to the office for the instruments and music book.

Ben watched patiently from outside the gate as she returned. "Yay, everyone! Here we go!" She yelled, holding the box of maracas, triangles, and jingle bells above her head. She deposited it on the center stools. "Music *tiiiime!*"

Back in early fall, she and Tony had requested donations of instruments and stepping stools from the parents. Moms and dads, thrilled with the daycare's new activities, donated generously, asking what else they might offer.

And right now, their enthusiastic children were bubbling over. Singing time was their all-time favorite.

One by one Emily offered the box to each child. "Try something different than last time." Once they chose, Emily offered the box of instruments to Ben. He chose the sleigh bells.

Emily did a fist pump with her own jingle bells. "*Now let's liven up the street!*" The kids copied with their own cheer.

Emily always made things fun. Tony could not imagine this job without her. Or having gone through those trials with his dad in the hospital last summer. She'd been there with Tony through it all.

Tony's prayers had pretty much been answered. He and his dad had reconciled. And yes, a near-death experience might produce that effect. But it happened.

But Emily—she had unanswered prayers of her own. And that's what saddened him. She deserved answers, but nothing had happened. After all her praying, Emily's mom and dad still hadn't gotten back together. Her mom was still mad at her dad. It seemed unfair. And by the looks of things…

"All set Tony?" It was Emily. The kids were settled back down—waiting for him.

Tony brought over his violin as Emily fed Ben's chair across the fence. She took her seat in the middle of the group and lifted Tony's music book so he could see it. Little hands shot up all around, even before Tony could solicit the first request. "Jingle Bells!" yelled Jimmy. The others echoed the same. Tony laughed and touched Jimmy's nose. "Okay, Jimmy—everybody—let's take it awaaaay!"

Joyful songs filled the playground and the otherwise quiet street.

But past the children's heads, a block away, a faded green Jeep approached.

Tony's smile twitched but he kept on playing. *Not them again.* That algebra-class kid and his black-haired girlfriend.

Wonnnnnnk! Wonnnnnnk! Tony jumped. His bow scritched across the strings. Children screamed and covered their ears. What was a train horn doing on the street? *Wonnnnnnk! Wonnnnnnk!* A second blast rattled the air and turned the joyful song into wails.

Tony stood and glared at the driver and his girl. He couldn't help but yell. "You've got to be kidding. C'mon, man, a train horn?"

Couldn't this dude act normal?

The Jeep passed by and circled into the parking lot across the street. It parked under a tree.

Idiots.

He took his seat again, thankful he hadn't said anything worse. "There, there, calm down, guys. It's just a noise." He and Emily gave hugs, patted heads and backs, and traded looks of disbelief. She frowned and shook her head as kids nearly jostled his instrument out of his hands. Others vied for Emily's lap.

One weeping girl stood apart from the rest. "I wet my pants," she wailed.

Tony turned again and glared at the Jeep.

Only a jerk enjoyed scaring little kids like that.

Something had to be done.

Moments before, Chad had steered his Jeep around the corner and headed toward the daycare. There sat his new Hershey-bar buddy, Ben, on a metal chair outside the fence, singing along with the violin and the kids. They all held instruments. He'd wondered why Ben had to sit outside the fence.

Then Electra had reached over and sounded his train horn. "Electra!" This was his vehicle. And there she was pushing that horn for all she was worth. He pushed her hand away. "Stop it, Electra!"

"Ha, ha. Look at everybody jump and holler. We stopped their whole show."

"Why'd you do that?" He and his dad had installed the horn for a gag, but it was never intended to harass little kids.

"Are you kidding, Chad?" She pressed the horn again. "This is way fun."

He jerked her hand away. "Knock it off, Electra."

"Woo hoo!" she squealed. "I love it."

As the Jeep crawled by the playground, the algebra-class kid stood up and yelled. And if looks could kill, Chad and Electra would be dead right now.

Chad turned and faced her. "Now look what you've done. Kids crying, people hating us."

Electra twisted around and checked the chaos on the playground behind her. "Who cares? Those people don't scare me."

All Chad could do was stare at Electra as he pulled into the parking lot and turned off the Jeep. What was going on in this girl's mind?

She smiled over her shoulder at Chad. "It's my adventure-some spirit, honey-poo. Don't you like your women a little on the wild side?" She fluttered her long black eyelashes at him.

"Just please. Don't do that again. Ever."

She shooed him away. "Don't be such a fuddy-duddy. It's nothing." Then she sighed as if bored with the subject. "Well, aren't we going to take a little walk? Maybe we could go get our evening ice cream cone?"

There was no "we" in that. But maybe he should lighten up a bit to keep up with her antics. And no other guys with his zitty looks were getting this kind of attention from her. Best not to squander it. After all, the Jeep's horn hadn't physically hurt anyone.

"Yeah, I guess."

She scrunched up her face and smiled, touching her per-fectly manicured finger to the tip of his nose. "You are such a sweetie. Let's stroll over to Parchment and Quill. I heard they had some beautiful new pens and stationery."

Unfortunately, a stroll in that direction would force them to walk past the playground again. Not a place he wanted to get very close to right now.

The crowd at the fence had broken up, and kids were swinging and singing again. Others clustered around the teenage girl. The algebra guy had gone inside.

Chad could walk Electra the opposite way around the block, but that side was under construction, not a good choice. He could certainly drive, but there was the problem of using gas. The things he put up with to save a little money. And Electra was not making anything easy.

He took her hand and led her across the parking lot to the

sidewalk. Ben was still sitting in his chair outside the fence. He seemed like a lost puppy out there.

Chad picked up his pace as they drew near.

"Poor little retard," Electra said in mock sympathy, and plenty loud enough for him to hear.

Chad pulled her along. How could she say things like that? Next time he'd walk her past the construction zone.

Back in his office, Tony snapped his violin case shut and shoved the music into the zippered pocket on top. "I've had enough of those two," he said to Emily, who stood outside the door. She'd followed him to the door but kept her focus on the playground. When supervising, one couldn't afford to turn their back on the little ones. At the blink of an eye, anything could happen.

"There's nothing you can do about it, Tony. Let it play out. They'll get bored and find someone else to pick on—or pester and annoy."

Tony set the case on the floor and handed her the key. "Lock the gate behind me, Em."

"Where are you going?"

"Tending to business."

"Tony, don't do anything stupid. Please," she said, following him to the fence with a worried look on her face.

"It'll just take a minute." At least none of the kids seemed to be paying attention.

What would Tony say to the two hoodlums? He had no idea. Yet he marched after them, gaining ground fast. His thoughts blazed. What he'd really like to do was wring their scrawny necks. But he knew better than that—definitely knew better than that. What would that prove, anyway? Words only. But words couldn't express how he felt right now. And he didn't want to sound stupid.

Some twenty feet behind them, Tony finally spoke up. "Excuse me. Hold up a minute."

They turned as if surprised and let go of each other's hands.

The girl placed her hands on her hips. Her posture said, *Who do you think you are, stopping us like this?*

The boy, with his hands at his sides, seemed to pale. He glanced from the girl to Tony and back.

Tony drew up in front of them. "Listen, I don't care what kind of crazy horn you blow. But scaring the wits out of those little kids—that's got to stop."

The girl thrust out her neck and waggled her head. "Says you and whose army? It's a free country, jerk." She threw in some nasty words. For such an exotic face, she certainly had a bad attitude.

The boy held up both hands as if to apologize. "Hey, we're not—"

The girl interrupted. "You and that retard, you church-going pansies…" she threw in a selection of curse words. "Ya'll just leave us alone. We ought to call the cops about you harassing us and chasing us down the street. So get lost, punk."

Talk about the pot calling the kettle black. They were the ones harassing all the daycare kids. "You had all the kids crying. And don't bother calling Ben ugly names. He's harmless. And a whole lot nicer than you."

The girl shot him a rude gesture. "Who cares?"

"And speaking of cops?" Tony said. "I can sure file a

complaint about that horn. I think there's a city noise ordinance about that."

"Get lost," the girl said.

Tony pointed at her face and then at the boy's. "I'm telling you, knock it off. Don't blow that horn around our kids anymore."

She turned and pranced up the sidewalk, leaving her boyfriend behind.

The algebra kid didn't seem to know what to do or say. He opened his mouth—seemed to be searching for words—then glanced back and forth between Tony and the girl as if he were trying to make some kind of decision.

The boy shrugged. "Look. I'm sorry," he said, then shook his head and followed after the girl.

Tony stared after him. What was that all about?

He did a 180 and headed back toward the church, replaying the conversation over in his mind.

Up ahead, a good two blocks away, his friend Mike skidded up to the gate on his bike.

Emily met him at the gate with a box, probably the box of cookies a friend had left for him. It only took a few seconds, and Mike was gone. Too far away and too fast for Tony to catch up with him.

Must be on his way to work. Mike, now, he would make a great twin brother.

Tony dropped his head and said a silent prayer. "Lord, please, don't let it be that witchy girl from the Jeep. I'm begging you. Don't do that to me."

Vinnie's hands trembled as he leaned in and stared into the

refrigerator. He had to get his mind off that blocked phone call a few minute ago. The whispered message kept repeating in his head, *"I'm comin' to get you. I'm comin' to get you."* That little event plus the setting sun—a signal for supper—had driven him inside.

He rubbed the side of his face. Normally he could identify a voice. Any voice. But not this one—always whisperin'.

After the call came Nancy's text—tellin' him she'd gone off to choir practice and to go ahead and eat the chicken and rice and peas she'd left in the fridge. He let out a long sigh. She'd texted again, askin' him to join the choir.

"No," he'd answered for the millionth time. "Just... no."

He stared into the fridge, cold air pooling around his feet. And where was that kid of his, anyway? Oh yeah, yeah, yeah—that daycare job. He raised an eyebrow and nodded. Tony was doin' all right these days. Bein' real responsible.

He lifted out the bowls and slid them onto the counter beside his phone. The screen had gone dark. He massaged the bullet wound through his shirt, but that only aggravated it. Made it sore.

Shootings. Phone calls. Texts. He wished people would leave him alone.

His wife was the worst these days—findin' any excuse to text and expectin' an answer—just to make sure he was okay. Treatin' him like a baby.

Sure, he was okay. But c'mon—him join the choir? *Forgettaboutit.*

"I ain't got no air," he'd told her. "I feel like Bigfoot's standin' on my chest."

Oh, sure, Vinnie used to have a good set of bellows. But so does a whale. That didn't mean he could sing. He wouldn't say it to Nancy, but he did enjoy makin' a racket in that fancy new car of his with all that high-class surround-sound.

Best music he'd ever heard and sweetest car he'd ever owned.

Vinnie's dad would have been so proud of him twisting that Mercedes guy's arm. *What a steal*, he'd have said, and patted Vinnie on the back.

He could still hear Dad's voice, "It pays to know things about people. You can always gain the upper hand."

But somewhere in the back recesses of Vinnie's mind that sense of conquest had hit a snag.

He closed his eyes to picture his expensive vehicle—and to summon the delight he'd once felt over its acquisition. But despite Dad's would-be praise, Vinnie could not bring it back. The pleasure was gone. And that was the snag. All Vinnie got now was a heaviness—a lead weight in his gut. What had happened to him? He needed to re-evaluate. Figure this out.

He breathed deep and opened his eyes. He lifted the cover off the bowl of peas. For now, he had enough on his mind. One more dark cloud was too much to dwell on. Anyway, Vinnie was done with all that. All the arm-twistin'. *Sorry to disappoint you, Dad. Those were the old ways and the old days. The old me.*

He found a plate, heaped it high with chicken, rice, and peas and shoved it into the microwave to heat up. As the timer ticked down, he stopped it midway to cover the food.

"See there, Lusmila?" he shouted to the empty house. "You and me both know that wouldn't have happened before."

Lusmila, the maid, was long gone, though. Moved up north for personal reasons. They all missed her—real bad.

He pressed the *start* button again. "You'd be happy with my progress," he yelled again. Vinnie wasn't perfect of course, but he was proud of his improvements. The bell dinged, and he grabbed a Coke out of the box and brought it all to the table.

As he ate, his gaze wandered back to the empty kitchen. Lusmila's absence was so thick he could reach out and snatch a handful of it. Six whole months had passed since she'd left. He hadn't realized back then how much like a family member she was. Until she left. They should really find a new housekeeper. But how do you replace family?

As he scraped up a forkful of chicken and rice, he considered his little wife Nancy. She worked so hard. With Lusmila gone, she'd taken over all the housework. Yet she never complained.

His eyes cut sideways to the uncovered bowls he'd left on the counter. In the old days he'd have left everything out. Just like that. He shook his head, headed back in to tidy up, and returned to the table. Nancy didn't need to be cleanin' up after him.

Vinnie had to admit he was behavin' better, and it felt pretty good, but he wasn't sure what to pin it on. It could be that deep down he was just tryin' to help Nancy, now that the maid was gone. Or keep Nancy from worrying. She was so freaked out about him getting' shot again. Or it might just be his new walk and talks with Jesus. A, B, C, or D—all of the above?

He dropped his fork and bowed his head over the food. He'd almost forgotten. *Thank you, Lord for this good food. And—* he stared at his silent phone—*would you please show me how to stop these calls?*

I don't have a clue who it is or what I done to make 'em so mad.

Chapter 8

Friday Evening After Work

After the confrontation with the daycare guy, an angry Electra had pranced away into the dark, her elbows pumping. Chad followed a block behind. He'd hang back until she cooled off.

Those things she said back there—and boy could she cuss—were about as bad as anything he'd ever heard in a locker room.

Chad quickened his pace as Electra reached the front door of the *Stoppattamart*. He couldn't help but speak up. "Electra, wait."

She slapped her hand around the door handle and swung around to face him. "I hate those idiots," she said through clenched teeth.

He closed the gap between them. "What are we doing here? I thought you wanted to go to the Parchment and Quill."

Electra let go of the door. "Forget it. There's a new plan." She slid the handle of her big red purse down her arm, snapped it open, and fished around until she found what she wanted. She waved it in front of him. Too fast to read, but clearly a driver's license.

Chad raised one eyebrow.

"Go around back and wait," she said, pointing toward the corner of the building. "There's a rock wall."

"But—"

She clutched the driver's license to her chest and shooed him away. "Don't worry about it. It's my sister's, okay? She's twenty-four."

"You—"

She shoved his shoulder. "Just do it."

This certainly wasn't what Chad thought he'd be doing tonight. But he followed her command and slipped past the dripping ice machine's slimy puddle, and around the corner between the wall and a wooden privacy fence. A jungle of bushes and saplings met him.

He paused. She must know her way around back here. So, with a protective arm across his face, he plowed on through until he burst forth onto a concrete pad within a retaining wall on its opposite bank. Behind it stood a bank of thick, weedy trees. Sand had eroded from the bank around the end of the wall, and formed a shallow delta across the concrete. Above this, a streetlight glimmered through the foliage and cast long shadows over the cigarette butt-littered ground.

Quite a little smokers' den back here. How would Electra know about it?

He crossed the space and shoved away an overhanging branch to sit on the wall facing the back of the building. He crossed his arms. What was Electra up to in there?

A driver's license usually meant alcohol or cigarettes. He raked the side of his toe across the cigarette butts. Her surprises just never ceased.

He jumped as a cat skittered through the shadows and leaped up on a large green dumpster. A stack of broken-down boxes slumped against it next to the street. *Great space.* He'd passed it by many times and never noticed it.

The bushes rustled beside the store, and Electra burst

through. She held a bottle of pale pink wine in one hand and a pack of cigarettes in the other.

Chad stood. He hadn't noticed her smoking before. Or drinking. "What are you doing?"

"What does it look like I'm doing? Are you some kind of baby?" She held up the bottle. "I am sick and tired of do-gooders. That kid's not going to tell me off. And neither are you, for that matter."

She eyed him as she unwrapped the foil from the lid and pitched it into the purse. Was she going to drink the whole blamed thing?

She lowered her head and dug through her bag until she found a lighter. "That fruitcake-boy and that girl back at the church took me right out of my mood for shopping," she said and lit up a cigarette like she'd done it a million times.

Had he just been unobservant? But of course, Electra nearly always kept him at arm's length.

He returned to his place on the wall.

She sat nearby, crossing her legs and placing the cigarette between her lips. "I'm in a different frame of mind now," she said, motioning for him to come closer.

Those long legs reminded him once again of a long-legged Barbie. How'd he ever catch such a girl?

Her cloud of smoke settled around him, and he fanned it away. Kind of like he'd brushed aside her blowing his train horn.

The algebra kid was right, though. He could call the police about the noise. And not only that, Chad and Electra shouldn't have been scaring little kids.

"Electra," Chad said, careful to use the right words. No need to resurrect her wrath against him. "You know, we really shouldn't be blowing that train horn like we did."

She narrowed her eyes and crossed her arms. "Just whose side are you on anyway?"

"It's my vehicle. Remember? If there's a ticket, I'm the one who would get it. It would be on my record. There is a noise ordinance." Dad had put the horn on just for fun, for being cool, for riding out in the country. He'd warned Chad about using it in town. "Everybody knows cops hate those train horns."

"Cars, Jeeps, creeps. I don't care."

"You don't care if I get a ticket or not?"

She thrust the bottle against his chest. "Cool your jets, Chad. Take a big drink. Let's finish it off."

How would drinking fix anything? Chad was already stepping over the line by driving under age without an adult. No need to push his luck. "Not interested." Besides, he had no desire to kill off his irreplaceable and limited brain cells with alcohol.

Electra snatched the bottle back and slugged down a big drink. She offered it again. "Take some, I said."

The strength of her voice almost compelled him to take it.

The angel Strength stood guard beside Myrtle who knelt beside her son's bed. Today was the third day.

"Lord, I'm weak and tired. I can hardly go. Please give me strength to get through this fast."

Weariness cupped his hands and tried to yell through the bedroom window. *A three day fast! How foolish. Waste of time. There's cheesecake in the refrigerator. It'll spoil if you don't eat it. Besides, that's wasteful, and your blood sugar's getting l...*

Strength plowed his fist into the demon's jaw.

"Ooof!"

He pulled his fist away. "Get lost, you liar." The angel's other hand touched the woman's shoulder and drew away a portion of her burden.

The woman prayed on. "Father, you know what's going on with my son. I'm asking you to hear my prayers and send him help. Help him come to terms with his thinking. Give him wisdom and discernment. Cover him with your protection. Cover him with the blood of Jesus. Keep him safe and watch over him. And bring him home by Christmas, Lord. Please. I pray this in Jesus' name."

Brilliance caught Discernment's eye. "You feel it? Myrtle's finished her third day. Something's about to break through."

The boy's small glimpse into the spirit world the other night had not been sufficient. But after the fast, a new excitement rippled through the heavenlies.

A victory.

It came then. The command. Like a trumpet blast, it split the skies. "Open the boy's eyes."

Brilliance stood taller, and the three raised their arms. "Praise be to the Highest, to the Almighty who was, and is, and is to come!"

Discernment inhaled with a wide smile and leaned toward Chad. "Finally." He touched Chad's eyes with his thumb and forefinger.

Brilliance nodded. "That's all it takes."

Chad's gaze drifted from the wine bottle up to Electra's eyes.

He gasped. *Wha...?*

Once again, her eyes were black pools. No blue irises, just big alien orbs.

Just like the other night.

He shuddered. Blinked. Tried to focus in the dark.

But as quick as it had appeared, the weirdness vanished. Her eyes were blue again. Beautiful aqua blue under the streetlamp.

Had to be the twilight playing tricks on him.

"You're staring at me. Are you even paying attention?"

"Sorry, Electra."

She sucked on her cigarette then blew smoke out long and slow across her shoulder. "I don't get mad, though. I get even. That guy has a payday coming."

"Who do you mean?"

Electra laughed and tilted the bottle for another long swig. One third of the wine had disappeared. "Who do you think? That violin playing is so gay. Sitting around in that circle singing Christmas carols and all that Kumbaya junk."

What was wrong with Electra's thinking? "The place is a daycare. Normal little kids do stuff like that. And they were Christmas carols, not *Kumbaya.*"

"I'm talking about the guy." Electra's speech was clearly loosening up.

If she only knew Chad's facts.

Electra took a few more drinks. "Oh, hey, did you ever get that old quilt-thingy fixed?"

"Listen, about him playing that violin—you really should back off. You have no idea what you're talking about."

"I asked you a question."

"The quilt? I've asked around."

"I've told you before. Throw that old piece of junk away."

"It's sentimental to Mom."

"Mom, *schmom*." Electra gripped Chad's chin with the same hand that held the cigarette. He blinked as its embers glowed inches from his ear. She leaned close, and her breath, damp with wine, warmed his face.

He focused on her lips.

Her voice came out deep, like a man's. "You going to go *gay-ay* on me, Chad?"

One glance at her eyes, and he backed away with a choking gasp.

Her eyes, like shiny black billiard balls, stared into his own.

He twisted away and closed his eyes—to break the dominance of her stare. It felt as if a demon had taken over her being. "It—it's time to go."

She waved the bottle. "I wasn't finished."

"It's dark. Let's go."

She tipped the bottle to her lips, but he turned his back and strode out past the dumpster, the opposite way from which they'd arrived.

"And leave that bottle there," he said over his shoulder, not daring to look at her.

In their office, Tony tightened the lid onto the plastic money jar and rolled it across the desk. It hit the wall and stopped. "How much do you think is left in there, Emily?"

Emily swiveled around on her folding chair and peeked inside the door. At her feet played the daycare's one remaining child.

Emily eyed the bills inside the jar. "Not that much. Want to count it today?"

"Tony. Tony." Ben called from outside the gate. His voice sounded off.

Emily turned. "Uh oh. Better come see about this."

Tony stepped out. A bent and broken picture frame dangled from Ben's hand.

"Hey, Ben."

"I didn't get cut," Ben said as if it could defend the vandal.

Tony reached over the fence and took the frame. A sliver of glass dropped out and hit the sidewalk.

"We'll throw this away. But tell me what happened." The mutilated frame was clearly no accident.

"He wanted the remote."

Emily approached. "Open your hands. Let's see."

Seemed like everything was okay. "Well, at least your hands are not hurt."

"Wait," Emily said. "Tony. Look at his arms."

A row of small red crescents marked each forearm. Claw marks. Tony frowned. "You're going to need an antibiotic."

"Medicine?"

Tony crossed his arms. "Who did this?"

Ben hung his head and stared down at the fence. He shook his head.

Maybe Tony should have held his tone back a little instead of revealing his feelings about the assault. At the least sign of anger, even if it wasn't directed against him, Ben clammed up like this.

Tony lowered his voice. "I promise I'm not mad at you, Ben. You can tell me."

"I gave it to him."

"You gave it to him?"

"The remote." Ben brightened. "I picked up the picture, too. I've got more. Want to see my family?"

Tony sighed and turned around. What was wrong with everyone? First the two nutcases terrorizing the kids with train horns, and now a violent roommate down at Ben's. Was this how Ben got cut the other day? He turned back to Ben. "Maybe I'll come look some other time, Ben. Don't go back there right now. We'll walk you home." He turned to Emily.

Ben pointed to the curb across the street. "I can sit over there."

The handicap parking space hardly ever got used on weekdays. "All right. Sit tight until our last kid gets picked up. Or walk around the block. You warm enough?" Darkness had fallen, and a chill as well.

Ben nodded and shuffled away.

"We'll get you a new picture frame, Ben."

Ben turned and beamed. "You're a great friend, Tony."

Tony needed to have a chat with Ben's supervisor and try to find out what happened. There had to be something Tony could do to help his friend.

Friday Evening, 5:45 p.m.

Chad took Electra by the elbow. The alcohol was well into her blood, and it was a long walk back to the Jeep. She was now so wobbly, he practically had to drag her down the sidewalk. He guided her across the boulevard, then a block beyond, as far away from traffic—and people—as he could.

If he stuck to the back alleys and kept out of the streetlights, maybe no one would notice her unsteady gait. Underage drinking was not something he wanted to be arrested for.

Or aiding and abetting it. "You trying to get me arrested, Electra?" he hissed. "Walk straight."

She giggled and waved him off, stumbling. "No, silly, you're the best."

"Let's keep to the alleys. At least they're lit up."

A block later they passed a privacy fence on the left. Behind it the hoarse barking of a small dog grew louder and louder until they reached a fist-size hole in the slats near their feet. The snarling flat face of a pug-dog poked through, gleaming white cataracts and all. It growled and strained against the opening. Chad stepped to the right, thankful to be on the outside.

"Oh, I know him," Electra said, stopping beside the fence. "Poor widdle fweabag. "He b'longs t' the neighbor." She reached down to pet the animal, and he went even wilder, snarling and pushing as if he might actually break through the hole and eat them alive.

Chad jerked her hand away. "Shh. Keep it down, Electra. We'll look like prowlers."

"Iz not me barkin'. Iz Blackie."

Chad tugged at her arm to move her away from the racket, but Blackie's commotion never let up until they reached the far end of the next yard.

"What do you mean, *the neighbor*, Electra? You don't live around here."

"Don't you know Jake?"

Wait, not the Jake that kept calling me queer. "The guy that drives a black Camaro? That Jake? He lives here?"

"'Course not. Up—over—" she squinted toward the streetlight ahead. "Now where's 'iz house?"

Chad scanned the area for Jake. He wasn't someone Chad wanted to run into.

"Oh, 'iz house is up ahead. I 'member now." In spite of the lights, Electra banged into a metal trashcan. It fell over and the lid clattered off. He should have been watching her closer—and just when they needed to be super quiet. Thank goodness, the thing was empty. He didn't feel like picking up garbage.

"Shhh!" He scooped up the lid and set the can aright. "Sorry. I didn't see that."

She giggled. "Don't worry. No nails broken."

"Wait, are you sure Jake—"

Off balance again, she grabbed at Chad's sleeve. "Yeah, we broke up last month… And…" she pointed with an unsteady finger. "There it is. I told you. It's right there."

To the left of the sandy ruts sat an old garage apartment. It had to be at least a hundred years old. Looked like an old carriage house, actually. Had to be, in this neighborhood. A light shined in the upstairs window. Underneath, just like she'd said, sat Jake's black Camaro.

Across the alley sat a well-kept two-story colonial brick home whose front Chad had seen many times from the boulevard. So that was Jake's. Chad stared at the building. Must be a million bucks sitting there.

"Pretty place, Electra. Why's he so nasty to everyone?"

"Yeah, and I hate his guts."

"Why? What did…?"

Then she caught the direction of Chad's gaze. "That's not his home." She tossed her chin toward the carriage house. "This is."

"He lives alone?"

"That one used to be his house," she said, leaning against Chad as she flipped her hand in the direction of the colonial. "His daddy kicked him out."

Chad scrunched up his face. This was all news to him.

"You 'on't know?" She leaned her head back and laughed. "Everyone else does."

"Shh. Let's keep walking. Don't make so much noise."

He led her to the end of the block, across the street, and hurried her down the next alley. A bigger dog snarled and growled, this one completely visible, and threatening to leap over a not-so-high chain-link fence. Chad yanked at her elbow. "Let's try to hurry."

Electra stumbled along, but picked up the pace.

Finally, at the next sidewalk, she jerked away, straightened her sweater, and walked at her own pace across the street.

"So, his parents kicked him out?"

"Come on. Don't you know anything, Chad?"

"Just tell me."

"Not now. In the car."

They walked another block to the parking lot. Electra tried to climb into the passenger seat, but her feet slipped around on the floor mats, and Chad was forced to lift her up. Man, she was heavy. If she hadn't drunk all that wine back at the *Stoppattamart*...

Finally, she was in. He buckled her up, closed the door behind her, and hopped into the driver's side. "You act like you're *trying* to get in trouble. Like you're trying to get *me* into trouble." He jammed the key in the ignition.

Her only response was a foolish grin that seemed to indicate that might be fun.

"All right, so what happened with Jake?"

"That's not why I hate his guts." Electra clutched the red purse against her chest.

So, she hated Jake. Why? He had to know. The Jeep moved forward.

Midway through the parking lot, she reached into the purse and pulled out the bottle again.

Chad stomped on the brakes, and she nearly hit the dash. "I told you to leave that bottle back there. Put it in your purse. Now." It was half empty, and she was way too loopy.

Electra giggled and shook the pink liquid in front of his face.

Her antics were going to land him in jail. What kind of mess had he gotten himself into? Here he was, in the Jeep, underage driving, with an underage drinker in his vehicle. Bad recipe. He shoved the bottle away from his face and drove out of the lot.

"No, you really s'ould try it. It's 'licious." She gave it another shake. "C'mon, Chad." Only she pronounced it more like *Shad* at this point.

"That's not funny. Your parents are going to kill me when they see you. They will literally kill me."

"Ha." Electra filled a long pause with sounds of more drinking then wiped her mouth.

Chad glanced around to see if anyone had seen her. "Would you please put the lid on that?" At least it was dark outside. "Just stop it, okay?"

"He beat up his brother."

Chad stared at her. "His brother? Jake did? What for?"

"Oh, my gosh, Chad. Didn't you hear? His brother was gay, for goodness sake. And Jake found out."

"And that got him kicked out?"

She tipped the bottle up.

"Please. That's not Kool-Aid!"

"Whadduz my dad care?"

"Are you kidding?" Chad's voice came out shaky and high,

like a ten-year-old's, but he couldn't help it. "He'll say I got you drunk. He'll have me arrested."

Electra flopped a limp arm across his chest. "Take me o'er to my friend's."

"Then *her* parents will have me arrested. I'll have two families and the cops after me."

Electra crossed her legs and gathered her bag against her chest. She used the hand around the bottle to point a finger at him. Was that slobber or wine on her lips? Her eyes were beginning to water. "Yeah, like they'll even know."

"Your friend's parents?"

"They're in the Bahamas, dummy."

Lucky for him. "What about your dad?"

"Ha." She took another long drink which left mere inches of liquid in the bottle now.

"Your dad. Tell me. Where is he?"

"Parties, *Shad*. With a new woman, too, prob'ly. Know why I'm o'er at my friend's tonight? He told me to go." She took another drink and stared out the window. "And you can *betcherbottomdollar* we all know why."

At the next residential section, Chad checked the rearview mirror for other traffic then snatched the bottle away. "Give me that thing. Your dad and mom would have a heart attack if they saw you drinking." He swerved the Jeep into the left lane, reached out, and dropped it onto the top of the hedges. No break, no harm.

Brilliance, Wisdom, and Discernment followed the Jeep.

Wisdom touched Chad's forehead. "My turn. It won't be long now."

"Hey—" Electra said. "Gimme back my bo'l. You 'on't have a right to do tha', Shad."

Swerving back in the right lane, he glared at her. "You've had enough. More than enough."

"Yeah, well tha's why I hate that stupid Jake."

"What do you mean?"

"Another time, Shad. Know where my friend's house is?"

This girl's trouble. Drop her off where you picked her up the other night.

"Pah!" She laughed. Spit flew out of her mouth. "Right past your mom's house. That ugly little ranch house."

"Your friend's parents had better be gone, or I'm cooked. And I didn't even buy you that bottle."

They reached Fifth Street, and Chad let off the gas as he passed his mom's place. He coasted by with his eyes glued to the window, where the blinds, still open, revealed her reading under the lamp, in her favorite yellow bathrobe. The scene looked like a painting.

Your sweet mom's in there reading her Bible.

Electra leaned across Chad with her eyebrows up. "Look at tha' bathrobe. And the curtains open. She's readin' in the dark? Turn on some lights, lady," she hollered.

Chad closed the Jeep's window.

Electra had no idea what she was talking about. Mom was simply cutting costs. Hence the open shades. He knew exactly what had happened. The sunlight had played itself out and she'd forgotten to shut them. Since Dad died, his medical bills had eaten them alive, and electrical use was a big deal.

Maybe Chad should be home helping her instead of

leaving her alone and running off trying to square himself away. Thinking it through now, it was all pretty selfish. Dad wouldn't have thought much of Chad's plan.

Mom was a good lady, and he shouldn't be putting her through all this.

Actually, without Electra's encouragement, Chad would probably still be home. Stupid dupe. What a follower.

He blew out a breath. These thoughts were wearing him out. He hated being analytical like this.

But truth be told, Dad would likely say Chad was running away from things. He'd call him a selfish jerk.

Looking back on it, the whole leaving to *get his head on straight* was pretty much a bust.

He could hear Dad's voice now, "How's that working for you?"

How much straightening out had Chad actually done? An average of nothing.

Instead, he'd only created more problems. And dangers. He'd spent a night with homicidal bikers, slept on top of a dried-up rat, nearly gotten fired, been broke, hungry, dirty, worried about his belongings, and now with Electra snatching him around, she might even get him arrested.

Not to mention breaking laws about underage driving. In addition, if he didn't get his act in gear, he might even flunk his mid-term exams when he got back to school.

Come to think of it, he ought to just forget all this baloney and move back home now.

Forget what Jake and the other jerks at school had said. It wasn't that he was living with his *Mommy*. Why would he be ashamed of living with her? Maybe if he was thirty-five-years old—but at fifteen? Come on. Dad would scoff at that idea. Mom was family.

At least at home, he could help Mom. And Chad would have someone to care about him, someone to love in return. And that was normal, not a crutch.

He sure missed having someone around that cared, especially in the silence of that stuffy old gas station.

Not that Mom didn't care about him from afar. Of course, she did. But it was something else long distance.

He needed people present. People to care.

Family to care.

Electra sure didn't have one.

Even with all her money. Her dad handed her off to friends—the way she existed, Electra might as well be an orphan.

She was pitiful, actually.

Compared to her life, Chad had nothing to complain about. Not rightfully.

Now if he could just get through this night without getting arrested for Electra's drunkenness.

How had he cared for his family in return? Not much when it came to Mom. Not much at all. And the quilt she'd asked him to bring back—that one simple thing. He'd failed. Hadn't returned the heirloom she cared about. Now the quilt was—

Wait, he couldn't go back home yet. Not until he figured out how to get it clean. He had to do that first. Mom couldn't see the quilt like that—he owed it to her.

What a crazy jerk he'd been. This was all a waste. A bad idea. None of this stupid stuff would have happened had he stayed at home and thought things through. He never should have left.

Electra swatted his arm. "Your mom's got a mess in that yard. Look at all those weeds."

"Marigolds, Electra. She's harvesting seeds."

"We've got a yard man."

"I bet you do."

Mom stood and closed her front shades. If she'd known he was out here, she'd have come running out to the Jeep.

"Ooh, frumpy," Electra said. "All I can say is she—"

Chad gritted his teeth and revved the motor.

She laughed. "Woo-hoo, Chad!"

He dumped the clutch and skidded his wheels, surely leaving a long black streak on the asphalt.

"Way to go. You tell her!"

Right Electra, those were for you.

Chapter 9

Late Saturday Morning

Late the next morning Chad returned to the house where Electra was staying. After her insults last night, he wasn't even sure why he was returning. He climbed out of the Jeep and knocked on the door. After way too many knocks, Electra finally answered the door in her sleeping shirt. Her hair was unkempt and she wore a frown. She held a hairbrush in her hand. It didn't look like she'd had much sleep. Not good.

"Feel like taking a stroll over to AutoSpot with me? I need to order that tail light."

She gave him a fake smile and formed the word *no* with her lips.

"You sure? A walk would make you feel better."

She glared at him.

"How about a ride?"

"Maybe," she whispered, "wait here."

In a few minutes she returned. Shielding her eyes from the sun, she dug through her purse and came up with an expensive pair of sunglasses. She put them on and pulled the front door closed behind her. "My eyes are disgusting and red, and I feel like a train plowed over me."

What could he say? He jingled his keys and kept his mouth shut, afraid something ignorant would pop out of his mouth—like she shouldn't have gulped that bottle of wine last night.

"Please don't do that."

"Do what?"

"My head is killing me."

Oh, the keys. All last night he'd tossed and turned inside his sleeping bag trying to figure out what Jake could have done to make Electra hate him.

A debate raged in his brain. One voice screamed, *Electra's an alcoholic.* The other one said, *Nah, Electra's not a regular drinker.* Last night was the first time he'd ever even seen her drink at all. How well did he really know her?

By morning light, the voices said maybe her drinking was a one-time fluke, a freak event. She had only been upset.

Besides that, Electra looked normal. Wasn't alcohol supposed to bloat a person and break their veins?

"You're still beautiful, Electra."

Gripping the hairbrush, she tossed him a wordless glance and trudged toward the Jeep.

On the other hand, though, facial bloating would take time. How long would that take if last night's binge was a regular habit? If it were a freak incident, a one-time event, then what other things might send her over the edge into another drinking binge? Another disagreement with someone?

He should Google the question when he got a chance: *How long does it take to develop facial bloating from alcohol?*

Electra walked ahead and headed to the Jeep. She turned her back to him and crossed her arms, tapping her foot. Sort of like a temperamental six-year-old trying to make a point.

Chad caught up. "Sorry. Thinking about something else." He pulled the door open. "Hop in." He helped her into the Jeep, and they headed toward the AutoSpot. She probably did feel pretty rotten today.

"Chad, why are you bothering with AutoSpot?"

"What do you mean?"

"Just order the dumb tail light online."

He kept his eyes on the pavement ahead. How could she be so out of tune with his living situation? She'd come up with the station idea, given him the key, and even walked in and looked around. She knew he had no electricity or water. How could she expect him to go online?

So, come on.

And UPS required a real address for a delivery. What was Chad going to use for an address? An abandoned station?

Clearly, her blood alcohol level was affecting her. "No Internet, remember?"

"My friend's got Internet."

Of course, she did. "So does AutoSpot. I'll order it there. It's just a tail light."

She slumped against the door with nothing more to add until they arrived at AutoSpot. As he pulled into a parking place, she mumbled something that sounded a lot like, "Just the way I wanted to spend my Saturday—at the good old car-parts store."

"Want to sit here or go in?" The order would only take a minute.

She flapped her hand. "Just go."

"I'll be quick."

Getting an order delivered during the Christmas rush would likely be slow, but since he'd gotten paid yesterday, he might as well start the process. That red plastic tape over one light was the pits. Dad, always conscientious, would have disapproved.

He hustled to the door. A bell tinkled overhead as he shoved it open, just like in the old timey days. Awesome. He'd never been in this AutoSpot. He and Dad always bought their auto parts at the larger one across town.

Overhead speakers resonated with "I Heard the Bells on Christmas Day." The central sales counter was deserted.

"Hello, anybody home?"

"Up here," a girl said.

He scanned the aisles and stopped at a pair of turquoise-studded cowgirl boots perched high on a ladder's metal rungs. A pair of long legs in snug little jeans extended above them.

"Comin' right down," she said, shoving a strand of wavy blond hair around her ear and peering down at him. "Hold on a second."

He sucked in a breath.

She climbed down, bringing her clipboard with her, and laid it on the counter. Her dimpled smile lit up the space. "Merry Christmas and welcome to AutoSpot. How can I help you?" If words were candy, hers were melted caramels.

"Uh." Heat rose in his cheeks. He scolded himself. Electra was right outside.

A sudden tightness took hold of his throat. He choked down some saliva then fought to command some kind of control over his voice. "I... I need to order a light."

"Headlight?"

"Tail. Jeep. No, sorry, I mean tail light." Boy, did that ever come out stupid.

"Well, come on over here," she said and opened a fat catalogue on a countertop pedestal.

He stepped nearer. "Eighty-nine Jeep Wrangler." What would this girl think of him with such an old vehicle? Old or new, though, Jeeps were always manly. Especially a rebuilt one like his and Dad's.

Maybe Chad was the sentimental type, after all.

He tried to focus on the pictures and numbers as the girl's tiny fingertips traced through the columns. Her short nails were painted hot pink, and he couldn't tear his eyes away from them.

The warmth in his cheeks rose by several notches.

Brilliance took his place near Wisdom at their post inside AutoSpot. With arms folded across their mighty chests, they waited, feet apart, on either side of the door observing but not interfering with the boy's interactions with the salesgirl, Becky.

A sly smile spread across Wisdom's mouth, and he caught Brilliance's eye. With an almost imperceptible tip of the head he indicated the door between them. His arms moved to his side, and he unsheathed his sword.

Brilliance returned the grin and unfolded his own arms. "Wait for it."

"Bull in a china shop." They laughed at their own use of the human cliché.

As he stood at the counter, Chad ignored the bell that jingled over the door behind him.

"Chad?"

The boy whirled to find Electra in the doorway. She was clothed in a demonic body suit—that of the demon Destroyer, which of course, was completely invisible to the boy. He could only see the girl. As the demon moved, so did Electra. In unison with Destroyer, she propped her hands against her hips. Four hands instead of two. She folded them across her chest and sauntered over to the counter. Four arms instead of two.

Obviously, the demon hadn't noticed Brilliance and Wisdom

behind him at the counter. The angels eyed each other. Electra's hangover seemed to have miraculously disappeared.

Becky glanced up from her counter. "Hello." Her sincere smile reflected none of Electra's attitude. Had Becky even noticed?

Electra's eyes drilled into the clerk.

Brilliance and Wisdom stepped closer to the counter.

Destroyer now spotted them. He gasped and loosened himself, pushing back from Electra. His scaly lip turned back with a snarl. "Whadda you want? This is my party."

Brilliance laughed, and clamped a mighty hand around the demon's throat. He gave it a strong squeeze. "That's about to end. Don't get too cozy."

Destroyer's yellow eyes bulged and his forked black tongue shot out like a blow-toy. Brilliance gave his neck another squeeze and then let go. The demon hissed and slithered around behind Electra.

Chad nerves lit up as Electra sized up the clerk across the counter.

He'd heard of this antennae-thing between girls.

The clerk turned the page in the catalogue. Maybe she was a good actress. "Be right with you, Miss."

Electra looped her elbow through Chad's and stepped closer. "We're together, honey," she said, the last word laced with the arsenic of a newly-minted southern accent.

Electra had never used the word *honey* before. Or grabbed his arm like that. He shuddered and glanced at the top of Electra's head. The way she was acting, her hair ought to be standing on end.

"That's the one, right there," Chad said, pointing to a squarish-round model and wishing Electra would let go.

"All right," the girl said, catching his eye.

His heart nearly stopped.

"I'll get this ordered. If you can give me your phone number, I'll just call you when it comes in. You can pay for it then."

Too embarrassed to say he didn't have a cell phone, he repeated his mother's number. He'd be back home soon anyway. Once he got the quilt thing straightened out.

Hey, maybe this girl would know something. He rubbed his neck. "Listen, since this is an auto parts store and all, and it's somewhat related, maybe you'd be able to help me with something."

She grinned and leveled her deep brown eyes on his. "I'll give it a try."

Was she really looking at him like that, or was she…? He tore his eyes away long enough to catch a look at her nametag—Becky. Was Becky trying to rile Electra?

Probably not. She appeared genuine, not that type.

Chad held his breath as Electra's irritation intensified. It radiated from her pores. "That's a nice cowgirl shirt you've got on, honey. Are you like a—a ranch hand on the side?"

Chad nudged Electra's shoulder. *Ranch hand? Come on.*

Becky shrugged and smiled. "Thank you. I like your sweater, too. So soft and pretty." Her comments seemed sincere next to Electra's.

"What I wanted to know was," Chad spoke up, "have you got any tricks for getting dirty car oil out of fabric?"

Electra jerked at his arm. "I thought you'd have thrown that raggedy piece of junk in the trash by now."

Becky kept her doe-eyes on Chad's but furrowed her brow. "I'll have to give it some thought. Maybe I can come up with an answer by the time you come back in."

"I thought ranch hands knew everything about cleaning and cooking," Electra said under her breath.

Chad's face grew hotter still. Very subtly, with a trembling hand, he unwound Electra's fingers from his arm.

"All right. Thank you, Becky. I'll be checking back."

"Should be in by Monday. If I don't see y'all before then have a Merry Christmas, now."

Electra pivoted and muttered something about hating ranches.

Brilliance and Wisdom stepped ahead of them and formed a high wall between Destroyer and Chad.

Chad hurried toward the door and opened it for Electra. The look she tossed back was one that could kill.

She paused to let it sink in, then flounced out the door. He sighed and tossed a quick glance back at the counter in time to catch Becky's eye.

Wait—was that a wink? Had the girl actually *winked* at him?

Tony dialed and leaned against the handrail outside the church. He pressed the phone against his year. *C'mon, pick up, Dad.* Practice was about to start.

"Hello?" Dad's voice. Sleepy and probably medicated.

Naturally Dad was home. He never left the house these days. And the likelihood of him cooperating was probably zero. But Tony had to try. Nothing ventured, nothing gained. He dove right in. "Hey, Dad. Morning. Listen, just this once—and after this I won't mention it again— would you please stop by the church and watch us practice. Please."

No response. Tony plowed on. "It's like… Think of it as a music recital. A great chance to hear Robert. And don't you want to hear me too—onstage with others?"

Silence on the other end.

Tony pictured Dad shaking his head on the other end. Every time he pressed the man to meet Robert, Dad was more adamant than the time before. Why was he so all-fired resistant? Robert meant him no harm. In fact, it was just the opposite.

Tony persisted. "You know where the church is, Dad, so come on down. Come hear us. Please? Him and me. Both at once. You don't even have to stay for the whole practice. It's the real deal. Better than Zoom or Facetime. And besides, Robert's only here a few more days."

"No. And don't bug me about it again."

Tony closed his eyes. "I promise, you'd absolutely love it."

"I'm sure I would. But I have no desire to meet your friend Robert. Now. I don't wanna be rude, but quit pesterin' me. I gotta go."

Tony lowered the phone, allowing Dad to disconnect. He nodded.

If Dad wouldn't come to them, then Tony had one more trick up his sleeve.

Knowing Dad, though, he hoped it didn't backfire.

Very Late Saturday Morning

Across from the church, Chad parked his Jeep under his favorite tree. He aimed his wadded burger wrapper at the bag on the floorboard. He'd splurged and bought two small Burger King meals, fries and all. "Your headache gone yet, Electra?"

"Yeah." She pointed a bent fry at him. "So, why don't we take that walk now."

Great, they could walk to Tuscawilla Park and see the migrating birds. So many these days.

"We never made it to Parchment and Quill, did we?"

Not that again.

She raised a hand between them. "But first, there's the bad news."

"Oh?"

"Dad texted me last night. He got a call. His job came through."

"That's good. For him, I guess," he said as he climbed out and circled around to open her door.

"Sure, it is." Electra pulled her bulky red sweater tight around her shoulders and slid out of the vehicle. "But he doesn't care a hoot about me and what I want. It's just him grabbing for more and more money. He doesn't have to do it, and he doesn't care that we have to move, move, move. I'm so sick of it all." She slammed the door. "I wish Mom was here."

Chad stepped back as she shouldered her purse.

"I'm sick of him. I'm sick of Mom and her stuff. I'm sick of Jake. His family. Sick of it all."

Of course, Chad would be sad if Electra moved, but

considering the way she'd been acting lately, it might turn out for the best. At least, he wouldn't be in danger of getting arrested all the time. "I'm sorry. Electra."

"Let's go."

"By the way, you never told me why you're so mad at Jake."

"Not now."

Okay, then, forget it. They'd just go take that walk then.

The construction zone on the far side of the church wasn't a good route to take, but dag nabbit, Electra, with her sour mood, wasn't going to vandalize the kids' projects again, not on his watch.

With Electra's hand in his, he cut to the left, in front of the church itself. Many times, he'd noticed the beauty of the tall clapboard structure with its high Gothic windows and matching red door. It always captured his interest, but he'd never actually been inside. Quirky or not, it was still something he wanted to do. And since they were exploring today…

Faint notes became recognizable as they drew near. "Silent Night" grew in volume as they approached the front steps. A chalk sign next to the banister reminded musicians of today's noon rehearsal of Christmas music.

Above them, one half of the twin doors hung open, dividing its large Christmas wreath down the middle. Maybe today was the day.

Chad tipped his chin toward the door. "Come on. Let's go in and listen."

Electra withdrew her hand. "Nope. Not interested."

He reached for it again. "It's Christmas. Humor me."

"Oh, please." She crossed her arms. "That is so fuddy-duddy."

"Be nice, Electra. I've had no Christmas this year at all." Of course, that was his own stupid fault—soon to end.

The song finished, and she turned away. She tapped her foot, impatient for him to move along. Chords from "O Holy Night" began to fill the air. Man, this was one of his all-time favorites. He had to hear this one. But something beyond curiosity pulled him toward the sound, and he moved up the steps. If Electra didn't care to follow him inside, that was her choice.

His fingers gripped the door's edge between the split wreath, and he glanced back. "It won't take long. Just a minute or two. Sure you don't want to come inside?"

She ignored him.

"Suit yourself," he said and pushed through the interior door.

The hinges whispered shut behind him, slicing between the harsh light of the outdoors and the dark of the sanctuary. Flames danced and flickered in the sconces along the walls. He blinked, adjusting his eyes to the dimness as musicians played their song. He studied the deep reds and greens of the velvet seats and mahogany podium. This place, rich with the scent of candle wax, old wood, and Christmas greenery, had to be a hundred years old. *Nice.*

Up front, a simple combination of organ, flute, and two violins filled the room with a sweet rich melody. One of the violinists was extremely talented. Professional, probably. But not from around here. Hmm. And the other was the guy from the daycare. Not bad. Not bad at all. So he played in the orchestra. He probably wouldn't appreciate Chad being here, but he'd lay low. They hardly seemed to notice him.

The wooden floor creaked underfoot as Chad made his way up the side aisle. With one eye on the musicians, he settled into a padded pew near the back of the near-empty sanctuary.

He scooted over to make a space for Electra in case she

changed her mind then leaned back and closed his eyes to listen. The song washed over him, filling his cells, his breath. It finally felt like a real Christmas.

Brilliance shifted to block the musicians' view of Chad. They needn't see what would take place. He frowned toward the Gothic arch of the church's entryway, wrinkled his nose, and glanced back over his shoulder at Wisdom. "He's right outside. I can smell him."

Wisdom stood tall, a full twelve feet, and raised his arms over Chad. He lowered them, and a flickering column of diamond-light remained above the boy's head. The angel stood back.

"The peace and wisdom of the Holy One is here," Brilliance said. But even as he spoke the door opened. A black form darkened its space. A putrid smell of dead-meat rolled into the room. "Here it comes."

Wisdom snorted. "*It* is right."

Destroyer prowled in with his fingers in his ears. Eyes to the floor. His scabby elbows extended outward as he tried to block the holy music. Disguised in Electra's body, he moved in sync with the girl.

"That's some costume," Brilliance said. But the creature avoided his gaze. His neck and elbows twitched as he tried to hide his eyes from all things holy. "Must've been hard to come inside a church, huh?"

The demon grimaced and approached the end of the pew. Brilliance chuckled. The creature hadn't blocked out all the sounds and certainly couldn't block out the angels' own light.

Wisdom gazed down at the top of Electra's head. "Poor child. No one is praying for her..."

Brilliance nodded but didn't respond. Maybe someday. But for now, they had no orders concerning her.

With hands ready, he waited as the girl paused at the end of the pew.

The last notes of the song ended as another person plopped down beside Chad. He turned. *Well, well. Electra.* He smiled. *Good decision.*

But Electra did not return his smile.

Okay, so she was mad. So, why'd she come inside?

The first notes of "I Heard the Bells on Christmas Day" began, and though he turned back to the musicians her fidgeting soon distracted him.

She crossed her legs to the left. Then she crossed them to the right. She twisted. Hugged her purse. Set it beside her on her seat. "This is so *pfff*," she said, a look of disgust on her face.

Why'd she bother to come in, then? He put his finger to his lips. "Shh. I'm not ready to leave yet."

She shot him a glare, probably expecting him to jump up and leave.

Sorry, Electra. Not this time.

Her fidgeting continued. Finally she glanced up front and noticed the violinist. "That's your playground guy up there, isn't it?" She shook her head. "So gay."

"What? Shhh!" This was incredible. He'd had enough of Electra's negative stuff. He pointed to her red purse and whispered. "How much money have you got in there?"

Electra frowned, clearly with no idea about what he was going to tell her. "Plenty. Maybe a hundred dollars."

That figured.

"Good." He pointed behind them. "See that door? If you don't like it, go outside and call yourself a cab."

Her jaw dropped. "Are you kidding?" She screwed up her face and crossed her arms over the purse again. "No." Then she fixed her eyes on the musicians. "I'm just tired of all this gay stuff."

Gay stuff?

The algebra kid, that guy up front, he was just like Chad. Nothing about him said that he was gay. Yes, he was a musician. And he worked with children. But like a man, he stood up for what was right. How could some self-righteous clown think a person's creativity or musical skills dictated their sexual preference? How stupid.

Chad leaned in, "Listen, Electra." He searched for the right words, kept his voice low. "Playing music is not gay. Not one of those people up there is doing anything gay. It's sin that makes people gay." He tipped his thumb toward the musicians. "That—is not gay. It's music—something you could use a little more of." His jaw clenched and unclenched as he waited for her response.

She shook her head as if to say Chad was wasting his breath.

Then it hit him. He leaned back. *Bingo.* That was the answer. *Talent.*

The very thing those musicians had. And Chad had. Darn good talent.

It was too late now to change what he'd done. He shouldn't have burned those trophies. He huffed. What a dumb mistake. But better late than never on figuring things out.

He should quit letting Jake yank his chain. Laugh in his face. Stop running away. Stop worrying what losers like Jake thought and embrace his real self. Really embrace it. Use that talent. Why did he want to please some bully? And no matter what Electra or some jerks at school said, it did not mean Chad was gay, or anything of the sort. They didn't have, or couldn't have Chad's talent—so they hated him for it.

Chad sucked in a deep breath. The truth felt good.

Jake's problem was jealousy. Plain. Old. Jealousy.

Electra's too. She hated what she couldn't have. She hated a whole list of things. She hated others' skills. She hated stability. Children. Daycares. And mothers. And she was jealous of anyone who had these things.

Oh, she could put on makeup—that was the sum of her talents.

Everything about her was destructive.

Inside the church, Brilliance stepped close to Destroyer as Wisdom placed a hand on Chad's shoulder.

The demon cringed. Trembled. The girl's lips moved in sync with his as he snarled and spoke. "Who cares, Chad? So what?"

Chad leaned toward her. "Let me tell you something else. King David played strings. And he killed lions and bears with those same bare hands."

Electra pressed her fingers into her ears.

Chad kept going. "You think that's gay? No, you don't. Because that's as macho as it gets."

"Oh, aren't we the Bible scholar?" she said, dipping her chin and sneering up at him with her bitter look. The marble-black eyes had returned.

One glance at their alien depths and the boy turned away.

"Let's leave." Her voice came out deep like a man's.

Chad crossed his arms. "I'm staying."

"*Humph!*" She turned away from him and faced the aisle that led to the front of the sanctuary. "Rest room break. Back in a few," she said, and pranced away.

Destroyer tossed a grin over his shoulder and made a rude gesture toward the angels as he accompanied her down the right side of the pews.

Brilliance raised an eyebrow at Wisdom. "Thinks it's in the bag, doesn't he?"

Wisdom nodded and grinned.

Several more songs played. Minutes ticked by. Chad glanced toward the hallway. The boy seemed more interested in Electra's absence than the music.

He shifted positions. Moved closer to the aisle, watched down the hall for her.

He started to rise, but when she appeared down the hallway he settled back into the pew and scooted back to his original spot.

Electra crept back to the seat and plopped back down. Destroyer twisted her mouth in a scornful grin, but the blue of her eyes had returned.

She rested one arm on the pew in front of Chad, the other on the back of his. "You know...? I just don't care for your attitude anymore. So, how about these apples, Chad? You're no longer welcome to stay at the gas station."

Wisdom cupped a hand around the boy's shoulder. Chad leaned back and studied her face. "That's fine. I don't need your gas station. I've slept in my Jeep before, and I'll sleep in it again. No big deal."

Destroyer jerked his eyes toward Brilliance and squinted hatefully. Electra opened her demon-sheathed hand in front of Chad. "Hand me the key."

The boy reached into his pocket and paused. "Can't you wait 'til tomorrow so I can get my stuff out first?"

Destroyer twisted Electra's lip, and shook her head in slow motion. "A sleeping bag and that dirty old rag of a quilt? Don't be ridiculous." Her upturned hand waggled like a witch's claw. "Hand me the key."

He shook his head, unclipped the key from its ring, but held onto it. "You didn't answer the question."

"You'll get it back."

"Are you sure?"

"Promise."

Brilliance balled his fist. "Liar."

The demon ducked and snorted, but, bound as he was to the girl, he couldn't escape. Brilliance slammed the demon's scaly head. A hollow thunk filled the room. A strand of snot flew over the pews.

Brilliance grinned. "I've been looking forward to that."

Wisdom lifted his sword with a grin and swatted it, broadside, across the demon's abdomen. "Loser." The demon howled and doubled over.

"Chad's not yours," Brilliance said. Give it up."

Chad dropped the key in Electra's hand.

Destroyer lowered his head like a buzzard and peered up from the slit of one yellow eye.

"Now," Electra continued, reaching under her bulky sweater and extracting a large animal cracker jar. She held it up by its red lid and gave it a shake. "A little surprise for you." She shoved it toward him.

Chad backed away. Coins and bills—ones, fives, and tens—showed clearly through its plastic sides. Not a whole lot of money, but it wasn't theirs.

Brilliance and Wisdom shifted, shielding Chad from the musicians' eyes up front.

"Where'd you get that? You stole it, didn't you?"

Electra's grin widened, and those large black pupils returned.

"Wouldn't you like to have gay-boy's money jar? I found it on the desk beside his violin case."

"You didn't."

She shoved the jar across the padded pew and up against Chad's side and stood.

Chad pushed it right back. "Are you crazy?" he whispered. "Get this thing out of here."

She thrust it back. "And as for your stuff...you'll find it in a dumpster."

Once again Brilliance reached back his fist. The demon hunched, whimpering in anticipation.

His blow loosened the demon's head. It bopped back and forth like a punching bag.

"Go put this back," Chad demanded.

A slow demonic sneer spread over her face. She backed out of the pew. "And by the way, Chad, if you follow me out the door, I'll scream bloody murder, or *worse*," she said, and headed toward the exit. "And you know what I mean. Then you'll see what jail-time is like."

Chad stared down at the stolen jar of money. Acid shot

through his veins as the reality of his predicament sank in. What had Electra done?

He couldn't walk up to the front of the church and hand this thing over. They'd detain him and call the cops. All the while he'd blubber like an idiot trying to explain what happened. Forget it. They'd never believe such a stupid story.

If he left it here in the pew someone would steal it. That wouldn't be fair.

He could return it down the hall. But not without getting busted first.

He glanced toward the musicians. They played on, paying him no attention.

If he did make it outside with the jar what would he do with it? He could bring it back to the guy and girl at the daycare on Monday, but once again, they would call the police. So, back to square one.

Everything in him wanted to scream, "I am not a thief." Instead, he put on his best poker-face and eased the jar to the floor.

The space was tight, and his cheek brushed against the holder and pink envelopes on the back of the next pew. Wait. Offering envelopes. He grabbed one and lifted out the small pencil that went with it. The least he could do was scribble out a note. Leave an explanation.

With a hymnal for a desk, he scratched out his note. *I did not take this, and I'm sorry about it ending up here. Please return the jar and money to the guy who works in the daycare. I heard it was his. Thank you.*

He laid the note on top of the red lid. With all these church people around tomorrow, surely someone would be honest enough to deliver it.

The melody from "We Three Kings" began to play. Perfect tune to leave on.

Chad rose and crept down the aisle.

Not an eye turned.

He pushed through the door and into the sunlight.

Electra had disappeared. At least he wouldn't have to deal with her big screaming mouth.

How'd he ever get mixed up with her?

He trudged down the steps.

All he had to do now was find the right dumpster. Before a garbage truck did.

They didn't run on Saturdays. Did they?

Saturday

After the rehearsal when most musicians had packed up and headed home, Tony stopped by the rector's office. He knocked on the doorframe and stuck in his head. Brother Ed was in the midst of pulling a dark blue sweater over his head.

"Hi, Tony." He finished up, smoothing his collar and hem. His briefcase sat in his chair.

Tony spoke up anyway. "Looks like you're headed home. Got a minute?"

"Absolutely. What's up?"

Tony slipped inside. "I know you've had a long week. But it's Ben. You know about his cut hand and the rest of what's going on?"

"Yes, yes, yes. I can't let him in until the paperwork clears, though."

"That's not why I'm here."

"Well, Mrs. Sanders—"

"No, sir. I just want to find out what else we can do for Ben."

"But we are doing something, aren't we? Once his background check is finished, he can come in and volunteer. And do it the right way. He'll be a part of our little community in here."

"No. Not that. There's something going on at the residence. Ben's getting picked on. His stuff is getting destroyed. He had fingernail marks on his arm."

The rector stared at Tony. "Is it another resident? Why didn't somebody come to me before this? I might have intervened."

"It happened late yesterday afternoon, and I can't get Ben to say who it is. It's a guy, though."

"Well, you could go talk to his director if you like. Nicely." Brother Ed set the briefcase on the desk. "But if you're going to go flying off the handle like you did with that boy and his girlfriend yesterday—then don't go."

How had the rector heard about that? "I did go down there. And I was very nice. But they claimed nothing at all was going on with Ben. Blamed it on the townspeople outside the facility."

"Gather more information from Ben before you go back to the group home again."

"We—"

"And, yes, if it doesn't clear up, we might have to go to the authorities. But you have to stay in control, Tony. You're no better than them if you copy their attitudes. So, no more Mr. Tough Guy."

The rector was right. And there had to be a better place for Ben. That residence was certainly not family. Ben had nobody to look after him.

Tony stepped out and headed back to where Robert waited in the sanctuary. Right now, he needed to get on home and see if he could try that one last trick with Dad.

Vinnie, in his oldest, most beat-up swimming trunks, stepped out his back door. He ambled toward the pool, his favorite place, with an armload of stuff—his Coke, his phone, a towel, and his gun—safety off. He nudged the chaise into the sun with its back to the French doors.

Nowadays he always faced the wall. One eye on the wall, one eye on the gate by the car. Kept the whole thing in view. Nobody was comin' after him. He'd shoot and ask questions later. Settling into the chaise, he set his pile of stuff on the left. He stretched his neck and eyed the ugly pink scar on his chest. So far it hadn't browned up like the rest of him. He'd been working on it. But either way, it was a battle scar. Somethin' to be proud of. He arranged the towel across his trusty pistol. Gotta keep things fair and square, right? A guy had to look out for himself.

"Dad!"

Vinnie twisted around. That would be Tony comin' in. With Vinnie's back to the door he couldn't quite see him. The door closed and Tony's footsteps approached.

Vinnie reached for another chair, but it lay just out of reach. "Sorry, son." He was tryin' to be nice these days.

Tony circled around with his violin in hand and pulled up the chair. He sat there with the toes of his shoes against the concrete and his knees jiggling and studied his dad with a grin.

Vinnie couldn't resist. "The way your knees are dancin'

you either gotta go to the bathroom or you got somethin' important to say."

"You busy right this minute?"

Vinnie shrugged and spread his palms as if to say, "See for yourself."

"Well—you couldn't come down to the church to hear me play, so I brought my music to you. You wanna hear me now?"

Vinnie hadn't wanted to avoid his son, he just didn't want to get involved with that Robert fella. "Sure. And I didn't want you to—" *Nevermind.* "Okay, son. I'm all ears. Play away."

He leaned back in his chair. Why was the boy so all-fired interested in showin' off his music? He practiced in his room every day. 'Course Tony kept his door shut. But he also knew Vinnie wasn't deaf.

Tony lifted the violin to his chin. His bow touched the strings. Out flowed the notes of *O Holy Night.* Vinnie closed his eyes. He knew this one.

Vinnie'd heard his son through his closed door, but this wasn't the same. It sounded so good up close. And Tony hit every note right.

Vinnie nodded with pride as the music flowed out of his son's instrument. Then came the *fall on your knees* part. Vinnie's favorite.

He tipped his ear toward the violin—he could almost swear Tony was playing two violins.

Vinnie placed his feet on either side of the chaise and leaned forward, his elbows on his knees. Eyes squeezed shut in concentration. Why hadn't he paid attention to his son before? This was the most amazing music he'd ever heard. *Beautiful.*

The notes rose and curled in waves, surrounding him and gliding through the crispy air like calligraphy—or sharpened swords—or gently drawn pinpoints—how could he even describe them? Tears seeped out and rolled down Vinnie's cheeks. He opened his eyes and gazed at his son. So many notes from one violin?

Tony lowered his bow and instrument and bowed his head—*but wait.* The notes hadn't stopped.

Wha—? Vinnie twisted around. Who was back there? From behind his chair emerged a second violinist—a young man with dark hair—and the kindest eyes and smile Vinnie'd ever seen—the real source of those amazing notes. He stepped around on Vinnie's left. His gaze, riveted on Vinnie, never faltered as he played through the rest of the verses.

Vinnie wiped his cheeks. *This couldn't be Robert.* No wonder Tony raved about him.

Lost for words, Vinnie grappled for the towel and plastered it over his eyes with both hands. What a baby. He never used to cry like this.

The song came to a close. Vinnie lowered the towel and startled. He backed away. There knelt Robert beside him in his fancy silk pants and starched shirt. Inches from his face. Vinnie swallowed. There was no way Vinnie could grab his gun down there by the man's knees.

"See? I don't bite." The man smiled. His soft voice, spoken as one would to a frightened animal, blended with the music still echoing in Vinnie's head.

Vinnie's guts jittered as he let out a matching sigh. "Robert?"

A nod.

Those eyes. Those dark brown eyes—like sunshine.

What had Vinnie expected? An angry ogre? A small helpless child still covered in blood? What about these legs?

Robert's right hand rested on the armrest, his chin just

above it, the violin and bow cradled in his left. "I forgave you long ago, Vinnie. I tried to tell you. Remember the letter?"

How could Vinnie forget it? It had turned him inside out with fear. He thought it was a— His thoughts returned to the useless gun down there on the concrete. But like Tony claimed, Robert held no malice. That much seemed plain.

"Won't you accept my gift, my forgiveness?"

Vinnie glanced toward his son. But Tony had left. Good. Tony didn't need to hear about all this.

Vinnie twisted away from Robert's gaze. Inched to the right. But with one foot on the left and one on the right he couldn't move too far.

His left shoulder tingled with Robert's face so close. He squirmed, wanting to rub a hand across the spot, but refrained. He hung his head. The man's gaze cut right through him as Vinnie studied the weave of the chair.

But Robert's intensity—his *gentleness* melted Vinnie like butter in a microwave. The jitters in his guts grew stronger and stronger until he couldn't take it anymore and he doubled over. Burying his face in his hands he bawled like a baby. Snot drained all over the place. He pinched at it with the towel but kept his head down. "I'm so sorry. I'm so sorry for what I've done."

A gentle hand gripped his shoulder.

"If only I could fix it," Vinnie blubbered. "Undo it. But I can't. I can't." He shook his head. His mouth contorted as sobs wracking his body.

Robert's hand never left.

When Vinnie could weep no more, he scrubbed his face with the towel. But he couldn't sit up. Nobody was going to see him like this.

The hand patted his back. "Is that a yes?"

He couldn't face this man. "How could you possibly forgive me?" he mumbled into the fabric. "How? How?"

"Because," Robert said. "I decided to." His voice was still gentle. Appealing. "I care more about Vinnie—that teenager of long ago—than holding a grudge. What happened to him—is all I've thought about—all I've worried about over the years. Sure, he crossed a line. A line he hadn't planned on. But we all cross a line somewhere. We all make stupid decisions. And what happened to my poor little friends who saw it. Those little guys. What happened to them?"

A fresh sob filled Vinnie's towel. "I'm so ashamed. I should be begging you to forgive me. Not the other way around."

Robert gave him a firm double pat, then pulled his hand away. "So, yes, you will you accept my forgiveness?"

Vinnie's breathing slowed, in, out, in, out, as he pondered what to say. Of course, he wanted forgiveness. His lifted his arm to peer out, but his eyes encountered the starched blue cuff of Robert's sleeve. "You're sure?"

Robert took him by the elbow. "Sit up."

Robert stretched an arm around him. Vinnie felt like a little kid right now. How could this guy hug him?

"Take it," Robert said. "Forgiveness is a gift. Clean slate, Vinnie. Clean slate. Let it set you free."

Vinnie couldn't very well return a hug, seated like this, but he wanted to. Careful of the violin, he hobbled off the chaise on half-numb legs. Robert, the boy who'd become a man, stood. He met Vinnie at the end where they embraced. This time Vinnie wept for joy. He wiped the back of his hand across his nose then pushed away. Didn't want to look funny. Or sissy. "I don't deserve this. I could never make it up to you." He nodded. "Thank you, Robert."

"No, you can't. But God's made it up to me. In so many ways."

Vinnie raised his arms and took in a deep breath. He felt so free. He spotted Tony behind his chaise and gave him a grin. He paused in front of Robert then sank back into his chaise. "So, this is how it feels. To be free." He had to let this sink in.

He cast another glance toward Tony. Had Robert told him what had happened?

Robert, shook his head, as if sensing the thought. "I've never said a word, Vinnie. And I won't. That's up to you."

Vinnie dropped his head. He started to speak, but Tony had stepped near with his violin. He laid a hand on his dad's good shoulder.

"Look, Dad. I know something happened. Way back. I do. But I have no idea what. Nobody's talking. It's probably none of my business. You can tell me now, tell me later, or don't tell me at all. I don't have to know. Whatever it is, I'll still be your son." He patted Vinnie's shoulder. "And I'll always love you, Dad. Always. No matter what."

Vinnie blew out a mouthful of air. He didn't deserve all this. Not after all he'd done.

Tony moved around and stood next to Robert. "One more song," he said, then the two violists raised their violins under their chins. Their bows lifted. "Now, Dad, you might want to stand back up for this one. You might even know the words."

"Whatcha got?" Vinnie's knees were shakin' like leaves in a windstorm, and he wasn't sure if he could take any more.

From down on the concrete under his towel came faint vibrations. His phone. He ignored it.

Singing along with their instruments the two violinists, belted out the first of several rounds of *We Wish You a Merry*

Christmas. Vinnie nodded and joined right in. At the top of his voice. He didn't care what anyone thought.

Between lines he peeked at the phone.

His blood ran cold. *BLOCKED CALL.*

He sang another verse and pressed the passcode. No need to hear the whispered voicemail. Its transcription was clear. *I'm coming to get you.*

A cold sweat broke out across his brow. The caller couldn't be Robert. So, who was it?

Saturday, Mid-Afternoon

Chad parked his Jeep behind the old Texaco station and sucked in a deep breath as he climbed out. He'd never met anyone that could set him up like Electra could, or get him into so much trouble.

Somehow, he'd escaped from the church and left the money jar behind without getting arrested.

And now Electra had a big head start to throw his stuff in a dumpster. It wouldn't bother him if he never saw her again.

Then again, maybe she'd lied about it. He had to see—make sure the quilt wasn't still inside the station.

He stepped around to the back door. A piece of notebook paper, slit down the middle, rested loosely over the knob. She'd been here all right. Must have come straight over. By taxi probably. He gritted his teeth and reached for the note.

Go find your junk in the dumpster.

No surprise there. He wadded the paper, and threw it against the door.

But was it really true? Or was the quilt inside?

Without a key there was no way for him to look inside. Not with all those newspapers plastered over the front windows.

He wouldn't put it past Electra to leave his quilt locked inside and laugh herself silly while he went on a wild goose chase hunting through all the dumpsters in town.

He'd have to trust that she'd actually followed through. She *had* been here, that was a fact. What else would she do here besides get his stuff? So, odds were the quilt was indeed lying on top of some fly-infested garbage in a rusty dumpster somewhere. But which one?

He left his Jeep parked behind the station and jogged around the street corner to the Greyhound station—as good a place as any to get started. He crossed over the two lanes of cracked pavement, passed the urine-scented palmetto hedges and palms. They'd served him well by obscuring his goings and comings at the Texaco. He didn't look forward to plundering the station's dumpster. But this one, the closest one to the Texaco station, seemed a logical place for Electra to throw the quilt. But who was she to be logical? Maybe he'd get lucky and find it on the first try. He didn't care about the bed roll. It was easily replaced.

In back of the building, the choking stench of urine grew stronger. Homeless men and women, likely drawn to the cheap food at the train station's hot dog stand, were known to camp here.

A lightweight creature bumped against Chad's shin. He glanced down. A cat. It meowed and moved away to rub against the rusted corner of the dumpster.

He called out, "Kitty, kitty," but left it alone as he crossed to the dumpster and lifted the lid.

"Hey, kid!"

Chad startled at the muffled voice but kept his grip on the lid. He turned. Scanned for its male owner.

"Wha' are ya' doin'?" The words, slurred from either drinking, drugs, or sleep, came from a mound of flattened cardboard boxes to the left of the dumpster.

"Who…?"

"That's my dumpster."

The cardboard wobbled, and fell. Out peered a toothless old man. His scrawny torso, draped loosely in a filthy short-sleeved shirt, reclined against the bricks. Gnarled fingers gripped a bottle inside a greasy brown bag. "You're trespassing."

The scent of alcohol and body odor reached Chad's nose. "I'm—I don't want your dumpster, sir. I'm hunting for something."

"You fin' sumpin' in there, it's mine. You hear? That 'ere's my dumpster."

"Understood." Chad peered inside, moved around some cardboard. "Don't worry, sir. It's not in here." He dropped the lid. "You can have your dumpster back now."

He waved his bottle. "Now get outta here, and don' come back," His last few words faded away as if his energy had expired.

"Have a good day, sir."

As Chad rounded the corner a thought stopped him. He fished in his pocket then doubled back with two quarters extended between his fingers. It wasn't much, but it was something. "Here you go, sir. Maybe you can use it."

The man's wrinkled brown arm, as frail as a bird's wing, extended for the coins. His wide grin revealed three teeth.

It was the least Chad could do for the old guy. Whether he drank or not, the guy still had to eat. If he even could.

After darting back over to the station, he drove his Jeep to its usual spot at the parking lot near the church then set out on foot. It took nearly an hour to search every stinking dumpster on the south side of the boulevard. How could one street have so much trash?

Despite the December weather, sweat drained down Chad's face. His arms ached. He needed a break. He sneaked a drink of water from the water hose behind a ladies' tea restaurant and slumped against a tree, disgusted that he'd found nothing.

That quilt had to be somewhere along this route. But where?

If Electra's friend had picked her up, the boulevard was a logical path to the girl's house. And pulling over on the right side of the road would be easier than cutting left across traffic.

But then, Electra wasn't logical. And she could have lied. She could have taken the quilt home and burned it in her dad's barbeque pit. Or left it at the gas station after all. He wouldn't put it past Electra with her mean streak.

Why'd he ever get mixed up with that girl? First the dirty oil, now this. It seemed like a lost cause.

But he stood to his feet, stretched out the kinks, and kept moving. At the end of the boulevard rose the brown and orange Baskin-Robbins sign. Electra's favorite place. Uh huh. He'd be sure to check that one. Then he'd search the other side of the boulevard. That would take him back to his Jeep.

He trudged on. One thing was certain, this town was full of dumpsters. If all else failed, he'd pick the lock at the old Texaco—just to make sure.

After searching every dumpster along the boulevard, Chad called it a day. At AutoSpot he pulled in beside a shiny blue truck, its cab nearly hidden by a stack of green hay bales. Nice truck. Someone had money.

Before he turned off the engine a realization hit. He should have cleaned up before coming down here. Two hours of dumpster diving had him sweating.

He raised his arm and sniffed underneath. Gah!

No way could he go inside smelling like this. What was he thinking? What would the cute blond girl think?

He reached under the passenger seat and felt around until his fingertips found the deodorant. There. He coaxed it out. He'd been doing pretty good lately, alternating between the hose behind the VO and the bathroom sink at work.

He lifted his shirt and rolled on the deodorant—then paused. What he really should have done was stopped by a gas station and used the bathroom to wash up first.

He thought of his hot shower at home but dismissed it. No time for that.

Right now he had to think. Would the girl be able to smell him? He rolled on one more coat, took another sniff, and tossed the tube on the floor.

Forget this. Too risky.

Back to the VO for another hose bath—equally hazardous in the broad daylight.

At least it wasn't chilly.

Once again Chad parked near the deserted VO. He climbed in the back seat and scrounged around for some clean clothes. He'd pretty much kept them separated, but the clean ones were getting scarcer and scarcer. He hoped the AutoSpot girl never caught sight of the mess back here.

He found some things and stuffed them under his arm. With the bar of soap in his hand, he made the cautious trip around the side and behind the Christmas tree house once again. No activity. No barking dogs. Probably at work. Or taking a nap.

All the same, he'd better make this quick.

This time he dragged the hose into the hedges and turned on the water. He knotted the hose around a limb and stepped out of his clothes.

Brrr! The water felt colder today than the other night. Good thing for mild weather. He scrubbed as hard and fast as he could, raising a good lather before rinsing, and relishing the feel of clean skin. Not half bad for a cold-water shower.

Yeah, buddy. Off with that dumpster scum.

With the water still pouring, Chad dried off with his dirty clothes, folded them, unknotted the hose, and pulled it over toward the VO and turned it off.

Back at the Jeep, he did a fist pump and climbed in. He'd barely spent thirty minutes.

It felt good to be clean.

No wonder dogs acted the way they did after a bath.

Within minutes Chad was back in the same parking space in front of AutoSpot. *Oh yeah.* He turned off his engine, reached under the seat, slapped on some deodorant, and climbed out.

The name *Becky* played across the marquis inside his head. What a beautiful name. Very nice. *Becky. Becky.*

Inhaling deep, he blew a breath out through his mouth. Somehow, with Electra out of the picture, a load had lifted off his shoulders. Maybe he should feel sad. But he didn't. He felt free.

And hopefully Miss Becky was at AutoSpot today.

Would she remember him?

What about the rude scene Electra had made earlier when she'd grabbed at his arm and acted snotty? Did Becky believe they were an item? Maybe so. How could he straighten that out?

But then there was that wink. It was a wink, wasn't it?

He hurried up to the glass door. But one glance at his reflection, and he stopped short. He spun up against the stucco wall.

His shirt.

Becky couldn't see him in this thing.

How could he be so dumb? He'd put on the shirt Electra gave him. No way could he wear that thing into the store. And come to think of it, after what Electra had said about it, she probably stole it. How had she phrased it? *A gift from the mall.*

His mind raced back through the inventory of clothes he'd just sorted through in the back of the Jeep.

Swinging open the back-passenger door, he pulled off the contemptible shirt and threw it inside. Using both hands, he dug through the laundry scattered over the backseat and floorboard. Everything needed folding.

A tan t-shirt caught his eye, and he pressed it against his nose. Not too bad. He yanked it over his head, grabbed the offensive shirt, and slammed the door.

Wait. His hair. He climbed up in the front passenger side and plowed through the glove compartment.

His comb, looking pretty much new and unused, was wedged between some papers. Time to give it a workout.

He twisted the rearview mirror toward him and raked the comb through his damp but curly mop.

He shook his head. *Time for a haircut. Way past time.*

And—he patted the pocket that held his meager earnings—it would happen today. Good plan. He grabbed the shirt again, stepped out, and slammed the door.

With one eye on the AutoSpot door he scampered across the parking lot to the dumpster near the street and flipped Electra's shirt under the lid. Halfway back to the door he stopped. Glanced at the dumpster.

Nah. Electra would never come here to toss his quilt. She hated this place. Hated Becky.

Moving on, he stepped up on the porch and reached for the handle.

What if Becky didn't even remember him?

Maybe he was being presumptuous about this attraction for her. And that wink. It could have been a twitch.

Worst of all—he gave the door a push—what if Electra had ruined it for him?

The overhead bell tinkled as Chad stepped through the AutoSpot door. He'd almost forgotten about that.

There stood Becky behind the counter. She glanced up from her clipboard and grinned. "Hi. Didn't think I'd see you so soon."

Wow. She did remember him.

This time, she wore a ribbon at the end of her braid. It matched her pink cowgirl shirt. Her fingertips brushed against her chin, still the same little pink nails that she had before. Chad could hardly breathe.

"W—I—was just checking on the order," he said, glancing around for something safer and more boring than Miss Prettiness to calm his nerves.

"Our delivery is fast." She smiled. "But not that fast."

What a stupid thing for him to say. Now, she'd know he came in just to see her. His cheeks were on fire. His whole head must look like a giant version of Rudolph's nose.

The front door bell tinkled again. Chad turned with a sense of dread, half expecting to see Electra. But it was only Ben, his Hershey Bar buddy.

Ben grinned. "Hi, Chad. Hi, Becky."

Chad nodded, still focused on what he should say to Becky. Somewhere along the way his brain had turned to scrambled eggs.

"How's it going, Ben?" Becky said, then turned back to Chad.

As she met his gaze the heat in his face rekindled. If he could just control himself.

Becky leaned forward, "Tell me again. What kind of cloth was it you wanted cleaned—that thing your girlfriend said to throw away?"

He tried to swallow, but it felt like a sock lodged in his throat. This girl was so different from Electra.

What had Chad seen in her, anyway? A pretty face? That was about the sum of it.

"N—not my girlfriend." Whew. There. That was out in the open now. He took a deep breath. "And, uh, it was a quilt."

"A quilt? You're trying to get dirty car oil out of a quilt?"

"Hi, there, Ben." An older lady emerged from between the rows of merchandise in back. She came out from behind the counter and hugged Ben like an old buddy. "How are you today?"

Becky leveled her big brown doe-eyes on Chad's. "The quilt?"

"It's my mom's quilt. My great-great grandma sewed it, and—"

The older lady had taken Ben by the arm. "Here, Ben, have an RC." She guided him to the drink machine near the door. "Pick something out."

"It's a long story how the oil got on the quilt and all—I just have to get it cleaned. Have to. I can't let Mom see it like this. She'd be—really upset."

"Bring it in. Maybe I can help you."

Chad leaned against the counter. "It's a little complicated, but right now I've got to find it first."

The older lady stepped close now, her attention on Chad's story. Ben followed her with his RC.

Chad kept talking. "The girl, the one who's not my girl-friend, she got really mad at me and threw Mom's quilt in a dumpster."

Becky frowned. "Can't you just go get it?"

"I wish. But I have no clue which dumpster it's in. And who knows what kind of grunge a dumpster will add to it."

"I see."

Ben waved good-bye to the group and moved toward the front door with his RC Cola in hand. "Bye, everybody. Thank you for the soda." The bell jingled as he exited.

Given the store it was attached to, Chad could learn to like that sound.

"I love that kid," Becky said. "He comes in all the time just to say hi and hang around. Left kinda quick today, though."

"I like him, too," the lady said. "What a sweetheart. He'd do anything for you, too."

"So," Becky patted Chad's arm, "when you find that quilt,

and I'll pray that you do—want me to try to clean it?" She turned to the woman. "It's got a big black oil stain on it."

"Oh, dear. That's too bad," she said.

"It—it's an heirloom," Chad said. "But I don't really have the money to pay you. How about you tell me how to do it?" Then it hit him. "Or we can cancel the order for the tail light, and I'll just give you that amount for trying to clean it. Unless it's more."

"Oh, honey, you don't need to be doing that," the lady said. She and Becky traded a look. "Cleaning quilts is pretty tricky even without a stain."

They both nodded.

"Chad, this is my mom, Mrs. McGregor. Sorry I didn't introduce you."

The furnace fired up in his cheeks again. "Nice to meet you."

"You, too, honey. I think it's nice how you want to clean the quilt for your mother. You must care a lot about her to do something like that."

Yeah, he shouldn't have taken the quilt to begin with. And right now, he could have crawled under the counter with both of them staring at him like that.

"Tell me how big the stain is and how long ago it happened," Mrs. McGregor said. "A fresher stain is sometimes easier to deal with."

She nodded, frowning intently as Chad explained.

"Honest," Chad said, "if you just tell me how to do it, I can clean it. I've done laundry before."

Becky and her mom exchanged looks again and shook their heads in unison with a look of *oh, no* on their faces. "You just bring it in, honey. Let us worry about cleaning it."

"Thank you. I appreciate you all trying to help me," he said, then headed for the door. He turned and gave a nod. "I'll keep looking for it."

Now that Chad had all this help and attention—where was the quilt?

Chapter 10

Monday After Work

Quitting time at Tires-R-Us. At least for Chad. He clocked out and washed up in their grease-stained restroom. He rubbed his hand across his new haircut and studied the reflection in the cracked mirror. A quick trim on Saturday had turned out pretty good. For once the barber hadn't scalped him. At least now, when he visited the AutoSpot, he'd be halfway presentable.

His shirt's reflection reminded him of his increasingly desperate laundry situation. He sniffed his armpits—not too bad—deodorant would fix that—and headed out into the dark for his vehicle.

He dragged his hand across the back door of his Jeep as he passed by. His miniature home these days. And weren't people building doghouse-sized homes these days? *Tiny houses* they were called. Nothing like living light. And he had the whole system down pat. Anybody who could sleep on a pile of laundry in a Jeep's back seat knew what they were doing.

Not that Chad had to live in the Jeep, though. He had a good home and a mother waiting for him to return. It wouldn't be long now.

But first things first. He'd be returning with Mom's quilt in hand. Clean, too. And no need jumping the gun and bothering her with all the embarrassing details while he got it straightened out. After the fact was best.

He climbed in the Jeep and turned his key as the back door of Tires-R-Us creaked opened and shut again. He flicked on his headlights, started his engine, and peered into his rear-view mirror.

Jim, one of the tire men, crossed behind him as he headed for his own gold beater next to Chad's. He gave the man a wave and waited to back out.

Jim tossed his battered lunch box in and nodded toward Chad's taped-up tail light. "Better get that there tail light fixed. Ain't much light comin' out through that red tape, you know."

"Yeah, I know. Thanks. I'm actually on the way now," Chad said, putting it in reverse. "Seeing if my order's in."

"Have a good one, man," Jim slid in, and cranked up. Chad let him back out first.

On the way to the AutoSpot, a single thought nagged at Chad. What if Becky always acted friendly to everyone? What if that wink she gave him the other day wasn't really a wink. Maybe she winked at everybody. Look how she acted with Ben, all super friendly and such. Chad was probably just another Ben. One of many people she liked.

All right. Enough worrying. Chad would tone down his expectations. That way he wouldn't be disappointed. Or set himself up for a letdown.

All that red-faced embarrassment the other day—what a waste of energy. He nodded. Decided what to do. Today he'd go into the store, get the tail light, and get back out.

Down the street the AutoSpot, sign came into view. Once again Chad pulled in beside the blue truck. No hay in the back tonight. This time he took the time to read the sign on the vehicle's door. Blue Skies Ranch. Hmm. Somebody from there was a frequent shopper. What was a ranch person doing here? But hey. He pushed the Jeep's door open and shrugged. Ranchers had to need auto parts too.

His sneakers hit the concrete, and he shoved open the AutoSpot door. This time he was ready for the bell. And there stood Becky grinning at him. She must have been watching him through the little hole-covered window dressings—the ones where people could see out but not see in. How did that work, anyway? He made up his mind that he didn't like them. They were an invasion of privacy.

Becky acted like she was up to something with those dimples and big grin. She didn't give him a chance to think. "Hi, Chad. Welcome back."

His heart flipped. His chin dipped. He gazed at the floor. Tried not to look at her as he gained control of the fire in his face. What was wrong with him? He had told himself not to do this again. "Hi. Just checking on that order of mine."

"You didn't want to call first and save yourself a trip? I hate to say it, but the part you ordered didn't come in today."

She had him there. He peered up, and her dimples deepened. "Well, I—I was just in the neighborhood."

A football-player sized jock came from around the counter with a mountain of boxes in front of his chest. Who was this? Had to be six-two, at least. The guy nodded at Chad, but instead of going on about his business, he held Chad's gaze with a long unsmiling stare as he bumped through the gate and unloaded his cargo in front of a display near the door.

What was that all about?

"Thank you, Bobby," Becky said. "Could you line those up on the bottom racks for me?"

Football player didn't answer, just grinned at Becky as if they had some kind of cute little secret between them. He pulled a box cutter out of his pocket, and… *No way.* Was that a wink? Had Bobby just winked at Becky?

Chad turned back to Becky but the gnarly sensation in his back told him the guy's eyes were still on him.

Becky leaned her chin on her knuckles and looked at Chad with those big brown eyes. "Well, I've got some big news for you."

A metallic squeak drew Chad's attention to the aisles behind Becky. Ben emerged between two and three pushing a broom. Ben had a job? When had he started working here? The broom scuffled along the edge of the counter, and Becky hopped over it as Ben headed up the next two aisles.

"You gave Ben a job?"

"Yep." She pressed a fist against her lips as if to hold in some kind of excitement. "But that's not all. There's something better."

What? That she had a new football player boyfriend? That dude behind Chad? The grinning idiot staring a hole through Chad's back? Had to be that, the way he'd just winked at Becky. The way he and Becky kept smiling at each other like they had a secret. Had to be that.

And that truck, that stupid Blue Skies truck out there, that probably belonged to old Bobby too. He'd been in here the other day with that truck out there. And those muscles. Old Bobby probably got 'em by working as a big dumb ranch hand. *Ox.*

And it was just Chad's luck to bust into the middle of a relationship like this—third man out. Chad should never have come in tonight. How stupid of him. And, of course, his tail light wasn't in yet. He'd end up having to come back.

Chad felt like a shrimp next to this massive jock—he could eat Chad for breakfast.

He sighed.

"Don't you want to guess?" she said.

He glanced up at her big brown eyes. "No, you better tell me. I'm fresh out of ideas."

"Well, Ben, here, knows. Tell him, Ben."

Ben leaned the broom against a shelf and came up to the desk. His face glowed. "Your quilt? I found it for you. I found your shirt, too."

The quilt?

"Just after you left on Saturday," Becky said. "Ben took it upon himself to hunt through the dumpsters."

Chad gripped the counter and leaned toward Ben. Forget the jock back there. "You found the quilt?"

Ben nodded, obviously pleased with himself.

Chad nearly yelled. "I knew it would turn up!"

"And not five minutes after you drove off," Becky said.

"That's awesome," Chad punched the air, emphasizing the last word. "Man, I owe you, Ben. I've looked everywhere for that thing."

Ben must've remembered the quilt from that day at the store. What if Chad hadn't shown it to him?

Ben grinned, clearly pleased with himself.

"You have no idea what this means. Do you still have it?"

Before he could answer, Becky's mother emerged from around the end of aisle five. "Hi, Chad, honey. I couldn't help but hear y'all talkin' back in the office. I see why your mother liked that quilt of hers. That Texas Star pattern is such a classic."

"I hope you don't mind, Chad," Becky said. "We took it straight to the ranch and got started on it."

Ranch?

Becky's mom pointed a finger at him and grinned. "Chad.

That's a mighty fine name, son. Manly." Then she strode back down aisle five.

Fine name?

Becky blushed then busied herself with merchandise under the counter. When she set an empty carton on top of the desk her face was still rosy.

Becky lived on a ranch?

"You…"

"Don't worry, it's all under control. It should be done pretty soon. We're using a strong dish detergent on stains that can't be brushed out with a wet rag."

"You have a ranch?"

"Have you ever heard of Blue Skies Ranch?"

Chad's head nodded. "So, that's your blue truck out there?"

His comment couldn't have sounded any stupider.

Bobby, who had finished loading up the display, had returned to the counter beside Chad with a knowing look. "Oh, and she washed your shirt, too."

Nooooo. Not that shirt! The one with the bass and the rhyming word. *Electra.* Everything about her was trouble. He felt the blood drain from his face. *Busted, boy, you are busted.*

Bobby's mouth stretched into a wide and stupid grin. Sausage-sized fingers scratched an itch on his bull-sized neck.

Now that Bobby boy had successfully humiliated Chad, he was probably a happy camper. He'd probably enjoy flattening Chad with his meaty fist, too.

"Bobby," Becky said, "could you be a sweetie and go get the shirt out of my truck? It's all folded up in a bag on the front seat."

Sweetie? Chad's heart sank. And sending him out to her truck? Football Dude had to be her boyfriend.

Chad somehow managed to thank Becky and get his embarrassed hide out the door and back to the Jeep. Football Dude followed him outside in the dark and smirked as Chad backed out of his spot.

Chad glared back at him. *Get lost. Look at the guy. Chad's scrawny self vs football dude? Forget it.*

Chad stomped the gas and screeched away from the AutoSpot.

Well, at least his problem with the quilt was resolving.

Chad's thoughts turned to mush as his foot pressed the pedal. He shouldn't be wasting gas, but he drove around anyway, burning energy. Stewing. He soon found himself near the Greyhound station.

While he was there, he might as well finish that other bit of business behind the station.

He pulled in by the old Texaco, backed around the side of the building, and pulled to a stop next to the burn pile.

This shouldn't take long. He grabbed a flashlight from the glove compartment and climbed out.

In the burn pile he found a half-burned stick and raked through the ashes. "Lord, let me find something in here, at least part of my stuff."

There. He leaned in and pulled out a half-burned trophy and set it aside. He dug out another.

The trophies were worthless, but not the engraved metal plates, the most important parts. He ran a thumb over a scorched plate. It showed promise of polishing up.

"I guess that's it," he said and headed for the back of the Jeep with his hands full.

He opened it up, lifted the edge of the box, and laid them underneath.

Vinnie, in tropical-style swimming trunks, unloaded his Coke, his phone, two towels, and his loaded pistol—safety off—on the concrete by his chaise. Then he settled in, angling his seat just so with its back to the door. Had to keep an eye on the wall and the electronic gate. Didn't want no replays—not with all those blocked phone calls.

A crisp black night had settled over the town beyond his home. But you couldn't tell in here. Looked like midday in the Bahamas. The pool and patio of his Mediterranean home were awash in floodlights.

No more meditatin' out here in the dark enjoyin' the stars and crickets. Not since the shooting.

He eyed the rolled-up towels on the concrete beside him and tried to decide whether to use them or not.

Nah, he could take it. Sixty degrees wasn't too bad.

His Nancy should be back pretty soon from choir practice. She hadn't wanted to leave him tonight. Felt guilty about it. But he'd insisted. "Go on to choir," he'd said. "I'll be fine."

His gaze drifted across the illuminated waters and new twelve-foot wall he'd ordered while he was laid up in the hospital. It replaced his wrought iron fence and hedges. "Yank them all out," he told 'em. And they had. Even the statues.

Too many hidin' places.

He dropped his gaze to that point in the wall. He squinted. *Right there.* Right behind that wall there the concealed shooter had aimed his gun—just months ago now—between the iron bars and foliage.

He averted his eyes. A shudder rippled through him as he rubbed his fingers across the scar on his chest.

A block wall was nothing beautiful. But it was necessary. And it solved the problem. Vinnie had a safe little cave in here.

Yeah, he could still sit outside at night. If all the lights were on.

There'd be no more meditatin' out here in the dark, though. Even though they'd caught the shooter.

Somebody was still out there tryin' to get 'im.

His gaze drifted down to the black screen on his phone.

If only it would stay that way. If only that idiot would stop those blocked calls. And quit buggin' him.

Yeah, that was it. He oughtta bug the phone. Sure. Sure. Vinnie'd call the police tomorrow. Set it up. Or was it the FBI?

He didn't deserve them threatening calls. Not anymore. Vinnie'd changed.

It wasn't something he'd set out to do. It's just that bein' nice was getting easier—and, well, a bit enjoyable. He crossed his feet on the chaise and took a swig from his canned Coke. Nobody had ever told him how much fun it was to be Mr. Nice Guy.

Goosebumps rose along his arms, and he set the drink down to unfurl the towels over his body. He tucked one around his chin. Didn't matter that he'd given in to the chill. All was well on this perfect December night. Gotta love Florida.

This would feel like summer to the folks up north.

He squinted up at the sky. What a shame he couldn't see the stars anymore. He'd just have to bask in the glow of the floodlights and enjoy the smaller things. At least the crickets still chirped. They sang much slower now, with the cooling temperatures, but combine that with the sounds of an occasional slow-moving car or incoming train, and you've got some excellent music. Enough to put one to sleep. He closed his eyes. Let his body relax.

Boom ba da! Boom ba da!

Vinnie jumped. Bolted upright—eyes wide. His chest vibrated. His chair vibrated. The air vibrated. He scanned the empty patio—then blew out a breath and settled back down. All but the slam of his heart.

He glanced down at the gun by his phone and let it lie.

No worries. Just a vehicle with a jacked-up radio.

The racket faded into the distance, and his eyes closed again. He tried to imagine positive things—to slow the crazy horse-race in his chest. He cracked his eye and peeked at the pool. Yeah, he wished everyone owned a pool like his—to sit beside and enjoy.

But as his heart settled, a niggling thought took over. A thought he had once pushed away. It crept now to the front of his brain and demanded full attention.

His claim about that radio—and his car. Not a month before the shooting.

Best sound he'd ever had. Best car he'd ever had. And for a steal, too. Like he'd always said, it paid to know things about people. You could always gain the upper hand.

And for a steal, too. The words screamed in his head.

He'd ripped that guy off. Cheated him.

That ain't right.

Vinnie knew what he had to do. He had to fix this.

He tossed the towels aside and climbed to his feet. Yeah, he had dirt on the car guy. Vinnie had dirt a lot of people. But so what? Vinnie had garbage of his own. Lots of it.

Vinnie was changed. He didn't need to be holdin' dirt over other peoples' heads.

Wasn't there a word for that? *Extortion.* Yeah. Extortion.

He dove inside the house to find his checkbook. To make things right.

He scratched out a $30,000 check plus another one for $5,000. *Kind of a bonus. That oughtta do it.* Within a few minutes he'd made out a stamped envelope addressed to the Mercedes car dealer.

Something new—a thrill—filled Vinnie's chest. Made 'im wanna dance.

Vinnie locked up the house and climbed into the car. He slid the envelope between his tropical britches and the seat. As he cranked her up, the radio, already on, blasted out the beginning notes of *Sleigh Bells.*

Vinnie grinned. Just the right song.

He headed out of his driveway toward the post office downtown. Vinnie couldn't wait to get that money out of his hands and into the box.

"Just hear those sleigh bells jingle-in' ring-ting-tinglin'," he bellowed at the top of his voice. At least he knew those few words. He caught a few more words here and there, and danced in his seat, careful not to bust loose those fireworks in his chest. Then *Feliz navidad, feliz navidad, feliz navidad, prospero ano y felicidad!* blasted out. He gave that a shot, too, twistin' and turnin' even more. "This one's for you, Lusmila!" he shouted, singing all the way there, and all the way back—filling the vehicle with his new joy.

The car rocked and rolled down the road.

He laughed. So what if people thought he was crazy.

Chapter 11

Tuesday Morning, Two Days before Christmas

Out in the parking lot of Tires-R-Us, Chad kicked the tire on his Jeep. "Cramminy!" The boss had just taken some of his hours and given them to Nick, the new guy.

Chad needed that money. Every bit of it. And he'd already been written into the schedule.

And Nick, a father with his bunch of kids, had just let it slip to Chad that he was the boss's nephew. This was all so unfair. And there wasn't a blasted thing Chad could do about it. Not one thing. He'd better keep his trap shut if he wanted to keep the scraps he already had.

He climbed into the Jeep and slumped in the seat.

"Now what?" he said out loud and to nobody in particular. Minutes ticked by as traffic whizzed along on the boulevard in front of the business. His mind raced. Might as well try to find a second job. But where?

Ha! Maybe they'd hire him down at AutoSpot. He imagined himself stocking shelves—side by side with the grinning Football Dude.

He shuddered. Forget that.

Well, at least he could ride over there and check on that tail light order. What else was there to do?

Hopefully Football Dude wouldn't be working today.

In and out, that's all he'd do at the AutoSpot. Get in there, find out about the light, and duck back out. No hanging around to be made a fool of again.

His hand moved robotically to the key and gave it a twist.

But Becky was a magnet that he couldn't resist. And Chad was glad for the tail light order. It was the perfect excuse to see her. Well, like Dad always used to say—make yourself available. Don't hide in a hole.

If Becky changed her mind about Football Dude, then Chad, with his friendly face, would be next on her mind, and hopefully, in a positive way. He'd show her he could work on cars. Be friendly. Put on a tail light.

And whatever else broke.

So, that was the plan. Be available. Be pleasant. Keep working on the Jeep, buy more parts at AutoSpot, and see more of Becky.

Within minutes, Chad found himself sitting in front of AutoSpot's big sign-covered window. "Now or never," he said, and turned off the engine.

The bell jingled as he entered. There stood Football Dude, smack in front of him, ringing up a customer.

"Hi."

Dumb cluck.

"Be right with you," Dude said, dropping merchandise into a bag and handing over a receipt.

If Becky was in the back, Dude probably wouldn't tell her Chad was here. Wait. Was her blue truck out there? He'd forgotten to look. Chad turned toward the door as the customer passed by on his way out. "How can I help you?" Bobby called out. Like before, there was that idiot grin on his face.

"Uh, well. Uh, I ordered a tail light and was just checking in to see if it was here."

An amused expression crossed Dude's face. "What was your name?"

This guy knew his name. Why was he acting dumb? It wouldn't do to show his true thoughts. Just play along. "Chad Montgomery."

"I'll check in the back. Hold on a minute." He turned toward aisle three. "We might actually have something for you." He disappeared in the back. "Becky!"

So, she was here. Great. Now if this doofus would just scram so he could talk to her.

Becky skittered down the aisle and came to a grinning halt when she spotted him. She raised her hands and let out a high-pitched squeal that said *I'm-so-glad-to-see-you* in the way that girls can do.

He was just Chad; so how did he rate that?

Especially in front of Dude boy back there. And where had the guy gone off to? Maybe he'd stay gone.

Becky's mother emerged from the aisle behind her. "Chad, honey, so nice to see you." Then to Becky, she said, "Do you want to show him?"

"Sure." Becky gripped the edge of the counter with her little pink fingertips and ducked down behind it. Then her fingers disappeared. She returned with a large white box and laid it on the counter.

"Becky and I worked and worked on these stains, Chad," her mother said. "Take a look." She opened the box.

So soon? He leaned in to see.

Becky stood back, apparently pleased, and watched him.

"You got it dry and everything? Quilts are thick."

"Oh, there are ways," her mother said, her eyebrows up. "Believe me. Where there's a will, there's a way, honey."

Where there was a will there was a way? Maybe he'd will Becky to be his girlfriend.

"I don't know what to say except... thank you. Thank you very much." And now he was sounding like Elvis.

"Don't be so quick, though," Becky said. "Show him, Mom."

"Well, like I said, we worked hard on it. It's still not perfect." She unfolded the quilt. With all the packaging and tissue paper, it looked like something from a fancy gift-shop.

Becky's mom laid the tissue paper over the counter. "We don't want it to touch the counter. No telling what all's on there."

Becky touched her finger to one of the quilt's geometric pieces. "There it is." It had a brown tinge, but it wasn't bad. Not black like before.

"It looks fine to me," he said, "It's just a small brown spot. The rest of it's great."

"We're just so sorry we couldn't get it back to its perfect color."

"Mom's gonna love this. You don't know what this means to her."

"How special is it?"

"Remember Robert E. Lee? The Civil War? His wife was friends with Mom's family, back in Arlington. Some of the pieces came from her."

She lifted her hand to her mouth. "Oh, no, Chad, you should have told us that. We would have been even more careful."

"Maybe even too scared to work on it," Becky said.

"I just appreciate getting it back, and it's clean. I had no business taking it to some stupid picnic."

"Well, you'll have to tell us about that picnic story some-time," Becky said. "But Mom, don't you have...?"

"Yes. Chad, honey. I'm just so impressed with you," she said. "I told all my quilting club ladies about you."

Chad watched as Becky leaned under the counter again.

"The ladies were so touched—like I was," Mrs. McGregor

continued, "that a young man who would go to such lengths to care about his mother and her quilt."

Chad took a deep breath. "Stupidity was the biggest part in it."

"Nevertheless, you cared about your mother and her feelings."

Well, he did care. Of course, he cared about Mom.

"The ladies talked and talked about you, and one of them came up with an idea."

Becky placed another large white box up on the counter. She folded Mom's quilt back into its own container.

Mrs. McGregor took the lid off the second box. All Chad could do was stare at the beautiful red, white, and blue themed quilt top, another Texas Star pattern as she lifted it out and unfolded it all the way.

He touched the fabric. "Wow, these colors. They're so rich. It's like a piece of artwork."

"So, you like art?" Becky said.

"Look at these designs."

"Honey, this quilt top is special for several reasons. The pieces are from a lot of places. Our quilt groups trade fabric. We donate, mix and match, even across state lines. This is one of our fun projects from last year. Each member contributed a star of red, white, and blue, and nobody knew what anyone else's star looked like. The main requirement was they had to use rich colors."

"It's fantastic."

"We talked it over and decided you were the perfect red, white, and blue American boy with all the values we love. You honored your mother. So, we're giving this one to you."

Chad's mouth opened, but words wouldn't come out. "Thank you," was about all he could manage. "This is—awesome."

With Becky's help, Mrs. McGregor folded the quilt with its tissues, and placed it back in its box.

"It's just a quilt top, understand. They didn't have time to finish it before Christmas. So after Christmas, you give it back, and they'll finish it up. But Merry Christmas."

"How can I thank them—these quilt ladies?"

"Mom?" Becky smiled and pushed the box over to Chad.

Mrs. McGregor winked at him. "Here's how, honey. We're having a big Christmas dinner bash at the ranch. All the ladies are going to be there. Becky and I would like you to bring your mother and come join in the fun."

Becky and I? So, Becky wanted him to come? "Wow, I—I'd like that. Thank you." He glanced at the floor. Couldn't help but think about Big Doofus Boy back there with the dumb grin. Maybe Becky and her mom were just inviting everyone they came across. "Do you mind if I talk to Mom about it first? I'll get back with you."

Becky and her mom grinned at each other. "Just let us know," Mrs. McGregor said as Becky stacked the two quilt boxes together. "We would love to have you."

Becky headed around the aisle corner and almost bumped into Dude Boy. "Bobby, hey. I didn't know you were there. Would you mind helping Chad out to his car?"

Had Bobby Boy been eavesdropping around the corner?

The two boxes filled Chad's arms.

"Let me help you." Bobby raced around behind him with a shipping box and brown bag. He shoved open the door. "You almost walked out without your tail light."

"Thanks, man. Uh, by the way, are you invited to this shindig thing?" The words were out before Chad could stop them. *Why wouldn't he be there? He's the boyfriend, knucklehead.*

"Wouldn't miss it for the world."

Chad cut his eyes toward the guy's cowboy boots.

If Chad showed up at the party, he'd somehow have to come up with some boots, too. Maybe Dad's old black ones. He'd polish them up. Chad could dress like a ranch hand, too.

Bobby reached the Jeep first and with exaggerated helpfulness, swung open the passenger door for Chad.

"Thanks." Chad said, tossing in the boxes. He took the door, slapped it shut, and brushed past Bobby.

Bobby popped him on the arm. "See you at the bash, dude."

Dude? Who was calling who *dude*?

After dark, Chad steered toward the bay at Tires-R-Us. Nick, the new guy, was in his bay pulling lug-nuts off a tire. Chad pulled close and leaned out of his window. "Hey, mind if I park her for a few minutes and use some tools?"

Nick barely glanced up. "Suit yourself. Shop's nearly dead right now. Most everybody's done bought their new tires and headed out of town." He tightened a nut on a wheel. "If this keeps up, boss says we'll close tomorrow."

"Yeah, that stinks." Nick's Christmas Eve hours had once been Chad's. Among other. Chad pulled to a stop and turned off the engine, still sore at his boss for double-crossing him. Nick probably had no idea.

Robbery's all it was, and it was about to break Chad. He snatched the tail light box off the front seat and slammed the door. Good thing he was moving home soon, or he'd be elbowing the dumpster divers out of his way.

Best to get in and out of Tires-R-Us before he said something he'd regret. He stepped in the bay and set the shipping box on the workbench. The package appeared to have been re-taped. Wielding a screwdriver, he cut through the tape and lifted the flaps. Packing peanuts scattered over the floor as he flipped it over and slid its plastic-wrapped contents onto the bench. He frowned as the lobby doorbell rang. A customer had entered the showroom.

Nick groaned and stood, wrench in hand. "Looks like I'm it."

Chad held up two new tail lights. "This can't be right. I only ordered one."

"Who you talking to?" Nick said, heading through the door.

Chad waved him on, dumped the box upside down, and scrabbled through the packaging for a receipt. Where was it? The only thing under the peanuts was the stained brown wood of the workbench.

He slapped his forehead. "No, no, no, no, no. How did I get this out of the store without paying for it?"

Grabbing fistfuls of peanuts, he stuffed them back into the box with the tail lights. He shut the lid, snatched it up, and darted to the Jeep where he tossed it inside. He headed for the office where Nick stood casually ringing up his customer at the register.

The rules forbid off-duty employees from going behind the counter. But what else could he do right now?

"Nick, I need to use the phone. And phonebook."

Unmoved by Chad's emergency, Nick pointed a ho-hum thumb over his shoulder and continued his business. Chad flew around the counter, seized the book, and threw it open. If Nick would keep his mouth shut, Chad wouldn't get fired. But if he didn't...

He fumbled through the pages. *A... Au...* His finger stopped on *Autospot.*

His hands shook so bad he could hardly dial. Now if Auto-Spot didn't have him arrested for shoplifting…

He took a deep breath. Swallowed to get control of his voice as the other end rang.

"AutoSpot. Can I help you?"

Oh great. Football Boy.

"I—I was just in there." Oh man, he was squeaking like a twelve-year-old. He cleared his throat and lowered his voice. "This is Chad Montgomery, I just bought a tail light…" Aw, forget it. "Is Becky there?"

"Naw, she's already gone. Why don't you let me help you?"

Stop, breathe, inhale. "Well, I bought—no—I didn't actually get to pay—for the lights. Two of them. But I only ordered one tail light. My box has two tail lights." Oh, man, this wasn't coming out right at all. "I started looking for the receipt and couldn't find it. Then I realized I hadn't paid…"

"Well, it sounds like you'd better take this up with Becky since she's the one you dealt with, right?"

"I don't want anyone to think I'm stealing a box of tail lights."

Dude Boy actually chuckled. "You wanna just call her tomorrow?"

The last thing Chad wanted was to stay up all night worrying about getting arrested the next morning. "Why don't I come down and pay you right now, just to get it straight."

"No, no rush. We're about to close. You can just take it up with her since she helped you."

"Well, don't anybody go call the cops and say I walked out with merchandise without paying. I'm not trying to steal anything. Plus, I only ordered one. I need to bring one back." How had he ended up talking to this guy, anyway? Bobby was the last person Chad wanted to be chatting with.

"Oh, I wouldn't worry. If you can't get Becky tomorrow, just call the McGregor house. It's Blue Skies Ranch. You can't miss it. But there's no way you're going to get her right now or later this evening. She's out shopping with her mom."

Okay, so he'd call her tomorrow. "Just don't go calling the cops," he said as he hung up.

He set the phone down with a sigh. Stupid. He should have asked for Becky's cell phone number. But he wasn't about to call the store again. Dude Boy would think he was stalking her. Forget it. He'd just call tomorrow. In the meantime, those tail lights would remain in the box.

Chad put the phone back. The customer had left. "Whew. Thanks, Nick."

Nick frowned as if to say, "What have you gotten yourself into?"

But Chad ignored the look and headed back to his Jeep. He'd move it under a streetlight beside the building and clean it up a little. Because down at the church tomorrow Chad had a little matter to get straightened out between him and that algebra class guy. If the guy didn't have the day off.

Dark surrounded Emily's home in the historic district. Up on the porch a single bulb shined down on Eldon's shoulders. They sagged right now as his one and only daughter kissed his cheek and went back inside, her dog at her heels. His ex-wife, waiting beside the door, slammed it in Eldon's face. Charlene's message was clear—he was unwelcome inside— and should not press his luck.

He turned away.

Well, at least Charlene was allowing him visits with Emily

on the porch. She could have refused. Emily and her praying had somehow gotten through to her.

Bless Emily's heart. More than anything she wanted them all back together again. She'd pressed and pressed for it. Emily was quite a little prayer warrior, too. Eldon was proud of his daughter.

And just like her, Eldon wanted his family back.

To her mother, though, he was still just a drunk. An alcoholic. Charlene had extended him lots of grace over the years. Worried over him. Spent all her hope on him. And when he'd drained her dry, she'd given up on him. Left him.

He'd changed over the last year and a half, of course, but he didn't really deserve Charlene. Or Emily.

At least God heard Emily's prayers. His own seemed to fall flat.

He climbed down the steps, his shadow preceding him, and ambled through the broad patches of streetlight toward his small duplex apartment a few blocks away and down this hill.

As dark as it was, he might as well make himself a baloney sandwich, and climb into bed. Dark came early these days. It weighed down his eyes and made them heavy—fooled his body into thinking it was bed-time already.

He passed by the neighbors' glittering Christmas trees and strings of lights—things that made up for the dark. Cancelled it out. Made the neighborhood feel like home. Like hope. He formed a half-smile.

Hope. He'd never give up on Charlene. Even though his prayers fell flat, he'd keep on hoping—keep on trying.

Eldon wasn't naive, though. It would take an awful lot to convince his ex-wife to take him back. He still loved her. Always had. And he loved his daughter with all his heart.

He regretted the way alcohol had sunk its hooks into him. Gained the upper hand.

But no more. Jesus and AA were really helping. And he was trying every way he could to be a good man.

He'd never go back.

Charlene struck a blow when she walked out. The worst thing in his life. Yet it woke him up—the best thing that could have happened. Otherwise he'd be dead by now—alligator food at the bottom of Orange Lake.

But the heaviness remained. After all this time, the ripping away of his family was still an open wound. An iron weight in his chest. He needed a miracle. One he didn't deserve. It wasn't his family's fault. How could he expect them to stay while he drained the very life from their souls?

He sighed, shook his head, and hoped it all worked out. These thoughts churned in his mind as he rounded the corner. Up ahead his duplex-neighbor stood sweeping her already spotless front driveway. Like his, her drive was empty. Neither one of them had a vehicle. He hoped to get one. One day.

As usual, the woman—some kind of tall foreigner—wore a fancy turban and robe. Like others in the neighborhood, her duplex window and hedges twinkled with Christmas lights. A sparkly wreath decorated her door. Eldon's apartment, a mirror image of hers, sat dark and bare.

He drew near.

"How ah you, sir?" Her warm accent was liquid caramel. She stopped her sweeping as he ascended his driveway.

"Merry Christmas, ma'am—doing great. Nice lights you got there."

"Thank you." Her smiled widened. "Such a feeling of home—even of hope, yes?"

"Very much." He reached in his pocket for his key. "I was just thinking the same thing."

"Just like fresh-baked cookies, you know. I should bring you some of my spicy fruit-cake ones." The lights reflected off her gold teeth. "One day I bring you some. One day soon. You are having a good day, yes?" Only it sounded like she said, *Youah*.

He nodded, his mind still tangled around his own bare window with its lack of lights, the weight in his chest, the mountain of his worries. and how he hoped God would fix it all.

"You have family, yes?"

He stuttered around, mentioning his ex-wife and daughter. The woman's eyes grew large, and she raised her brows, a pleased and knowing look. "Ahhh. A daughter." Only it sounded like *dawattah*. "A wonderful thing. Is your daughter a praying girl?"

He nodded and tilted his head. "Morning, noon, and night. I'm really proud of her."

"Ah, yes. You are both wanting de same thing from de Lord?"

How did she know?

Her black eyes twinkled. She trained them on him and smiled.

Of course they were praying about the same things. He nodded.

"Would you happen to be praying along with her?"

He turned that over in his head. Praying with her? Wasn't that the same as praying about the same things?

"*Youah dottah* should not have to fight *dees* alone."

This woman didn't even know him, yet she was giving him advice. "I—I; she's not fighting alone." He was doing all the right things. Going to church. Getting his life straight.

"You are expressing your desires to the Lord?" To his ears it sounded like *youah deziahs*. "A child of de Lord must know he can come to his Heavenly Father with his desires. Don't just hope for de thing, but tell your Heavenly Father what it is you need."

"I try to avoid being selfish when I pray."

She tipped her head back and laughed. "Oh, no, child. 'Come boldly to de throne of grace,' de Word says." She spread her arms wide. "Your heavenly Father loves you, Eldon!"

Eldon couldn't remember telling her his name.

She lowered her arms and winked. "You know, some people say, *Whatever will be will be.* Have you heard dat one? Fate is not a safe plan, child. While you are just sitting around hoping—well, de devil come in like a roaring lion to take over your life."

Had she read his mind?

"Eldon, what do your Father's Word tell you?"

He shrugged. He hadn't read the whole Bible yet. But he was working on it.

"Philippians four, and verse six tell you this, my friend Eldon, *Be anxious for nothing; but in everything by prayer and supplication with thanksgiving let youah requests be made known unto God.*"

Eldon took a deep breath and nodded. He hadn't been praying that way at all. "Thank you." He turned the key in the knob, eager to get down on his knees and get that straightened out.

She laughed a big rich laugh. "Youah goin' to be all right, Eldon. Youah goin' to be all right."

Eldon flipped over on his thin mattress. He tugged the blanket up under his chin. His bed, more like an army cot, was as hard as a floor. He'd become a light sleeper. Especially tonight. A niggling thought, or a voice—plenty loud— nudged him toward consciousness. His brain grappled for a landing.

Was it a dream? Or a voice in the room?

He tensed. His eyes parted as he frisked the darkened room, a space lit only by the numbers on the clock beside him: 2:20 a.m. Nobody there.

He closed his eyes and slid once again into that weightless vortex of sleep. Had to be the neighbor next door.

"Check on youah wife!"

His eyes flew open. There it was again.

He sat up. Threw off the blanket. Sounded just like the Jamaican woman. How'd she get in his apartment? His ankles cracked as he tiptoed through the empty rooms.

Empty. Not even a cockroach.

He craned his neck at the kitchen window. Peered out. Nothing. The branches of the trees hung limp.

A chill ran up his spine. He should get a dog. Put up some window shades.

He crept into the living room. Through his curtainless window his front drive, a streetlight, and the house across the street stared back. Nothing out there. He tried the front door. Locked. Like a phantom he eased open the latch and gave the door a push. He stepped flatfooted onto the concrete.

Jamaica's lights, next door, were out.

He padded down the drive, craned his neck, checked up and down the street.

All quiet and still. Except for the drumming between his

ears. And him in his bare feet. He opened his empty hands. *Stupid. Should have at least grabbed a broom.*

He eased through the wet grass around the side of his building. Nothing. Just the bare wall.

It couldn't have been a dream. Impossible. Too loud. And why would he dream a thing like that?

Old Jamaica must have gotten to him.

He wasn't going to check on his wife in the middle of the night. Not for some dream. She'd call the cops.

Front porch visits with Emily were one thing. Stalking and prowling around in the middle of the night was another.

Besides. They lived in the historic district. A nice neighborhood.

Eldon went back inside and locked the front door. He wiped his feet with the bathroom towel and crawled back in bed. His eyes closed and he drifted off once again to the tic of the clock.

Ta daaaaaadaaaaaaaaaaadaaaaaaaa! His eyes flew open. A trumpet blast? "Check on youah wife. Go now!"

The voice was clear this time. And wasn't he awake? He bolted upright in bed and threw off the covers. What in tarnation was going on?

Okay, okay. His feet hit the floor.

Axelrod rubbed his lips together. Tonight was the night. The one he'd been waiting for. He was about to get even with that bossy woman in the two-story house. Settled on his knees in the dark, he peered over the tall weeds of the vacant lot across the street and took another bite of his cheese sandwich. He'd found it on the counter on the way out. Dear old auntie had wrapped it up for him and gone beddie-bye.

He'd waited for a while. Watched an old Hitchcock movie. Then a half hour ago he'd left her snoring in bed with her mouth hanging open. He'd crept out the back door with his sandwich. He'd be back soon enough. And she'd never miss him, not in the middle of the night like this.

He stuffed the crust into his mouth and wiped the grease on his black pants. Cat-burglar clothes. They matched his black shirt.

He wiped his mouth across the back of his arm and studied the dark windows of the historic home. Not a thing stirred. This would be easy.

He reached into his pocket for the small kit—the lock-picking kit he'd sent off for with his aunt's credit card. Being at juvie had taught him a wide range of skills. He reached in this other pocket for his aunt's black leather gloves. Didn't have to hunt for those. Pulled 'em right out of her coat pocket. Nice leather ones.

Axelrod stood back in the shadows of the cedars and pulled the gloves on. They were extra-snug, but stretchy. They'd work. He stuck to his path and made his way up to the sidewalk.

This way, instead of cutting straight across, he could take his time and check things out along the street. Come up from the east.

Just to keep an eye open for that old guy.

He didn't want to get the stew beat out of him again. Not like last summer.

Eldon's heart pounded as he yanked on yesterday's clothes and stepped into his shoes.

In all his life, he'd never done anything so weird as this—prowling around in the night. He wasn't a burglar. Or a peeping Tom. Normal people didn't act like this. Crazy people did. Maybe he was crazy after all.

But that voice—three times in a row. In an empty room. Just like when God spoke out loud to that prophet Samuel.

He blew out a mouthful of air.

Forget that. Eldon was no prophet. Far from it. Anyway, the voice was female.

Then that trumpet thing—

Eldon could be cracking up. But better safe than sorry when it came to his family. He pressed his hand around the knob and gave it a twist.

Was it an *angel?*

An odd sensation crawled up his spine as he stepped out. He gave his neck a rub and scanned the street—twice. Not a thing stirred. A warm cloud—a presence—hovered around him. He squirmed his neck around, tried in vain to shake it off, then dug in his pocket for his key. He latched the door—paused—then unlatched it.

Just in case he had to run for his life.

Talk about crazy.

He stuffed the key back in his pocket and descended the slope with a shudder.

Where his own drive met the asphalt, he turned. Scanned woods behind his place. Not a leaf or limb stirred. His eyes returned to the dark street with its blackened windows and unplugged Christmas lights. He scanned the shrubbery. If he was alone right now, it sure didn't feel like it.

On silent feet Eldon headed toward the stop sign at the end of the street. His ear strained for the snap of a twig or a second pair of footsteps. That feeling of being watched followed.

But all remained silent.

At the intersection he reached for the stop-sign pole. Rested there as he gazed left and right up the empty street. Seeing nothing, he turned and moved up the hill to the right.

There might be something to those voices.

And if so, whoever was out there, whatever this was about, it wasn't about him. Charlene or Emily could be in danger. His wife and child.

Whatever it was. Whatever it took. He'd just have to deal with it. Nobody was going to hurt his girls.

His legs, trembling, carried him up the hill as he glanced one more time into the quiet darkness behind him.

If the cops found him sneaking around, he'd probably lose his job. And that would be the end of this good life he'd started.

But if that voice he heard was real—and his wife was in danger—he didn't care. He had to go.

Axelrod approached the sidewalk in front of the two-story house. He peered left and right. This time of night the street was his. And now the crickets had stopped singing. Not a dog barked. Nobody but nobody was out on the streets at this time of night. Not a body stirred.

Body. Or bodies.

He snickered.

And nobody would figure this one out. Or pin it on him.

He crept forward, his pale sneakers a mere whisper against the sidewalk, and turned down the front walk of the house.

He shivered. This was the very same front sidewalk Miss Ruffled-shorts had come down.

A quick check across each shoulder, then he slipped up the concrete steps and crossed over the wooden porch.

In the shadows he lifted the kit out of his pocket. He'd practiced plenty at his aunt's house, and the lock would only take a minute to do. He paused. *Rats.* He'd forgotten his flashlight. A shadow of the porch's fat column covered the front door. He'd have to pick the lock in the dark.

He squatted. One, two, three…*click.* No big problem. He stretched tall against the door's dark frame and turned the knob.

The door cracked open, and out flowed the interior air. He slipped inside, pushing it nearly closed again.

Now all he had to do was finish the job at the top of the stairs.

Eldon strode up the sidewalk toward his ex-mother-in-law's house on wooden legs. Legs that belonged to someone else. He passed by homes, light poles, hydrants.

Balling his fists, he shot another glance across his shoulder.

This whole thing might evolve into a big mess. A big big mess.

Then it hit him—that thing he'd asked God about last night. He'd asked God to direct his path. Maybe this was it.

But a voice in the middle of the night—and a trumpet? This was over the top scary. And just when things were getting better. Life was settling down for him.

Even though Charlene hated him, he'd still made progress.

He pictured her house and what he might find.

A robber? No problem. Eldon had no fear of busting chops.

But what if the danger was inside the house? What if Charlene was sick? Hurt? What if she couldn't come to the door? How was he supposed to know?

He could kick the door down.

There it was—his worst-case scenario—not being sure whether to break in.

He sucked in a breath and wiped his brow.

Oh, God, help me. What am I supposed to do?

He approached the small orange grove adjacent to his mother-in-law's house. The trees filled half the block and prevented him from seeing the house. He'd have to get right up on the yard.

As he passed by the grove the threat of being handcuffed and thrown in the back of a police car grew more real.

C'mon, c'mon. He craned his neck as he approached the last tree and stepped among its branches where he waited, eyes on the house, and blending in with the dark foliage.

He traced the outline of the house. Searched for any sign of movement or irregularity. *Oh, God, help me to see.* The streetlight threw leafy shadows across the home's white paint and dark windows. Eldon's heart slammed a hundred miles an hour as he scanned the downstairs windows. Nothing at all.

Oh, man, the very thing he feared.

He grasped his jaw and swallowed hard. He'd better check around back. Otherwise he'd be ringing that doorbell.

He eyed the door's dark frame—and the front column's fat shadow that lay across it.

Wait. He squinted. Hard to be sure in the dark, but—he squinted even harder—and his veins ran cold. Had the front door *opened?*

And that flicker at its base—that small, pale flicker—

Like a foot.

It may be Eldon's eyes—his overblown imagination—but something there had moved.

Energy shot through him. He bolted over the grass.

One. Step. At. A. Time. Axelrod approached the stairs. He paused to stuff the tools back in his pocket and climbed up, sticking close to the rails to keep from squeaking.

At the landing he stopped under the round window to flex his gloved hands and admire the handsome black leather. *Meh. Too dark. Nevermind.* He'd take a look later. He clenched and unclenched his hands. His hands felt so good. The leather made him strong. He could get used to this. *Practice, practice,* just like his teachers always said. *It makes you perfect.* He snickered.

Then a quick gasp.

Did these guys have a dog?

The only thing he hated worse than that old guy—was a mad dog.

Emily turned over in the bed and snuggled the comforter under her chin.

Grrrrr!

At Pup's growl, she rolled back and dropped her hand over the side of the bed to the dog. His head quivered as she scratched behind his ears. "Shhh, now. It's just Grandma." Grandma's snores, loud and clear, came right on through the closed door.

The dog settled down, and Emily curled her hand under her chin and drifted back to sleep.

Eldon, muscles taut, leaped every-other-one of the front porch steps. Adrenaline surged through his veins. Strong now, his hesitation gone, he crept across the planks on cat-feet. He drew up tall beside the door.

He didn't need to wonder now. The door hung open—with a two-inch divide between it and the frame. Cool air and a hint of this morning's fried bacon seeped through the gap. Something was definitely up. And Eldon was going in.

Call the cops if you like, Charlene. Someone's after my family and I'm taking him down.

Axelrod hesitated in the upstairs hallway. He studied the two open doors and the closed one behind him. Loud snoring poured out of the left one—probably the old lady. He aimed toward the door on the right—the woman's—he hoped. One step inside. Silence. His foot sank into the rug. Another step. Another. He squinted at the sleeping face. People looked so different from under the chin. Especially in the dark like this.

His hands flexed, eager to do their job. He crouched. One more step. Just to be sure. He leaned over the face and stared straight down. This had to be the woman—not Miss Ruffled-shorts.

But she'd be next. Then the old one.

Eldon pressed a finger against the front door. The gap widened in silence. Like a panther he slipped inside, thankful for oiled hinges.

Oh, they used to squeak. Back when he was the son-in-law.

Bill must have done it. Charlene's other ex. *Sorry-no-good character. Happy prison, bub. Nobody goes after my baby girl.*

Eldon gritted his teeth. That was all his fault. He should have been here.

His eyes searched left and right for any sign of the prowler. Then up. *There!* A pale flutter—top of the stairs. A shoe. A heel. Same thing he'd seen in the shadows. It wasn't his imagination after all.

Eldon grimaced at how close he'd come to missing this guy. One second later at that orange tree, and he'd have missed the whole thing.

This ends right now. He grabbed the bannister and pulled himself up the stairs.

Right behind you bud, right behind you.

His brain sparked. *What if this was some boyfriend…*

Nope. Nope. He shook it off and peered up. But the landing's right angle blocked his view.

Up he crept.

No, not a boyfriend. Charlene wouldn't…

But she'd gripe about him coming inside—that's for sure.

His soles pressed against the risers. The stairs held quiet as his palm slid up the rail.

He'd explain. But she'd give him a hard time about those voices.

Eyes up, he passed the landing. Energy surged through his arms, his legs, and his chest. Eldon was the Hulk—a mass of strength.

You're goin' down, bub. Goliath himself couldn't stop Eldon.

He reached the top of the stairs. Nobody there. Where'd the creep go? He peered into his mother-in-law's room. She snored away, oblivious to the world. A dog growled behind the closed door on the left. The dog was about to break out barking—and wake up the house. Eldon was about to do the same.

He crossed the hall. The door on the right had to be Charlene's.

He peered in the door—and his blood turned cold. A black figure hovered above Charlene, his sleeping wife, his face just inches away from hers. The man's fingers, like black widows, opened wide—and in slow motion glided together above her neck.

Not on Eldon's watch. He tightened his lips and scanned the place for a weapon. Not a thing.

He stepped inside. The growls behind the door grew louder. More frantic. Now a bark. Scratching. Another snore. God bless the dog. Bless Grandma. And God bless their racket.

Eldon crept forward. Placed a foot between the man's.

The creep's fingers opened, hovered over Charlene's throat.

Eldon clasped his hands together—swung them high to the right—then down hard to the left—*bam!* Right across the ribcage.

The intruder spun, arms splayed out like a rag doll's, and smacked the nightstand, dragging phone, lamp and books crashing to the floor. He landed face-down, like a heap of garbage on top of a landfill. He made one effort to raise his head—make sense of his world—but dropped it like a brick—*bam!* For the time being his lights were out.

"That oughtta do you for a while, punk!"

Charlene roused, yanked the covers around her neck and sat up. "Wha-what's going—*Eldon?* What are you doing in here?"

Eldon brushed his hands together and nodded his head. "Protecting my family." He pointed at the body on the floor. "Intruder. Better call 911."

She fumbled around on the trashed floor and retrieved the phone and its base. The land-line's dial tone filled the room. She eyed the stranger as she dialed, trembling now apparent in her hands. She darted a look at Eldon. "You'd better explain this. Quick."

"Well, it's a story, that's for sure."

The dog bounded in, snarling and snapping at the unconscious intruder. He didn't bother with Eldon. Eldon grinned. Even the dog accepted him.

Emily burst in behind the dog. "Daddy?!"

She took a step back and stared in horror at the body. "How—what's he doing here?"

"I've seen this kid before, Eldon," Charlene said.

Eldon set a foot beside the guy's head and stared down into his face. "Same guy I beat up last summer. I thought I ran him outta town." He glanced over at Charlene. "I followed him here."

"But how?" Just then the 911 dispatcher came on the line. Charlene held a hand up for Eldon to wait, then filled them in. And no, she did not want to hold the phone. Everything was under control. Just send the police.

She hung up, grabbed her robe from the foot of the bed and stood beside Eldon to get a better look at the guy. "I—I saw this same guy the other day. I'm sure it's him. Hiding in the palms over by the school. Very creepy." She let out a sigh and sank to the edge of the bed. "I chased him off. Almost had to pepper spray him."

Grandma's snores still reverberated from the other room.

They all traded looks. Nobody dared laugh. Some other time it might be funny. But not tonight.

Bless her heart. Eldon had to give Grandma credit. Her snores might have saved the day—or rather, the night.

He thought better of mentioning it, though. At least not for a long, long time. "Got something to tie his hands together with?" Eldon asked.

Emily darted back to her room, and Eldon looked back at Charlene. "He was about to choke you, hon."

Charlene's hand trembled as she touched her neck and stared at the body. Emily returned with a colorful sash. Tears now filled Charlene's eyes.

It was all Eldon could do to keep from taking her by the hand. Or wrapping his arm around her. This wasn't the time to push his luck. He'd pushed it far enough.

He took the sash from Emily. "I guess you're gonna want this back, huh?"

She nodded and pointed at the intruder. "I've seen him too, Dad. At the art booth at the farmer's market. He was pestering me, trying to guess where I lived. I didn't tell him. I didn't."

Dad yanked the guy's hands together. "You low-life stalker," he said between gritted teeth and gave the scarf a yank, tightened it even more. He didn't care if the guy had a whole rack of broken ribs. He dropped the knot and stood. "They'll trade this in for handcuffs," he said to Emily. "Make sure you wash it good after they give it back."

She frowned. "Ewww."

"Cootie factor," he said. "Guys like this are chock full of cooties."

Charlene reached out and touched his hand. "Eldon. Thank you."

The front doorbell rang. The police. That was quick. It helped being so close to downtown.

The police stayed a lot longer than Eldon expected, but finally left with the guy the back of the cruiser. Turned out he wasn't a stranger to the system.

They drove away, and Eldon stood on the front porch with his grateful ex and Emily.

"I'd better get going," he said. "It's almost morning—time to get back to work."

"Eldon," Charlene said. "I think there's a little more to this story. Something you want to tell us. Something you haven't said."

"There is."

Behind him, Emily motioned to her mom as if to say, *c'mon, c'mon.* Eldon pretended not to notice, but his peripheral vision was plenty good.

Charlene ignored her antics. She cleared her throat and looked up at Eldon. "Well," she sighed, then cleared her throat again. "Would you like to—I mean would you care to come to dinner tomorrow night and tell us the rest of it?"

Eldon turned and caught Emily in the middle of a little jig. She grinned. *Busted.*

Charlene rolled her eyes.

Eldon smiled and headed down the front steps. He'd better leave now—before something changed. "I'll be here."

Chapter 12

Christmas Eve Morning

At the daycare, Tony slouched on the bench beside Emily. He tapped the toes of his sneakers together. She hadn't stopped talking about her mom and dad and their improved relationship—or that stalker last night.

He was glad for Emily. Her prayers were finally being answered.

But that stalker—Tony wished he'd been there. Caught the guy himself. At least they'd thrown him in jail.

Thinking about him gave Tony the heebie-jeebies, and he'd like to get away from here—go hang out with Emily somewhere. After all, it was Christmas Eve.

Ten feet away, the last two children, a brother and sister, swung high on the swings. The rusty metal-on-metal squeaks, audible for a block or two, cut through the crisp morning air. "What are we doing watching these two kids?" Tony grumbled. "Daycares ought to be closed on Christmas Eve."

"Knock it off, Tony. If our clientele wants chocolate-flavored sand, they'll get it. And you know that."

"At least it's a paycheck."

"And good tips, too. So, quit complaining. We're only here a few hours today, anyway," Emily said.

He nodded. The tips were great, actually.

She turned back to the kids. "Okay, then."

"Hey, what's your problem? Don't you ever grumble?"

"Ha ha." She shoved an elbow at him. "Try following me

home. I still have to do chores and wrap presents. And help Mom with *dinner.*" She dragged out the word to emphasize the news of her dad coming over. She fake-fanned herself like Scarlett O'Hara in the old movie, and put on a deep Southern accent. "Oh, Rhett, how I *do* hate wrappin' presents at the last minute."

He grinned.

The bell beside the gate tinkled. Very few ever used it.

Tony twisted around. "Wha...?"

There stood the Jeep kid from school. Tony hadn't even heard him drive up. Of all people, what did this guy want?

"Hi, mind if I come in?"

Tony stood. "Well. I'm shocked to see you here. What's up?" Maybe he'd come to get even.

"Thought I'd come by and patch things up. Can I come in?"

Tony hesitated. "We're not allowed..."

Emily pointed out the silver Mercedes pulling into the parking lot. "The parents just arrived. I'll get the kids signed out." Checkout was inside near the rector's office. She called to the children, "Your daddy's here. Hop off, guys."

With happy yelps, the children leaped off the swings and raced behind her.

"Okay, then," Tony said, unlocking the gate. "Come on in. We're not allowed to have visitors except for parents. At least with kids here. They're cracking down on guidelines."

"I won't stay long. I know it's time for you to leave."

Tony walked him into their little office and sat behind the desk. "Have a seat."

Chad dug in his pocket and pulled out a ten-dollar bill. He laid it on the desk.

"Thanks, but what's this all about?"

"Put that in your wallet."

"Ten dollars? I don't get it."

The boy settled in the other folding chair and leaned forward. "Look, I know Electra was rude to you the other day. We blew that horn, scared the kids, and acted like jerks."

Tony nodded.

"I'm not happy with all that was said and done, and I want to apologize—for both of us."

Never in a hundred years had Tony expected to hear such a thing. Especially after following them down the street and telling them off. But okay. He nodded. "Apology accepted."

The boy straightened. "And there was that little matter of the money jar..."

"Yeah, about that—"

"I didn't steal it," he said, holding up his hand. "But at the same time, I can't be sure the other person—the one who took it—didn't take anything. She could have, so I hope this money covers at least part of it. I can get you more if I need to—later."

Mighty strange. A scrawny little jackrabbit like this— paying someone else's debt. "That's awful generous when it wasn't you who took the jar."

The boy sat back. "Maybe nothing was missing, but hang on to the money, anyway. I hate the way things have been going. It's not the way I am. So please keep it. Along with my apology."

"Like I told you, apology accepted." Tony stuck out his hand. "I'm Tony, by the way, and this lovely lady," he turned to Emily who had just appeared, "is my girlfriend, Emily."

The guy nodded and shook his hand. "And I'm Chad. Nice to meet you both. Under these positive circumstances."

This seemed to take a load off the kid's shoulders.

"And thanks, man, I do appreciate it."

There was still something Tony ought to tell the guy, though. "You don't need to worry. We played back the security tapes. We know who did it."

Chad raised his brow. "Really?"

"We rewound the tapes and watched her kick the plants over, too."

Chad grabbed his head as if he'd forgotten that. "Yeah, I'm sorry. I didn't have a clue she would do that."

"And then we played it forward and found you cleaning up the mess. Of course, your apology is accepted."

Chad nodded, clearly unburdened. "I know I said it before, but I appreciate all this. By the way, I heard you guys at rehearsal the other day. You and that other violinist. Man, you do a pretty nice job with that violin."

"Thanks. I've had it for a few months. Been really working hard. Gonna learn to play it if it kills me."

"Believe it," Emily said. "He's serious. He practices hours a day sometimes. I don't know how he does his homework."

"Yeah, speaking of homework," Tony said, "you and I, we've got a big algebra test coming up."

Chad shook his head. "Don't I know." He returned to the subject of music. "With all that practice you must be doing something right. You've only played a few months? Sounds like natural talent. I'm impressed."

"Yeah, well, the music director made my parts simple, simple, simple. I play the notes, and they play all around me."

"Being at that rehearsal the other day—it did me a lot of good. Electra and I were passing by and heard you. Except for the money-jar incident, I'm glad it happened. The song got me to thinking. About things I need to do."

Chad stood.

But Emily perched on the desk. "What kind of things?"

"I've been living on my own for a little bit. It's a long story, but I'm going back home to Mom's where I belong. Starting tonight." He laughed. "I can hardly wait to eat real food again."

"Does she know?"

"Let's just say she'll be pleasantly surprised."

"On Christmas Eve?" Tony said. "She should love that." He motioned to Chad's chair. "Sit back down. Stay a minute."

"Wait," Emily said. "I've got something here." She reached in the desk drawer and pulled out a plastic zipper bag of homemade cookies. She dangled it above their heads. "Let's celebrate."

Chad eyed the bag and took his seat again. "Guess I've got a minute."

Emily passed around the bag. "So, whatever happened to your girlfriend?"

Chad raised a cookie to his mouth and shook his head. "Out of the picture. She was bad news."

"Can't say I'm sorry," Tony said, stuffing his mouth. "We weren't too crazy about her."

Ben's voice called out from near the gate. "Tony, Emily!"

Chad crammed the cookie into his mouth and spoke around it. "These are awesome."

"That's Ben out there, a friend of ours." Tony said. "Come on in, Ben. It's open."

Ben entered. "Hi, Tony. Hi Emily. Hi, Chad."

"Y'all know each other?" Emily said.

Chad grinned. "Yeah," he said through chocolaty teeth. "Sure do. Wanna cookie, buddy?"

"No, thank you," Ben said.

Chad turned to the other two. "We met at the *Stoppat-amart* the other day. And then"—he patted Ben's back—"Ben did something really special for me, didn't you? Found something important for me."

Ben nodded.

Emily passed the bag and Chad took one more cookie. "That's enough now, thank you."

"Our good old music director's been teaching Ben a little violin. He's all about helping people find their talent. And Ben's practicing hard."

"Do you have a violin with you?" Chad asked.

Ben shook his head, but Tony spoke up. "He's been using the music director's, but," to Ben he said, "you can use mine if you like. Want to show him your song?"

Ben grinned from the doorway as Tony readied the instrument for Ben. "With all the kids gone, I need to make sure this thing gets home tonight."

Ben, his hand still bandaged from the other day, placed the violin under his chin. "Ready everybody?"

Tony stopped him. "That hand doesn't hurt?"

Ben shook his head. "I can do it."

Chad leaned back as Ben scritched out a beginner's exercise on the strings.

When he was done, he bowed politely and everyone clapped.

"Good job," Tony said, echoing the others.

"I'm a good practicer, right, Tony?"

"That's a mighty nice violin," Chad said, brushing his hands along the side of his pants.

"Ben will earn his own instrument when he learns a little more. One of our church members died. She willed a lot of musical things to the church. Since Ben is always on the front row singing and clapping at every service, the music director made a deal with him. If he was willing, took lessons, and practiced, he'd earn a violin. Ben's working hard for it. He loves to sing. Loves all kinds of music."

Ben passed the violin back to Tony, but Chad reached for it. "May I?"

"You play?"

"A while back. Before some things happened, and I let it go."

"Please. Go ahead."

Chad's fingers glided over the wood like a stable master inspecting a fine horse. Then he held the violin to his eye and peered inside. Satisfied, he reached for the bow and re-tightened its hairs. After he tuned it, he began to play.

The notes of "Oh Holy Night" curled up and out of the violin. Like silver threads, they drifted into the night and up to the stars.

Wow. Tony backed up and leaned against the wall. *Man, what a sound. And the volume.*

The last note drifted away into silence, and Tony could hardly speak. Emily and Ben stood, open mouthed.

Finally, Tony gained control of his tongue. "That was fantastic. Where'd you learn to play like that?"

"So beautiful," Emily said. Tears pooled in her eyes.

Chad let out a long breath and laid the instrument back in the case. "Thank you, guys. That felt so good. You don't know how bad I've been wanting to do that ever since I stepped into the church last Saturday." He slapped his knees and stood. "Well, guess y'all had better lock up, huh? I'll get going."

Tony was still in shock from the sounds he'd just heard. He'd have to learn more about this scrawny kid. "Uh, well. Enjoy your family reunion with your mom. It was great meeting you."

On the way out, Chad paused to touch the poster showing Tony and Emily standing in front of the state capital. "Cool picture."

"Long story on that one. We're saving up for a project."

"Oh, yeah? Looks like you're individuals. Got your own ideas. I like that."

Tony followed him to the door. Maybe one day he'd tell him about the trip they planned so they could pray at the capital. Hey, he might even jump on board and go with them.

"That reminds me of something Mom once told me," Chad said. "Something related."

"About the poster?"

"No, no, not the poster, of course."

"What'd she say?"

"She said 'Never be ashamed to follow your own ideas. It takes courage to be different. But it's not the being different that's important. It's the being true to who you are that is.' I'm working on that one myself."

"Hmm, good thoughts, Chad."

He stepped out. "You'll like this, too. She said it's a mark of higher intelligence to stay true to your path, especially when others try to tear you down."

Tony gave him a thumbs-up. "Good reminder. I've seen what jealous people do to tear others down."

Chad lifted his hand. "Okay. See you. Sorry to hold you up. Have a Merry Christmas. You guys have really made my day."

"We'll forget about that other incident, okay?"

"You got it. Merry Christmas Tony, Ben, Emily." He disappeared through the gate.

The kid was all right. Wow, from a silent student in the

back of Tony's algebra class to this. Why hadn't he met this guy before?

Out in the parking lot Chad twisted the key in the ignition. "Let's go, Jeep. You know the way to AutoSpot."

Now that he'd gotten things straight with that guy, Tony, a load had lifted off his shoulders. Tony and his girlfriend were good people. They'd make good friends.

Right now, though, Chad needed to get over to AutoSpot and find Becky. Get things straight regarding those tail lights. Walking out with one was bad enough. But two?

And Christmas Eve was no time to get arrested for shoplifting and go to jail. Especially now when he was about to go back home.

He glanced over at the box on the passenger seat. No packing slip. No AutoSpot shopping bag. It even looked like he was shoplifting.

AutoSpot was only a few minutes away. But the speed limits in between were ridiculous. He reached Seventeenth, known for its beautiful chinaberry trees. Through their bare limbs he spotted the familiar red AutoSpot sign.

Chad slowed, swung into the parking lot, and coasted to a stop in front of the door. He squinted at its hand-written sign. Read it twice. "No way!"

Closed on Christmas Eve

He thumped the steering wheel with the heel of his hand. *Great.* That's all he needed.

He stared at the darkened glass, straining for any sign of life inside. Hoping Becky's form would actually materialize.

Yeah, right. In a closed store. What to do?

He drubbed an impatient rhythm with his thumb against the steering wheel. He'd like to thump it against Dude Boy's ugly head.

So, old Bobby. Reckon you're havin' a fine fat chuckle over this one, huh?

If he had a smartphone, he could look up Blue Skies Ranch. Give Becky a call. It wouldn't be long now before the party started.

Without wasting another second, he threw the Jeep in drive.

Think. Where could he get a phone? Not Tires-R-Us. They'd be closed for the day. There was the church. It wasn't too far. But Tony and his girlfriend were probably gone by now.

A flicker drew his attention. He glanced in the rearview mirror. Blue lights. Molten lava poured through his chest. *Not the cops.* This couldn't be happening. "That's all I need, another problem."

And how was he supposed to pull over around here with all these curbs? He didn't want to be arrested for ripping up lawns. An entire block of curbs with manicured grass passed by. He finally spotted a doctor's office and eased onto the apron of its parking area. Put it in park. Chad couldn't have been speeding. He'd been so careful. Everywhere he'd driven. And now *a cop*—right when he was about to get his act together.

He turned off the engine. What exactly did people do if they got stopped? Should he step out? Get his license out? Put his hands on his steering wheel? In the air? How was he supposed to know all this? It wasn't in the training manual. Or was that the part he'd skimmed over?

He aimed for the safest thing and placed both hands on

the steering wheel. He studied his wrists and pictured them in handcuffs. Better enjoy the view. It might be the last time he ever saw them against this same steering wheel.

What if they impounded his Jeep? Sold it at an auction?

Before he locked up the office, Tony wrapped Emily in a quick warm hug and planted a kiss on her forehead. She always smelled like strawberries. "Merry Christmas Eve."

He tipped her chin and kissed her lightly on the lips. The best day of his life was the one when Emily started paying attention to him last summer.

She grinned and tweaked his nose. "Happy Christmas Eve to you, too. Your nose is like ice."

"I know." He let go. "It's the cold front. And the rector's already turned off the heat in there."

She slipped on her jacket, tossed him his, and threw on her backpack. "That's what I thought," she said with a shiver. "Time to vamoose."

"You know," Tony said with a twinkle in his eye. "I think I smell a roasting turkey, don't you?"

Emily's mom and grandma had invited Tony and his family to their house for Christmas Eve dinner. They may or may not end up having to take Dad a plate. But who knew? Dad was changing daily. For the better. He might just show up.

She wagged her finger at him jokingly. "You can't be hungry yet. We've still got stuff to do this afternoon. Like, for starters, finding Ben that new picture frame."

Tony rubbed his grumbling stomach. "Such torture."

"Hold up, kids." Brother Ed called out from across the playground. "Don't leave just yet."

They stepped outside. The rector, wearing his red going-home sweater and holding his briefcase, held the main office door open with his foot. The man was ready to leave.

Okay, so they doubly needed to get a move on. Everyone wanted to get home. It was well into the day, and besides, the stores would be closing early.

"I'm letting you lock the gates today. The gate key is on Mrs. Sanders' desk. She said she'd be going out of town for a few days, so you're to hang on to it. Just in case anything comes up. And Tony, she's left you an envelope on her desk. Take that with you. And now, I'm out of here, and you two go have yourselves a very Merry Christmas. Don't forget to lock Mrs. Sanders' office door behind you." The rector saluted them, reentered the building, and walked away whistling past the windows.

"I'll tidy up the office," Emily said. "You go ahead and lock up everything."

The keys in Mrs. Sanders' office lay on top of an envelope. Probably a bunch of new rules and directives from her. He folded the envelope and stuffed it in a back pocket.

What kind of new rules had she thought of now? He'd get to it later—sometime before he came back to work. When he had nothing better to do.

The rector hadn't asked him to lock up very often, so with the key in his hand, he moved carefully through Mrs. Sanders' office, turning out lights, and checking the cord of her coffeepot and the computer in case she'd left something on. He didn't want to forget anything. After locking her door, he headed back to the playground. It only took a couple of minutes, but it was time well spent since the daycare would be closed for a few days.

Emily, using the time wisely, had nearly finished sweeping the sidewalk of the kids' pine-chip village. Tony grabbed a second broom and helped her wrap it up. Then they returned to their office.

"How much money should we take out of the jar?" she said.

"Why don't we take seventy and leave the rest here?" Ben's picture frame wouldn't cost that much, and they'd have some extra money, too.

"Wanna count it?" Emily said. "I'd like to know how much we've saved so far."

"Why not?" Tony dumped the jar onto the top of his desk. It only took a few minutes to count, but with tips and gifts, they had $150.

"I had no idea we collected that much," Tony said.

"Stick the jar behind something on the shelf there."

Tony nodded and covered it with a stack of aprons. As long as they remembered where they put it when they got back.

"Get your violin."

Tony scooped it up and slung the strap over his arm.

He stuffed the money in his pocket. "All right, let's get those bikes and go have Christmas."

"I've got to lock the front gate anyway, so why don't we go out that way today?" Tony said. They eased the bikes down the two steps and met Ben coming down the sidewalk with a small flat box.

"Man, I totally forgot, Emily. I told Ben to come by and show me his picture so I could get a size for the frame."

"I kind of wondered about that."

"Hi, Ben," Tony said. "You're just in time. Those your pictures?"

He clung to the box. "Hi, Emily."

Tony leaned his bike and case against the fence and locked the gate. Emily leaned hers, too.

Ben opened the box and held it toward Tony. It was an eight by ten; an easy size to find.

"That's my mom and dad."

Tony took the photo from him. "Wow, Ben, that's nice. What color frame do you think would look nice with this?"

"Blue. Like Mama's dress."

Frames didn't usually come in blue—or did they? Emily would probably know where they could find one.

"Your mom is beautiful." Tony patted Ben's shoulder. The woman's face seemed vaguely familiar, but Tony brushed it off. So many people looked alike. He'd never met Ben McDavid's mother.

"They're all gone."

"Who's gone?" Tony said. "Your mom and dad?"

"In heaven. And the lady," he pointed at the assisted living residence, "she told me I'm too ugly and nobody wanted me. Not even my own aunt." He shrugged his shoulders. "So I have to stay with her."

Yeah, fine thing to tell a kid. Or anybody else for that matter. Ben might not have good looks, but he sure had a heart of gold. Tony would have to talk to the old hag, probably the same one that lied and said the street people had hurt Ben. She needed a piece of his mind. After Christmas, he'd talk to Brother Ed again. But for right now there wasn't much anybody could do.

Then it occurred to Tony. Ben could stay at his house for Christmas break. Mom wouldn't care.

Chad checked his rearview mirror again, expecting to see an officer of the law marching up to his door with his little ticket-writing book. But the police cruiser blasted right past him with its lights still flashing. Two blocks away it made a fast left and disappeared.

Chad wrinkled his brow, stuck his neck out the window, and checked his blind spot.

Nope. All clear. He sucked in a deep breath.

"Okay, then." With trembling arms, he shifted into drive again. His legs were rubbery above the pedals. "Close. Too close."

Now he'd be even more careful.

He traveled back toward the church, and his new friends, five blocks ahead. There stood Tony, Ben, and Emily out by the gate. Chad coasted close and stuck his head out the window.

He hated to get right to the point, but time was ticking. "Tony. Sorry to bother you, man. It's really important. You got a cell phone I could use?"

"Sure, Chad." Tony handed over his phone. "Here."

Emily and Tony traded glances as he parked and climbed out.

"So, what's going on?" Tony said.

"Long story. Let me make this call first. I'll explain in a minute." Leaning across the hood of the Jeep, Chad found the number for Blue Skies Ranch and dialed. His hands shook like a caffeine junkie's. Nothing about him ever worked right when he was rushed. Or rattled by a near arrest.

Twice he punched the wrong numbers. If he could only stop this shaking.

He finally got it right and stepped around to the opposite side of the Jeep for privacy. After three rings, a male voice answered. "Merry Christmas. Blue Skies Ranch. How may I help you?"

Up to now, he'd imagined Becky picking up the phone. Was this her father?

"Uh, could I speak to—is this Becky's dad? I'm looking for the Becky that works at AutoSpot. She—she invited me to..." Man, Chad couldn't have sounded any stupider. He should have thought this through and planned his speech better.

From the other end, it sounded like a hand had been pressed over the receiver. A muffled version of the same male voice hollered out, "Becky!"

Wait, this didn't sound like a father. It sounded just like—like *him*, Dude Boy. Great. The guy was spending Christmas Eve with her, too? Stalking her? Why didn't the guy just leave Becky alone? How much worse could this get?

But then, if the guy was at her house, she had to be allowing it. She must actually like the guy.

Now Chad was starting to feel like a real third wheel. A dumb one. Maybe he should just hang up and wait till after Christmas. Then he could go down to the shop and straighten things out.

"Hello?"

Becky. Too late.

"Uh, hi. Chad here. You know, the one that ordered the lights down at the—"

"Hey there, Chad. I'd been wondering about you."

"I didn't mean to—didn't realize you had company."

"Company?"

What was the guy's name? Chad couldn't very well say Dude Boy, now, could he? Oh yeah. "Bobby, the guy from work. I didn't—"

She giggled, even covered up the receiver for a second or two. "You mean my brother?"

Chad's mouth fell open.

Her brother?

Words failed him. Unfocused thoughts swirled in his head.

Boy, what a dummy. Had Becky's brother let him out on a long string and yanked him around? He had to figure this out.

"Chad? You still there?" Becky asked.

"Yeah. Um, I—you know the box with the tail light? I never got to pay for it. I didn't mean to leave without giving you the money, it just—"

"Why would you? Merry Christmas. You like the tail lights?"

A long quiet breath eased out of his mouth. Did she mean what he thought she meant?

"Chad? You still there? You keep cutting off or something. I don't hear you."

"I didn't want you to think I'd stolen them, didn't want to get arrested for stealing tail lights."

"Didn't my brother tell you? It was part of the gift. You didn't have to pay. And it wasn't a mistake. There were supposed to be two."

That scoundrel. Chad was going to get even with that guy.

"Well, no, he didn't tell me anything like that." Chad kicked the tire on his Jeep. "He must have forgotten to tell me that important little detail. I was freaking out about it, I thought—"

"Oh, no, no, no. Don't let Bobby off the hook so easy. Trust me. He didn't forget. He knew exactly what he was doing. Bobby is a genuine stinker, and he's always pulling things like that."

A long breath flowed out of Chad's mouth. What could he say?

"Thank you. I really do thank you. The lights are awesome."

"So, are you coming to the party with your mom? I called the number you left at the shop to find out, and I spoke to her. She said she'd be there."

"How'd...?" Then it all came back. Becky had Mom's number from the paperwork. He hoped Mom hadn't told Becky any details, like about him being a jerk for leaving the house to get his head on straight. Becky didn't need to know about him living at that stinking Texaco station. Now that he thought about it, it was pretty embarrassing.

And what had Becky told Mom about him? Mom had to have figured out that he was coming home. She was probably sitting in front of the window watching for him right this minute.

But gosh, it felt good, knowing she'd be there.

"You still there, Chad? There's something wrong with our connection."

"Did—did you tell Mom about the quilt?"

"No, I figured if she already knew about it, she would have brought it up. So, you can surprise her with that. Say, we might go riding tomorrow. That is, if you want to and if you like horses and riding. And you don't have any plans."

His head felt like it was spinning. Party tonight, ride horses tomorrow? Whatever it took, he'd learn to ride. Even if she owned a zebra. And he'd learn to love it.

"Uh, sure. Thanks. I'll be there. Wouldn't miss it for anything."

Something told him he shouldn't try to learn to ride around Bobby, though.

Closing time had come and gone at the daycare. Mrs.

Sanders pressed her nose against the frame of the last hall window. Tony and Emily stood outside with Ben. And now the boy in the Jeep had parked beside the curb.

Brother Ed peeked out the other side.

"Stand back, or they'll see you," she said.

"No chance of that." Brother Ed leaned his back against the wall. "I can't see diddly from here, anyway. Just tell me. Does he have it?"

"Well, it's not on my desk anymore. He has to have taken it."

"Probably in his pocket."

"He couldn't have looked at it, or he'd have come back inside."

"Yeah, but not if he thinks we're gone. Which he does. No reason for him to come back in. Just keep watching. Tell me what you see," he said.

"Good grief. I wish he'd hurry up and read that thing. I want to see his reaction. And I need to get home." She kicked off her shoes.

Brother Ed grinned at her. "Mighty lonely there all by yourself, you know."

Certainly, widowhood was lonely. But he should butt out of her business. She glanced down at her bare feet and so did he. She flexed her toes "What are you staring at? Those heels were killing me."

"You did the right thing, you know, Mrs. *McDavid Sanders*."

"Don't call me that." She knew what Brother Ed knew. And he knew that she knew that he knew. And he'd keep throwing those little digs until she came admitted the truth. Her nephew needed her more than the group home, and she needed him.

But her concern about the two boys was not a diversion from the truth. Not totally.

Ed laughed, his wrinkled face reminding her of old Doc on Gunsmoke. "You and your animated flustering over those two boys. What you need is standing right out there as big as life."

And right in front of her, too. If Brother Ed would ever come to the realization…

She jabbed at him with the corner of her square leather purse. "Don't rub it in. It is important to me. Those two are a valid concern."

What Brother Ed didn't know is she'd already made up her mind. She wasn't going to let her nephew languish in that group home any longer. Not with him getting cut and battered at the hands of those bullies.

Ben was flesh and blood. Her sister's boy. She could deny him no longer. Her guilt at the wasted years had eaten her up. As soon as she could arrange it, Ben would be going home with her.

She heaved a sigh of relief and slipped into her shoes.

Brother Ed watched as she walked away. "What's the rush?"

Had he winked? "Nevermind, Ed. I'll see you later."

"Wait, now. Wait just a minute. Come back here and stand by me. I think there's more to come out there."

She returned with a sigh. Kicked off her shoes again and set them under the window beside her purse. "Well, I do hope they hurry up."

It was time to get home and get Ben's room ready. And put something under that Christmas tree.

Vinnie sat in the dining room and scraped the cherry pie syrup off his plate. It was midday on Christmas Eve, Nancy had gone off to help Emily's mother prepare for Christmas

Eve dinner. Sure, they'd invited him. But gunshots do funny things to people, and he couldn't quite get out in public like that yet. And until they brought him his plate of turkey and dressing this evening, he was on his own with these two pieces of pie and whatever else was in the fridge.

His mouth watered. He reached for the second piece of pie. But the phone rang. He growled and set his fork down.

Those weird calls had stopped since Robert left town. But it couldn't have been Robert after all. No. He was off the hook for that. They'd called Vinnie with Robert standin' right there in front of him. And right now, Vinnie hoped this wasn't them calls startin' back up again.

He was glad, though, it wasn't Robert making the calls. That boy was—alright. Better than alright. A good kid.

Vinnie glanced toward the phone. He hoped it was Nancy or Tony. So he could put this phone-call thing to rest for real. He'd sure been trying.

He'd almost gone to Emily's with Nancy this afternoon—to watch her help out. Almost.

The phone rang again.

Vinnie stood. "Okay, okay," He strode across the room and picked it up. "Hello."

"Thanks for da note. And da checks." The rusty voice wore a New Jersey accent-and sounded vaguely familiar.

Thanks for the checks?

"Dis is Carlo from da Mercedes place. I gotcha checks."

Vinnie nodded. *Of course.* "You're welcome."

"So aboutcha note ya stuck in there. Interestin', that Jesus-changed-me stuff."

Vinnie scratched his chin. Sure, he'd written the sticky note. He'd simply tried to explain to Carlo why he wrote the checks.

So he'd know what it was all about. Carlo, the guy Vinnie had all the dirt on. What a scum-devil. Carlo'd never done anything to Vinnie personally. Nevertheless, Vinnie would never trust him. He'd just wanted to make it right about the Mercedes and the way he'd cheated Carlo. "Yeah. Okay."

"Ya figured it all out, eh?"

Figured it out?

As Vinnie's brain mulled that over, Carlo said, "How 'bout this?" and whispered, "I'm comin' to get you." He followed it up with a crusty belly-laugh.

Vinnie gasped.

The blocked caller.

Carlo laughed again. "So, let's go fishin' sometime. And talk aboutcha Jesus experience ya had."

Vinnie tried to swallow but the spit refused to go down. He cleared his throat instead and spoke around it. "H—how about lunch instead?" He didn't want to be out in a boat with this Carlo.

Carlo's laughter blasted through the phone, and Vinnie had to hold it away from his ear. "You got it, fella. Meetcha at five tomorrow. Luigi's. No, wait. That's Christmas. They next day, okay? My treat. I wanna hear all about this."

Vinnie nodded, but Carlo had already hung up.

At least Carlo wasn't going to toss him to the sharks.

And maybe he did wanna know about the new Jesus thing with Vinnie. He glanced at the clock. Maybe he did have time to roll over to Emily's house.

Yeah. That might be fun after all.

Tony stood outside the daycare gate with Emily and Ben.

He moved his bike a little further down the wall—a few feet closer to getting out of here—as Chad made his phone call on the other side of Jeep.

Eventually Chad disconnected and came around, returning the phone. "I sure do appreciate this. You saved the day for me."

"Listen, I know you've got to go, Chad, but one quick question."

"Sure."

But before Tony could ask, a shiny black Camaro spun around the corner and skidded to a stop next to Chad. Its passenger window lowered, and there sat the girl who had kicked over the daycare kids' radish pots and stolen the money jar.

The criminal. What did she want?

Brilliance and Wisdom stood at attention. The ground vibrated as the Camaro drove up beside the daycare's sidewalk. Brilliance crossed over to the driver's side and reached down through the roof where Destroyer sprawled like a boss between Jake and Electra. With one hand he clamped the demon's mouth shut and lifted him out by his grisly head. "You'll be keeping your filthy trap shut."

Destroyer squirmed under the angel's mighty arm—and kicked like a toddler. Brilliance popped him on the top of his head.

His mouth opened and a muffled squawk tried to escape, but Brilliance popped him again. "Stay still."

Wisdom, over on the sidewalk, waited behind Chad at the curb.

Electra, in the passenger's seat, smirked out the window.

A look of disbelief crossed Chad's face. He bent to see the driver. "Sooo...Jake the Snake, picking up where I left off?" But the rumble of the engine consumed his words.

Wisdom whispered in Chad's ear. *After what you've just learned about Jake and his brother, you ought to be feeling sorry for him. The whole family has problems.*

Inside, Jake propped his left arm over the wheel and peered around Electra. "Well, hey, there, gay boy," he hollered. "How's it going these days? I heard you lost a little something in a dumpster."

Destroyer writhed in an effort to free his mouth, but Brilliance held his grip. The angel rapped his knuckles against the demon's scabby pate. "Settle down."

Jake peered up at Chad from under his brow. "Yeah, Electra here, she told me about the quilt. We had a good laugh over it."

Wisdom whispered in Chad's ear. *This kid has the issues. Not you.* Chad raised his voice so Jake could hear. "I—"

But Jake turned away and punched the gas. A thick black mark scabbed the asphalt. The stink of burnt rubber filled the air. Inside the car, Electra touched Jake's shoulder. The Camaro jerked to a stop then backed up.

Chad approached Electra's door again and squatted. Brilliance pointed, and Wisdom blocked Chad from getting too close, in case Jake tried to take off again. Christmas Eve would not be a good day for the boy to get run over.

Jake had turned away again. Brilliance reached his other hand around Jake's head and plugged both ears.

Chad tipped his head toward Jake and addressed Electra. "I thought you hated him."

"You couldn't possibly understand," she said.

Chad shrugged. "Try me."

Her red nails, chipped now, gripped the window frame. She talked low, yet loud enough for Chad to hear over the noisy engine.

"It's not really Jake's fault. It's his mother's. Jake and I are both in the same boat. Sort of like stepsister and brother."

Chad frowned.

"His mother. My mother. In Europe together? Get it, Chad? They're together. To-geth-er. Girlfriends. In the worst sense of the word. Now you see why his brother's messed up?"

Chad leaned back on his heels. "I—I never would have guessed that." He nodded. "It explains a lot."

Wisdom settled a hand on Chad's shoulder.

Chad glanced toward Jake. "Listen, Electra. If he ever lays a hand on you, you let me know."

Electra drew back, a look of amazement and shock on her face, like she'd never heard words like that before.

"Just sayin'," Chad said.

Several second passed as she stared at him, speechless. She finally found her voice. "Thank you, Chad, really. That's— that's very nice."

Wisdom whispered in Chad's ear. *You can't let Jake drive away without saying something.*

Still squatting, Chad craned his neck to where he could see Jake's face a little better. Brilliance removed his fingers from Jake's ears. But Jake, drumming his thumb against the steering wheel, stared through the front window and refused to return Chad's gaze.

"Look, buddy. I'm really sorry for all your troubles, man. I heard about it. But I'm not gay. No more than you are."

Wisdom patted Chad's shoulder. *You can only try. Whether*

it hits the mark or not, you have no way of knowing. But maybe Jake will quit taking out his anger on you.

Without a word, Jake gave his hand a mid-air twist and screeched away.

Brilliance dropped the demon like a football and punted him howling and flipping end over end across the daycare building.

Chad sighed as the Camaro roared and swerved around the corner. It felt as if all the problems of his last few months left with it. Today was a new day, and he didn't have the time or insecurity to cower and hunker down from that juvenile name-calling junk. Chad had his own life to live, and he wasn't about to dissolve into a pile of melted Jell-O because of a kid like Jake. The guy didn't even know him.

Never again.

These were Jake's issues. Not Chad's.

The Camaro sped around the corner and out of sight. Tony watched Chad as he gawked after it. He wished he had the right words to say to this new friend of his. He really had some crummy associates.

Chad turned with an embarrassed look on his face. "Sorry you had to see that. The guy's been a bully, and I needed to deal with it." He placed his hand on the back door of the Jeep. "And don't look at me that way. I'm not gay."

Tony stepped off the curb next to him. "Never thought you were."

"Oh, good grief, no," Emily said at the same time and followed him down.

"But I was about to ask—before those jerks showed up," Tony said, "why you stopped playing your music."

"Why? I'll tell you why." Chad thrust a finger down the street in the direction the Camaro had disappeared. "That guy right there and some of his buddies. I never should have let him yank my chain like that. They started in on me right after last year's school talent show."

"Sorry I missed that event."

"Yeah, him and his group, they put together some crude skit. Trying to be funny. It flopped. There were a lot of contestants, but I won First Place. Guess they couldn't take it. Or didn't have enough to keep them busy after the show."

"That's all?" Emily said.

"I was so messed up already. And Dad was…" He shook his head. "It just got to me. I shoved the instrument in my closet for a while. A really long while. Then I just forgot about it."

Tony made a mental note to ask about Chad's dad. The kid had enough going on right now. "I'm really sorry about all that, Chad. But I'd sure like to see what a pro my age plays. You got it with you?"

"Don't expect a thing. You've heard of bow bugs?"

"Bow bugs?"

Chad zipped his fingers through the air like scissors. "*Vzzt.* They'll chew the horse hairs right off your bow."

"Wait, just from leaving it in a closet? How do I keep from getting them?"

"No worries, man, not if you practice all the time. Anyway, the nearest luthier's in Gainesville. Long story short, by the time I pulled it out of the closet it was too late. It was money I don't have."

"A luth—what?"

"Somebody who can fix a bow."

"Can we see it anyway?" Emily asked.

Chad opened the back of the Jeep and laid his hand on the box's lid. "That's not to mention the new set of strings it needs. It was due for those when I put it away." He opened the lid, revealing a violin case inside. A strong odor wafted up.

Tony backed away. "I know that smell."

Emily pinched her nose. "Moth balls."

"Yeah, a fix that came too late."

"Why the cardboard box?" Tony asked.

"Insulation. I'm trying to keep it a steady temperature. It's why I park under the tree. You know how it is in Florida, hot, cold, hot, cold, and nothing in between." Chad pulled open the case.

Inside lay the violin, a glossy deep mahogany. The bow, clamped against the inside of the lid, was clearly ruined. Its pale horse-hairs, still attached at the top end, sprawled down over the violin's strings.

"It's a mess, all right. But the instrument's beautiful. You can bet I won't be stashing mine in a closet."

Chad laughed for the first time.

"Say, do you have music?" Tony asked.

"Thought you'd never ask." Chad snapped the lid shut and lifted it out in the box. Underneath lay a loose collection of sheet music and books. He grabbed a handful and handed it to Tony.

"Wow. What a collection. I'm just getting started on mine."

"It piles up. Won't be long, you'll have a bunch. Everybody does. Who throws away music?"

"Care if I look?"

"Help yourself."

Tony shuffled through the books and sheet music and reached for more. "Hey, what's this metal plate down here?" It was a small inscribed rectangle. He read it aloud. "*Teen Talent First Place Strings?* Is this yours?"

Chad took it, rubbed the soot off with this thumb, and gave a nod.

Tony nudged his shoulder. "You're kidding. That, too? What else have you got under here? I'm impressed."

Chad hefted up the pile of sheet music, and Tony peered underneath at the dozen or so metal plates.

"Wow." He sorted through them. He studied each label. "Good grief, man. You won all this? So why are these all burnt up?"

Chad shrugged. "It's a long story."

"You have a lot of those to tell." Tony smiled. "What was it, a house fire?"

"Not a what, but a who. A real dumbbell. I'll say that much."

"Whoa, now, I've got to hear this. Details and all."

Chad took a deep pensive breath then let it out. "Soon. But not today."

Emily, rifling through her own stack of sheet music, shook her head. "Unbelievable, Chad." Under one book she found a yellowed envelope. Her slow gasp drew everyone's attention. "Chad, what's this?"

Tony reached for the paper, but Chad beat him to it. "A letter. From my grandfather."

Emily slid the music back into the Jeep and pressed her fingers over her mouth. A squeal escaped, and her eyes connected with Tony's.

"Are you thinking...?" Tony asked.

She nodded frantically.

Nerves prickled all over Tony's arms. *Be calm, be calm. This may not be what you think it is.*

Emily practically shouted. "It's just like your envelope, Tony."

Tony's hand trembled like an old man's as he reached for the letter. "Could I, Chad? I know it's personal, but please? It's important. There's a good reason."

Chad frowned—but handed it over.

Tony lifted a torn letter from the envelope. It rattled in his hands. Its top left corner was missing.

Emily hovered behind Tony's shoulder as he studied it. She let out a squeak. "Give me the office keys, Tony! Quick."

He fumbled in his pocket and handed them over, as she raced back to the gate hollering, "Stay there, Chad. Don't leave!" and a long string of unintelligible words.

Tony hardly heard her as he stared at the words on the paper.

"What's going on?" Chad said.

For the first time, Tony took a good strong look at the other boy's face. He blinked, suppressing tears and the urge to wrap the kid up in a huge bear hug. This was so surreal. Yet how could Tony stand here like this and wait? Was this actually happening? He wanted to remember every detail of this moment. His own brother, right here in front of his eyes? What had this day brought? After all Tony's efforts and dead ends—

He sucked in a shaky breath and held up a trembling hand. "Just wait, Chad. If this is what I hope it is, you're not going to believe it. I can hardly believe it."

Emily raced back, her hair flying like a wild woman's. She took two steps at a time and stumbled at the bottom. "I'm okay. I'm okay," she said, her arms catching her as she fell against the Jeep. She climbed up and reached for Tony's violin case, where he'd propped it on the wall beside the bike. "I forgot you brought it out here," she said. She laid it flat, fumbled it open, and fished out Tony's own letter.

Chad pushed away from his vehicle, and approaching the case. "What's going on?"

Emily thrust Tony's letter into Chad's hands. "Read it. Read it, Chad!"

"Wait." Tony took it from Chad's hand. "Not yet. Over here first." He motioned Chad toward the front end of the Jeep. Spread the letter over its hood.

"Now open yours. Right here."

Chad laid his letter beside Tony's.

Identical handwriting. Identical words. But on Chad's letter the part about being a twin had been ripped away. The kid had no clue.

Tony directed him to the identical corner of his own letter. "Read mine."

Chad studied the words and his mouth fell open. He turned to Tony. "No. Way. Jose." He pressed his hands against his face and leaned against the Jeep. "All these years. I never knew. I never even knew." Tears rolled down his cheeks, past his hands. He scrubbed them off and lowered his arms. Shaking his head, he studied Tony's face and laughed. "Twins? How can we be twins? We don't even look alike, man."

A sob escaped as Tony grabbed his brother in a bear hug. "That's just the way it works sometimes."

"I can't believe this. I just can't believe it."

"I've been looking everywhere for you, bro. All over the place. And I found you. I found you."

Emily threw sky punches. "I told you so. I told you so. I knew you'd find him."

She grabbed Ben by the shoulders and bounced up and down on her toes. "They're brothers, Ben, brothers!"

"Let's all hug!" Ben shouted. And they did.

Eventually they settled down, wiping their noses and eyes on their hands and shirt tails. Emily pointed at Mrs. Sanders' letter in Tony's back pocket. "That paper, Tony, whatever that is you're about to lose it." He reached behind him and rescued it while Chad, still shaking his head in amazement, closed up his treasures in the back of the Jeep.

Tony opened the envelope. Might as well. A photo and a note. He pulled the out. In the photo were two little boys, about one-year-old.

He unfolded the note.

"Please forgive me for separating you and your brother," it said. "I've never forgiven myself. Please don't sue me. I was just trying to make sure you both got a home. I'm sorry I let them split you up. If I'd waited, maybe someone would have adopted you together—I'm so sorry for jumping the gun. Please believe me that I just wanted you two to have a home."

Tony frowned and handed the letter to Emily. She studied it, shaking her head.

With her heels still off, Mrs. Sanders gazed at the two brothers hugging out by the Jeep. Tears burned in her eyes. "Look what I've done. I've robbed them of so much."

"Tell me," Brother Ed said. "What do you see?"

Why'd he need to ask her that? Clearly, he could see what she saw. "They've found each other." She turned away. "But look what I've kept them from all these years. I'm—just a mean old selfish thing."

"Not anymore."

So, he *had* thought bad of her. She shook her head. The truth was supposed to set you free.

He gazed outside with a satisfied expression.

She grabbed her purse off the floor. "Merry Christmas, Brother Ed. I'm going home. I can't stand here thinking about it all day."

He tore himself away from the scene and gathered his briefcase. "Don't be so hard on yourself. You've done what you could at this point. It's in the kids' ballpark. You can't undo history. And back then you did what you did with the best of intentions."

"Maybe I shouldn't have written the note." Her comment was a diversion. What hadn't been mentioned was what she'd done to Ben. His wasted years alone. Rejected by his own aunt. There was no excuse for letting her dead sister's child live in that *institution*. Not even Ed could claim she'd done that with the best of intentions. It was all about her and her own inconvenience.

And now she had no one. Turn-about was fair play, she supposed.

"Maybe, maybe not. But what you've done is redemptive. It's better late than never, isn't it?"

Mrs. Sanders let out a loud sigh. "Let's just go. I can't stand myself. I need to get on home and get Ben's room ready. And put something under that Christmas tree." She clamped her fingers over her mouth. *Uh oh.* There went the cat out of the bag. She wasn't going to tell Ed yet.

"Can't stand yourself? I think you're a mighty fine little lady."

She brushed off the comment but felt herself blush. "Oh, pshaw!"

Slipping her feet into her shoes she glanced up and met Brother Ed's crinkly-eyed grin and wink. She couldn't help but grin back.

Maybe she should move forward. There was still plenty of time to hit up the grocery store and fix a special dinner tomorrow.

Ben would enjoy having a third person at the table.

And old Ed didn't have anywhere else to go.

Out by the Jeep Tony laughed and slapped Chad on the shoulder. "Bro. I like the sound of that. We're going to have to celebrate."

Chad punched him right back and practiced the sound of the word. "Bro. Bro. Bro. Has a nice ring to it. Yeah, I like it." They carried on like this for a full five minutes, with Ben still cheering from the sidelines, and Emily grinning and wiping tears off her cheeks.

Finally, Chad said. "Hey, listen, I've got some business to tend to, or Mom's gonna think I'm not really coming home. And it is Christmas Eve. You've gotta come over for five minutes. It's not far."

"Sure. Can you take Ben? We'll follow you over."

Ben wasted no time climbing into the Jeep.

Chad started his engine.

Tony hollered, "And Ben, you're coming home with me tonight. Whaddya say?"

Ben fist-pumped and let out a whoop as the Jeep lurched away kicking up gravel.

Tony grinned and waved as he and Emily picked up their bikes. "Slow down," he yelled. "Not so fast, bro."

Tony led the way behind the Jeep. After a few blocks, Emily pulled up even with him. "Hey, listen, what do you say we give Chad that seventy dollars?"

Tony nearly skidded to a stop as he processed the thought, but moved on again. They had to keep up. "Are you kidding?" he yelled. "That's an awesome idea, but—"

"He's your brother, after all."

They pedaled another block before Tony slowed. "You sure about this? I'm perfectly okay with it. He's my brother, yeah. But what about you? The money's yours, too."

"I like your brother. And don't you think he needs it?"

"Well, sure..."

"We could run back to the office after this and get a little more cash for Ben's frame. Easy."

"That's great. I can't believe you, Emily."

"Yeah?" She grinned, stomped the pedals, and sped away from him. "See you later, slowpoke!"

"Hey!" he yelled, and raced to catch up.

Chad snapped off the engine in front of his house and leaped out to open Ben's door. Not that the boy needed help, but Chad wanted to hurry things along. "Come on, Ben."

Ben clambered out, and Chad motioned for Tony and Emily to follow them inside. Ben followed close on Chad's heels.

Up at the house, a sweet aroma, like baked cookies, wafted through Mom's open windows. It settled around the doorway. *Ding, ding, ding, ding.* He jabbed at the bell.

Waiting was more than he could stand, and he snatched open the front door. "Mom, I'm home!"

"Chad!" The muffled but joyous response came from around the corner in the kitchen. Mom emerged, wiping her hands on her apron and beaming ear to ear. "Chad!" She threw her flour-speckled arms around him and leaned him left and right. "I knew you'd make it." She nearly squeezed the breath out of him. "Oh, it's so good to have you back home, honey."

Tears burned Chad's eyes as he repeated the words he'd been rehearsing all afternoon. "I'm so sorry I put you through this, Mom. I shouldn't have left home to start with. But I can tell you, I learned a few things."

"It's all right, son. It's all right. I'm just so glad to have you back." She half-laughed, half-cried, then backed away to wipe her eyes on her apron. "Hey, somebody's got to eat all this good food!"

Emily knocked, then she, Tony, and Ben eased in beside Chad.

Chad flung a hand in their direction. "Mom, you'll never guess who I brought home. Not in a million years." He grabbed Tony by the shoulder and nudged him closer. "Meet Tony. Tony, meet Mom. This, Mom, is my twin brother!"

"Twin?"

Emily and Ben hung back watching.

"Oh, I'm sorry," Chad said. "This is Emily, and this is Ben. I was so focused on my new brother and all. Didn't mean to be rude."

Mom clasped her fist over her mouth, ready to cry again. Emily stepped to her side. "Let's sit you down. And wow, have we got a story."

Ben followed them to the sofa.

"Oh, my goodness, this is all so…" Mom shook her head, "so unimaginable."

"You guys tell her what you can," Chad said. "I need to grab something out of the Jeep."

He darted for the door. A minute later he returned with two large white boxes. He set them on the coffee table in the living room.

"What in the world's all this?" Mom said.

"Open this one, first," Chad said, sliding the box with the antique quilt in front of her.

She lifted the lid and tipped her head. A question played over her features. "You wrapped up the old quilt?"

"For good reason," Chad said, "And it's such a story. The problem is, there's so much to tell you I don't know where to start. But for now, just remember two things about the old quilt. Be glad you have it back. And be thankful it's clean. All but a little—well, just a little something you probably wouldn't notice. You might want to call it a history mark."

Mom still appeared puzzled as she ran her hand along its surface. "Well, it is clean, as clean as I've ever seen it. And it's wrapped so nice."

Chad laughed. "I didn't wrap it. Someone else did. Now, this, Mom." He slid the old quilt away and brought the other box close. "You remember the cute—I mean you remember that girl—" Uh, yeah, Mom had already talked to Becky. He stopped to gather his thoughts. "Remember Becky, the girl that invited us to a party?"

"Yeah," Tony said, nudging his brother's shoulder. "We'd like to learn a little more about this cute thing named Becky. And the big shindig tonight."

Heat built in Chad's cheeks.

Mom nodded. "I baked cookies for it."

"Well," Chad snatched off the lid, "this is a gift from her family. Ta da!

"Oh, my, my, my." Mom gasped as she lifted its folds. "Isn't this beautiful? But why would they—"

"I'll explain everything, eventually. Every single thing. So, let me see, what do you need to remember about this quilt for now? Hmm. Oh, they like your son. Yeah, they like me, Mom."

"Oh? You must have made a pretty good impression." Mom shook her head. "Well, I'm just dying to hear about it." She removed her hand from the quilt and planted a kiss on his cheek. "And I like you, too. But for now, I'm just glad to have you home."

Tony and Emily stood to go. Ben did the same. "We've barely met your mom, Chad," Tony said, but you've got places to go, and you need to get ready."

Yeah, and he needed to find Dad's old boots. "You're right. But count on it. We're going to be seeing a whole lot more of you guys in the future."

"Y'all have fun," Tony said. "We'll see you soon."

Chad raised one arm to say good-bye, but dipped his head instead, and took a sniff. "Phew. One hot shower coming up." His stinky days were over.

Everyone laughed.

Even so, Chad grabbed his brother in another bear hug then stepped back to look at him. "Seriously, man, I'm so glad we found each other. Things will never be the same again. Never."

"You're right about that."

"And Mom," he said. "I was so stupid. But I can tell you, good things came out of this."

"I knew they would, honey. It was meant to be. And I'm so glad you're home. Tony, you all come by anytime. Anytime. You two don't look a bit alike, but I can't wait to hear about this twin brother thing." She hugged each one in turn. "I'll expect you back real soon."

Chad blew out a breath and shook his head. This was too much to take in.

Emily led the way outside.

"Oh, yeah. One more thing," Tony said, turning to Chad and his mom in the doorway. He pulled the wad of money out of his pocket and thrust it toward Chad. "Merry Christmas."

Chad stared down at the gift. "Wow. Are you kidding?"

"No kidding. Put that to good use." He lifted Chad's hand and slapped the money into it. "Get something you want. Or fix something you need, like your bow. That's from Emily and me."

"Man, Tony. Thank you both so much. I will. This is going to be my best Christmas ever." He pointed at his twin. "No, wait—"

Tony pointed right back, and they shouted together, "It already is!"

They howled with laughter along with everyone else and high-fived.

As the three walked the bikes past the corner stop sign, Chad watched from the sidewalk. Before Tony disappeared around the block he turned to wave.

Chad lifted his arm. "See you, soon, bro," he whispered. "See you soon."

Acknowledgements

Thank you, my friend, Marian Rizzo who helped me decide on the right title for this book, *Girl With a Black Soul*, and to Zandy Demets, for your smart advice on skidding jeeps and the effects of alcohol.

Mandee Wells Johnson, my valuable trauma nurse friend—thank you so much for your advice on gunshot wounds, recovery, and psychological issues that follow such an event. I never would have guessed.

Very many thanks to the wonderful Linda and Mickey Cruey and dear Sonja and Abi Lonadier, all excellent beta readers who knew how to zero in like honey bees on all the important points. You are my gemstones.

Thanks to all the faithful members of my Word Weavers team, who stayed the course through rain, shine or COVID: Diane Kitts, Elsie Bowman, Doris Hoover, Karen Skirpan, Pam O'Brien, DeVonna Allison, Robin Collison, Yeny Rowley, Leah Taylor, Jen Cason, Melissa Adams, Marian Rizzo, Delores Kight, and Sue Montgomery. You shined like stars with your perceptive critiques and suggestions. Thank you all.

Thank you, Mike Parker, may God reward you for what you have done for this industry and those in His service. And David Warren, artist extraordinaire, who always knocks it out of the park, thank you for your delightful surprises.

Most of all, thank you to my perceptive husband, who will always tell it like it is. I appreciate all your good ideas and thoughts.

About the Author

Jennifer Odom, a 40 year veteran teacher of elementary education—and her school's 2003 Teacher of the Year—has taught kindergarten through fifth grades in all subjects. She enjoyed the latter half of her creative career as a team member of Dr. N.H. Jones Elementary, a National Blue Ribbon School where students excel in competitions of math, science, technology, writing, and videography.

Jennifer writes human interest stories for her local newspaper, *The Ocala Star Banner*, and has also been published in national magazines including, *Splickety* and *Clubhouse Jr.* In 2015 she was honored to be named Florida Christian Writers Conference's Writer of the Year.

Girl with a Black Soul is the culmination of Jennifer's award-winning **Black** series, which also includes *Summer on the Black Suwannee* and *Stranger with a Black Case.*

Connect with Jennifer online at:

jenniferodom.com

Also Available From

WORDCRAFTS PRESS

Presence in the Pew
by Marian Rizzo

Gretchen and the Bear
by Carrie Anne Noble

Tears of Min Brock
by J.E. Lowder

The Mirror Lies
by Sandy Brownlee

House of Madness
by Sara Harris

www.WordCrafts.net

www.ingramcontent.com/pod-product-compliance
Lightning Source LLC
Chambersburg PA
CBHW021308190726
48288CB00003B/741